About the author

The author was born in Newquay, Cornwall and spent his first 18 years growing up with Lusty Glaze Beach as his playground and summer season work place, whilst he hired deck chairs and later became a beach lifeguard. Having worked in London for a year as a volunteer working with the disabled, he returned to Cornwall and became a Special Constable in Newquay, and later Launceston, before finally joining the Devon and Cornwall Police as a regular officer in 1990.

Having worked the beat for a few years attending everything and anything, he later joined the Armed Response Unit dual rolled with the Traffic department. As a Sergeant, he was an Operational Firearms Commander, a Firearms Tactics Advisor, a VIP protection officer and Pursuit Tactics advisor along with investigating many a fatal road traffic collision being regarded as an expert in his field.

Harry has 10's of thousands of followers on his award-winning Police Twitter account @ex_arv_sgt and Youtube channels 'Harry Tangye' and 'Frontline Chat'

Also, by Harry Tangye

#1 Best Selling autobiography, 'Firearms and Fatals' which led him to use his experiences to write his two novels, the highly successful, 'The Cornish Scoop' and now 'The Cornish Beat', gaining much of his ideas from very real events.

The Cornish Scoop reached the same very high reviews as his first book which was an expansion of his autobiography, using all those other anecdotes in the form of a Novel.

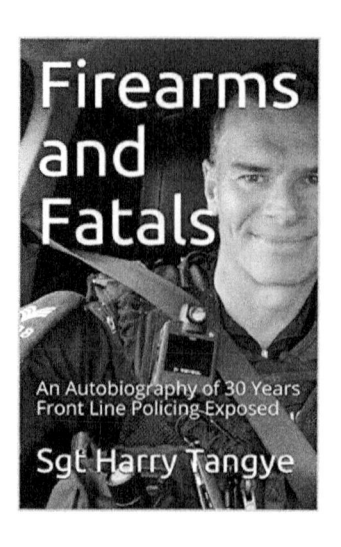

The Cornish Beat

The Author's second novel.
Based on true crime events
witnessed by former police sergeant
Harry Tangye

Copyright Harry Tangye 2021

The right of Harry Tangye to be identified as author of this work has been asserted in accordance with sections 77 and 78 of Copyright, Designs and Patents Act, 1988

All rights reserved. No part of this publication may be reproduced, stored in a retrieval system or transmitted, in any form or by any means without the prior written permission of the publisher, nor be otherwise circulated in any form of binding or cover other than that in which it is published without a similar condition being imposed on the subsequent purchaser.

Harry Tangye Ltd

This book is a work of fiction. Names, characters, places and incidents are either a product of the author's imagination or are used fictitiously. Any resemblance to actual people living or dead, events or locales is entirely coincidental

Dedicated to habibti, Noor...

Someone who came into my life when we both least expected it

but who has fulfilled it in every way.

Everyone needs a Noor in their lives... ♥

ACKNOWLEDG[

Thank you to Tanja Conway[
more by proof reading my boo[
her as always.

... and to my brother's Ge[
incredible support along with
been the loving arms every
Thank you, Mum, or Moira to [
with advanced dementia but is
still.

I want to add a special tha[
Bates, a wonderfully kind and c[
much respect from those he led
sergeant who influenced me as
on the beat and who kindly gav[
name in this book only last y[
Thank you, GGB and God bless

CONTENTS

1. A first-class robbery — 11
2. Love and lifeboats at the Huer's hut — 30
3. Turning up the heat — 49
4. The knockout punch — 69
5. Tea and medals — 84
6. Sun, sea and sinister endings — 102
7. Love on the Island — 123
8. Cash not in transit — 149
9. Pot and pursuits — 165
10. A fine day for a funeral — 184
11. Cliff rescues and sex — 201
12. Death on the doorstep — 220
13. Heroes in stockings — 238
14. Fast and furious — 255
15. Synchronize your watches — 274
16. The silent hero — 295

Chapter 1
A first-class robbery

Proud as punch and feeling quite the experienced Police officer by now, Treavey turned his burgundy BMW 318i, into the rear car park of Newquay police station. It was a late turn, and the early august sun was shining hot, giving him a renewed zest for life, but with a certain trepidation as it was his first shift having officially moved from the little Perranporth police station that had served him so well for several years.

It was 1996, a couple of years after his infamous drugs busts in Perran which had made him so well known in the area with the criminals and with his new colleagues. He knew he had to hit the ground running to keep his reputation, but he also felt just as much a fish out of water with being permanently based in Newquay on the North Cornish Coast. He couldn't quite believe he was being paid a wage to do this job, the same wage as a police officer working in Liverpool or in the centre of Birmingham. But here, he often had the blue skies and warm breeze on his skin.

Treavey carefully parked his car neatly between the lines as he knew he would be judged on it. He didn't want to have to put up with a stream of, "Nicely abandoned there, Treavey" as he walked in for his first day. He shut his car boot having removed 3 large bags and began making his way up the steps to the front of the station and caught the eye of the Inspector he'd never really liked that much. Inspector Levey was a gaunt looking man with thinning wispy grey hair and a strong Irish accent which pierced the air.

"You're that new Treavey lad, right," he shrilled as he leant forward towards Treavey, forcing him to stop in his tracks.

"Yes Sir, that's me. It's my first day and happy to be here."

Inspector Levey raised his eyebrow slightly and enquired, "You don't have one of those slim jims, do you Treavey?"

Treavey looked puzzled as it was a strange request to ask him as his hands were already full of bags. After all, a slim jim was used to slide down the window of a car door to hook the levers within and pop any locks open. A great mechanism for opening your car door when you'd locked your keys inside but also a favourite tool with the local scallywags who spent their time either stealing cars or removing tourists' property from within them.

"No Sir, but how can I help?" Treavey enquired with a tone which gave the impression he hoped it wasn't going to take too much of his time and effort as he was keen to get in and meet his new section.

"There's a guy in a car down there who's asleep. I've tried to wake him but he's out for the count."

"That's a bit strange Sir, I'd best take a look down there with you."

Both the Inspector and Treavey walked down towards where the man had been sighted by the inspector, with Treavey trying to quicken the pace as he was not happy with what he had heard. As they approached a rather nice-looking black Mercedes car tucked away in the corner of the car park, Treavey was hoping the car door would be opening soon, alleviating them of any further concerns. It remained closed, and concerns raised further within Treavey as he realised the heat would be intense inside so as he got to the window, he rapped his knuckles hard on the window, startling Inspector Levey who had, it seemed, spent too long in an office to remember any of his street skills if he had had any at all. Some of these bosses really pissed Treavey off as their feet didn't touch the streets for two minutes before they were being promoted through the ranks and away from any real policing. He often wondered what they joined the police for in the first place. Was it to police the streets and do some good for the community or was it to stay in an office and push paperwork around all day?

With no response forthcoming, Treavey had his secret weapon deployed, a spring-loaded centre punch seized from a prisoner of his which consisted of a centre punch with a spring mechanism to give it a contained force to very cleanly and simply smash the window against which it was pressed. The Mercedes window went in and Treavey had the door open, and in the same movement, the body of the man inside was being hauled out by his armpits onto the surface of the concrete car park and Treavey was instantaneously bouncing on his chest with his palms of his hands.

"Shit, it's the Superintendent. Superintendent Steer!" exclaimed the Inspector, who shuffled his weight from one foot to the other nervously, not knowing what to do with himself.

"Go get some fucking help... Sir," Treavey shouted as he continued throwing his palms on to the sternum of the rather heavily set man who was looking extremely pale and very much at the wrong end of his life expectancy.

The inspector hurriedly scuttled off towards the station to raise the alarm, and Treavey pushed some breaths of air into his lungs before continuing on his chest again. He had passed his Water Merit and advanced resuscitation at the local swimming pool growing up, and had spent a couple of seasons being a lifeguard on Lusty Glaze Beach so he was comfortable with what he was doing. He was simply happy to do it for real, as often he had practised with some colleague with simulated pushes on their chest with much larking about. Whilst at his life saving club it was always a bonus if he had dragged one of the good-looking girls out of the swimming pool before simulating CPR but when it came down to it, he was so shy about being caught staring at them in their swimsuit, he would often look away anyway. 'A wasted opportunity' he thought, as he continued his CPR, 'but an honourable thing to do, all the same.'

In only a few minutes there was the sound of scuttling feet behind him as others came to assist. One PC speaking in confident tones, said, "Okay mate, we have the ambulance coming, I'll take over the breaths if you like."

"Great, thanks mate, it may take a while if the Ambulance is coming from Truro." Treavey glanced across to see a fit and strong looking man kneeling beside him. He was in his late 40's quite pale looking and with very white hair, blue eyes and fair eyebrows which gave the impression of almost albino in looks. He had a full looking chest which looked strong enough to rip a tree trunk out by the roots, so it was probably just as well he was responsible for the breaths and not cracking every rib in the Superintendent's chest. His voice commanded respect with its depth and gravel-like tones and Treavey already hoped he was on his section, after all it was always nice to have some muscle to help you out of those scrapes from time to time.

There was a growing group of high-ranking officers growing around him, starting from the odd Sergeant to another Inspector and then the group addition jumped straight to a Superintendent from somewhere. Treavey had wondered from time to time what they were all up to, but he took it that any boss in a mile vicinity needed to show their face. He ignored them as they bustled and chatted until the paramedics arrived and there was more bustling and chatting whilst they took out the paraphernalia from their green bags and took over the procedure from an extremely grateful Treavey and his new friend who finally introduced himself as, "Jon. Jon Goodman."

It was over as soon as it had begun as his Superintendent was being moved onto the stretcher and being tied in by the paramedics. Treavey was keen to avoid the false adulation, so made a beeline for the station to carry on with his original plan for the day, but by now, he hoped he wouldn't be chastised for being a little late and looking a little sweaty.

He glanced out of the station window to watch the progress and was relieved to find the paramedics had Superintendent Steer secured on a stretcher and it looked as though the situation had improved somewhat. The sense of urgency was there but there was also a lifted spirit in the air. He had oxygen on his face, but no chest compressions any more. It seemed he had got to him in time.

"Diabetic" was one of the words flying around the briefing room as Treavey entered with some purpose with his head held high, now dressed in his black trousers, white shirt, black tie, and with heavy Dr Marten boots. His epaulettes were still looking shiny and new, even though they had already seen some adventures with him already. He longed for the day they were faded like the older officers who had been around the block a bit.

"Was he?" Treavey enquired.

"We think so, yes, according to the ambulance guys," replied Sooty, a friendly looking man, slim with blonde thinning hair already, even though only in his late 20's. Treavey was impressed with the air of experience and confidence about him. Some people exuded confidence. They just looked approachable. Treavey popped his pocket notebook and pen on the desk in front of him and took a rigid piece of card from the inside cover to neatly underline the date in it before sitting in readiness to see what his callsign was going to be for the day, and indeed who he was going to be crewed with.

"Good afternoon, all. Welcome to our new member today, all the way from Perranporth, PC 3908 Treavey. It seems he's already been quite busy saving the life of our

Superintendent today so well done you. It only goes downhill from here, hey Treavey?"

There were undertones of respect, but no one actually said very much to Treavey's relief, feeling slightly embarrassed at making such an entrance when he didn't really know anyone quite yet. Sergeant Andy Fox was a bean pole of a man, with jet black hair in no particular style and a bushy black moustache. He had the stature of a pencil, but he controlled the room. He had a kind face with dark eyes which glanced up from his notes and scanned the table of officers gathered around it.

"Right, quickly at it," Sergeant Fox shouted. "We have a firearms team sat up now at the post office. They have been at it all day and are waiting for the robbers to strike. I would have expected it to have happened by now but who knows what's going on. They were bristling with MP5s when they left here in their cars, and they are in plain clothes so don't go mistaking them for robbers will you? I suggest you stay out of their way if I were you."

Treavey was already happy he had made the move to Newquay. Even though he had had quite an exciting couple of years, he was excited to see what he would be involved in here in this vibrant holiday resort known for its beaches and surfing and its nightclubs and stag dos at night. It was the place to be as a young, keen, and fresh-faced cop.

Sergeant Fox turned his radio up and brought it towards his ear and listened intently to it. "They are requesting transport for some prisoners. The firearms teams have done a strike, and they need help with transporting their prisoners back. Treavey and Sooty, you take Golf 30 and head out there. I'd take the blue Escort if I was you, just to keep a low profile."

Sooty was up out of the chair grabbing his things together and clipping his Pye grey police radio to his waist belt and the top extension to his shirt tag. "Ready Treavey? We've got to go now."

Both officers were hurriedly walking through the corridor of the station swinging the door which leads into the reception area and out into the front car park where Sooty led Treavey to a pale blue Ford Escort looking rather weary and faded in the corner. "It's nothing much, mate, but it'll do. Chuck your bag in the boot 'cos we'll have passengers soon."

Treavey threw his bag of paperwork into the boot and slammed it shut, jumping into the front passenger seat, before Sooty spun the wheels of the little car through the loose gravel and headed left out of Newquay station cul-de-sac and towards the town centre post office on East Street. The two officers sat in silence for a moment. This was big stuff. They were actually going to pick up two armed robbers and take them into custody. What it must have felt to point those guns at criminals in the middle of a crowded high street on a mid-summer's day. What it must have been like to have loaded guns and your finger on the trigger. It was unimaginable.

"Why do they call you Sooty?" Treavey asked accepting it was down to him to break the silence.

"Sutton, my surname is Sutton. Not too much imagination with that one."

The car slewed around the corner of Mount Wise, a road whose entire length offered a view of Newquay Bay below it and was aligned with guest houses and hotels, but Sooty was only driving a little way along its length before he was careering down the long and narrow steep hill towards East Street. He squealed the wheels of the little Escort car around the bend to the right to head up towards the Post Office. The suspension wasn't quite up to the treatment it was receiving and was more designed for a weekly shopping trip to the supermarket by someone's grandmother, but police officers on the beat soon managed to adapt it in their minds to a high-performance vehicle. As they approached the location of the post office, they could see a melee grouped on the forecourt near the post office. The road was cordoned off with blue police tape, an impenetrable barrier in the minds of the onlookers who stared on in disbelief.

Sooty and Treavey got out of the car as nonchalantly as possible, trying to give the impression this was all in a day's work to them and if they were in the plain vehicle, they may seem more important than they actually were. He scanned the location in disbelief. There was still some disorder in the area with one man sitting handcuffed to the rear in the back of a police Ford Cosworth car with the rear passenger door wide open and a firearms officer in jeans and white T-shirt, with only a firearms police cap on his head to identify him from the robbers. Oh yes, and he had an MP5 machine gun strapped across his chest. Another officer dressed very similarly was pointing his pistol towards the back of another presumed robber who was lying flat on his stomach, straddling the pavement with his legs and arms open wide in a star shape. He wore a cheap looking tracksuit, had a bowl, curtain style haircut, and gave the impression of more of a sulky teenager than a hardened post officer robber. Treavey focused in on a handgun looking rather lonely on the ground a few metres from him, and the officer was telling him to remain still and not to move an inch. The stroppy teenager had decided to comply.

"Sooty, Jesus man, give us a hand will you and cuff this guy?" The officer was pointing the gun at the teenager still and shouted towards Sooty. Sooty jogged over, grabbing his handcuffs from his belt in readiness.

"You," the firearms officer pointed directly at Treavey with his free hand, "Go with the dog handler, he's picked a track up… he's headed down towards the Tram Track."

Treavey started running in the direction the officer had pointed in. His local knowledge of living in the town was going to be especially useful to him. He knew exactly where the tram track was. He skipped through the lines of people pushing each other for a better view. Treavey had popped his flat police cap on his head. He felt more authoritative with his cap, as he barged his way through a stubborn family blocking the way with pushchairs and surfboards.

He caught a glimpse of the dog handler disappearing down the small gateway which led to the tram track, a well-known local cut through along the coast where trams used to be pulled by horse carrying ore, coal, and other supplies to and from Newquay harbour. It enabled the traveller to move unseen through the town and contained a sorry tale of just a few years prior where police officers were chasing some suspects on foot through the very same place, but they were unfamiliar with the location and on seeing a waist high fence alongside, decided to jump over it to evade the pursuing officers. On doing so, they both will have had the fright of their short lives by then as they plummeted the 40 metres or so below to the waves below. Their bodies were recovered by police in the morning once the tide had receded.

Treavey skipped down the steps to the track and turned to follow the back of the handler who was being pulled by his dog towards the police station before diverting sharply up the very steep bank of the track. The handler was finding it difficult to negotiate so he let the lead out further so the dog could make its way without the hindrance of the dope on the rope at the other end, as the dog handlers affectionately called themselves when tracking with a dog. The dog is the intelligent one, after all.

"Dave, mate, you okay, how's it going?" Treavey had realised it was Dave from his Perran days as he covered large areas and it was good to see Finchy, his dog, working hard again.

"Hi Treavey mate, just as well he darted off up here...," he grunted as he negotiated a high wall to jump on to first to then climb further up a grass bank. "... cos any further along this tram track, the track would have been completely obscured by all the tourists. And one thing I know... no tourist has taken this route I am on now."

It looked as though the track headed towards the backs of some commercial premises and ironically in the same direction of the post office again. Maybe hiding in plain sight perhaps? Dave scrambled over the lip of the grass verge way above the head height of Treavey who felt obliged to follow. He knew he was going to get very messy as he dug his knee into the bank to get purchase, before heaving himself up and over the lip to follow Dave and Finchy.

Once on level ground again, Treavey had some catching up to do as he stumbled after Dave. Treavey had so much admiration for dog handlers and especially with those such as Dave who wouldn't let anything get in their way or stop them from getting their prey, because prey is indeed what they were. He marvelled at the dogs like Finchy, who was following the track of the Robber because he knew the reward of his dog chew would be awaiting if he were successful. That was the only incentive for the animal to pursue the criminal, often a dangerous criminal, but the dog was never perturbed and never put off by an obstruction or even a threat. He just wanted his toy.

The adventure continued through some abandoned looking rear gardens of some industrial looking buildings and then right up to the back door of what looked like an extension to a building which was separate from the main building. "This could be it", Treavey hoped as he and Dave approached with Finchy sniffing enthusiastically around the foot of the door, and along the base of the wall either side.

Dave wrapped his knuckles on the door to raise the attention of not only the occupant of the building but inadvertently, the surrounding neighbourhood too. Treavey updated the radio with where he thought they were, but it dawned on him he must be sounding quite vague as it was extremely difficult to judge the address of somewhere from the rear. To his surprise, Treavey saw the door open of the main building and a firearms officer ran through and right up to Dave, carefully negotiating Finchy as he did so. The door to the outbuilding eased open slightly and a sheepish looking character with the same dress sense as the man earlier peered through it. The firearms officer flung the door open and on seeing the gun, the man dropped to his knees and straddled on the ground.

The relief on Dave's face for finding the man was obvious and it was well deserved because to have a successful track in such a busy area was as rare as an honest thief, but the robber had done his level best to help Dave out by going in as few populated areas as possible.

Within ten minutes or so, more uniformed officers had worked their way through the front of the building to where Treavey and Dave were waiting with their quarry in their custody. Treavey had arrested the man to keep Dave and the firearms officer free and he knew it was an easy arrest as CID would be taking the job on anyway. This was a big job, and it was good to get a piece of it on his very first day in Newquay.

He ended up winding his way back to the police station in the back of a marked panda car, this time, sitting next to his arrestee. The young man was in his early 20's and looked thoroughly despondent and depressed. He saw the young man's relatively short adult life had been riddled with drugs. His yellow skin was sunken in around the structures of his skull. He did not look like your usual post office robber but as Treavey studied him, he felt for him a little. His life had gone in a bad direction and a lot of the time, people like this felt they had no other way out but to take a one-off risk to get money quickly, and to pay off the debt hanging around their necks, usually involving drugs of course.

Treavey booked the man into Custody, the Sergeant behind the desk treating the arrest like any other and showing little interest into the severity of the crime for a seaside town such as Newquay. It normalised the situation which relaxed Treavey, and once his man was booked in, he sauntered up the stairs from Custody back into the briefing and report room where he had started off his shift, and having selected a fresh sheet of statement paper, began writing his arrest statement.

He was not more than three quarters of a page down the front page when he saw a CID officer enter the report room. He was looking expectantly around and stopped his gaze on Treavey. "Arresting officer?"

"Yes, of one of them at least, I think his name is Daniel Squires." Treavey was feeling rather important for being an arresting officer of an armed robber. Even though it was the dog handler who found him, they didn't tend to want to get the arrest, so it saved them from becoming too tied up. They were always ready for deployment, and they could hardly say they were just finishing booking some chap in, when there was a badly needed track with a criminal at the end of it, waiting.

The CID officer looked satisfied as he gazed over the paperwork Treavey had started. "I'll be upstairs, I don't think I know you."

"Treavey."

"Good to meet you, I'm DC Adam Gee. Could you bring the statement up to me when you're done? Oh, and what was that chap's address in the end?"

Treavey scanned over the top of his statement and replied, "Flat 2b, 27 East Street," and continued to write, but his concentration was broken,

"It can't be. That's my main witness's address."

DC Gee stood in front of Treavey looking annoyed at the incompetence of Treavey giving him the wrong address.

"It definitely is. I know the address I followed the dog handler to, and that was it. Flat 2b, 27 East Street." Treavey replied with some certainty in his voice.

A puzzled DC Gee stared into middle space for a moment before saying in a particularly organic and gravelly voice, "I wonder, I wonder if our armed robber with a balaclava on his head showing on CCTV is actually the boyfriend of our post office employee witness? Well, well, well. Isn't it a small world?"

He ran back upstairs allowing Treavey to continue with his statement. Treavey quickly glanced around at the other officers left in the room. "How's the Super, anyone know? Did he make it?"

"Yes," came the reply. "He's believed to be stable now, reckon it was a diabetic coma or something." The officer continued writing his statement without turning his head.

It wasn't long before Treavey walked his two pieces of paper up the stairs to the CID office. This was considered the inner sanctum where much respect was laid before being invited in. Treavey had remembered coming into this office once before when he had just been in the job for a couple of years. He blushed as he remembered submitting a crime report for a burglary at a holiday chalet but with spelling not being his strong point, had spelt the word chalet as 'shalley.' It seemed sensible enough at the time but it wasn't sufficient that he had spelt it wrong just the once, the whole document had the word mentioned a dozen times, and so he had been summoned to the inner sanctum where the DS had swung his chair around to face him, peered over his spectacles and said, "PC TREAVE, could I suggest instead of criming this as a burglary, you, in fact, re-crime it as criminal damage of the English language?"

After a short pause, he broke into a smile and the room fell about laughing. Treavey had been relieved that much light-heartedness had been made of it, but at his expense of course, but it had made him feel accepted at the same time.

The welcome was a little more subdued this time as Treavey handed over the statement to DC Adam Gee who was half buried from an avalanche of paperwork. This is not what Treavey wanted to do for a job in the police, and he could never understand why some officers craved the role. He was far more interested in traffic work, and maybe even firearms if that was at all possible, but that was going to be sometime down the road.

Adam thanked him for his quick actions in arresting him and just as much for the statement. Treavey realised that if the dog handler hadn't got the track so accurately and just gone for it, even though there was little chance of success with the foot traffic in the area, then it could have been a nightmare trying to track the offender down, and if his girlfriend was involved, which it was very likely she was, then she could have got away with it as well as her boyfriend.

"It had very little, if anything to do with me though," Treavey insisted. "Dave and Finchy did the track and found him. He's sending his tracking statement to you in internal as he's got another job to go to now." He never saw the point in taking someone else's credit. He preferred to bask in any glory of his own, and only his.

Treavey's attention sparked up to the other side of the room where the DS was talking to another officer about the Superintendent who'd been found in his car. "No answer at his house, can't get hold of his wife and we have no idea where she is, either…"

Treavey was surprised to hear them talking as if something might be amiss. The DS, Geoffrey George Bates, was already a legend in the station and beyond. He was sitting back in his chair and Treavey noticed he breathed a deep sigh which seemed forced through his thickened neck. He was overweight, which seemed to add to his aura, and he had a bushy mousey coloured moustache with a simple tweed suit which rustled as he adjusted his bulk. It was known he enjoyed a bargain in suits but always managed to look smart. His voice was deep and gruff, and he came across as a formidable character, but he was very well respected by all who met him. He had a good tight grip on his team who were known as the most hard working in the station. Treavey was glad they were the ones on duty as he knew he wouldn't be fobbed off.

"The trouble is," the DS pondered as he looked up towards the ceiling thoughtfully before pausing and then,

"The trouble is, we can't be sure if it was an accident you see. Did he not take his insulin on purpose, but then why would he do it here if he had meant to end his life. Do we know what his marriage situation is?"

The other CID officer said he wasn't sure, but, he said, we owed it to him to try to find his wife as he was one of us and, after all, he would expect his colleagues to inform his relatives of him being in hospital, anyway. They discussed whether he had any close friends within the station or nearby, but the room was silent. There were no obvious friends or family to locate apart from his wife and no one knew where she worked. They would just have to wait.

Treavey risked being presumptuous by interrupting... "Or, or we could use his key on his car keys to enter his house to see if there are any clues as to where his wife could be? There's bound to be an address book, or something there, or maybe photographs of his wife which may help, for example at her place of work, if she's a nurse or such like. Maybe worth a punt."

The DS slowly swung his chair around at Treavey and stared at him for a second or two. The young CID officer waited next to him and glanced Treavey up and down disapprovingly, but DC GEE kept on writing without altering his gaze.

"We could do," the DS replied, "but then the question is, would we if it were for anyone else? If he's out of the woods, then what's the rush? No, we've put a note through the door for her to get in contact with us with the log number and we'll go from there. I'll leave instructions with Inspector Levey to organise someone to let themselves in if there's no answer by tonight. She could be away and on her way back, after all."

Treavey found himself volunteering before even realising what he was doing, "I can do that, Sarge. I'll liaise with Inspector Levey and get that sorted if there's no reply by then. I'm on Lates tonight."

Treavey ran downstairs jumping several steps at a time as he made his way back towards the report room to see if Sooty was there. He wanted to go out on the street as he was infused with adrenaline and motivation. Not knowing what was going to happen next was exciting and he couldn't wait. As he turned into the report room, Sooty was running out.

"You finished fannying about with CID yet, Treavey? Quick, move your backside.

We've got a job."

Chapter 2
Love and lifeboats at the Huer's Hut

Treavey about turned on his heels and followed Sooty back towards the car. It was hot still, and Treavey breathed in deeply to smell the summer day which had a distinct warm smell to it. There was the obvious coconut scented sun lotion, the resin of the wax used to rub on surfboards which was simply idyllic, although named 'Sex Wax' for a brainwave of a marketing ploy. Even the sand on the roads swirling about, added to the flavour and the atmosphere of Newquay, and the background sounds of chattering families laughing and giggling added to the summer theme of holidays and carefree times.

The car was baking hot as the windows had been closed so having jumped into the car, they delayed shutting the doors for a moment, before flicking the two-tone buttons on with the single blue light for what help it did to cut them through the traffic.

"Well?" Treavey asked.

"What?" Sooty replied. Treavey remained silent waiting for the penny to drop.

"Oh that. You want to know where we are going? Yes, we have a jumper on the cliff at the headland, just on from the huers hut."

Treavey remained a little confused. "Huers hut?"

"Yes, it's a white building, built in the 14th century don't you know." Sooty joked, as if everyone should know that. "It was used as a lookout to spot the shoals of pilchards in the bay, and then the locals would be guided out to them to catch them and land them on the beaches."

"Right," Treavey acknowledged, grateful for the history lesson, but more interested in the job, "So is it a popular place to jump?"

Sooty negotiated a group of slow-moving pedestrians meandering across the road minding their own business, his police car was hidden to them by some surfboards they were carrying so he gave them a burst of two tones. They visibly jumped and Sooty gave a little chuckle in response. "Not really, no, it's not very high there, but there are some very jagged rocks there. There have been a few anglers fishing from those rocks who have been washed in and they rarely make it out again. Fortunately, the lifeboat from Newquay harbour is always on hand."

Sooty gazed up at two puffs of smoke which disturbed the perfect deep blue sky, created by the Lifeboat maroons being let off to call the lifeboat men to arms. Treavey was well aware of them, having been born and brought up in the town. The maroons had been used for over a century by the lifeboat and they would always create a feeling of excitement with the locals who never got bored of searching them out in the skies. Especially if heard on a winter's night with storm force winds and rain battering the windows of the cottages on the top of the cliffs. Treavey had grown up above Lusty Glaze Beach, and his father, much older than the average father of Treavey's age one would expect, would take him as a 10-year-old into the middle of the storm at the top of the cliff to measure the force of the wind with a special instrument he had. It had a tube he pointed into the wind, and a flap which raised with the various wind strengths and the gauge could be read. Both Treavey and his dad always hoped for the 'hurricane' to be reached, but he couldn't ever remember it being achieved.

The panda car was screaming along Mount Wise as if it was complaining at the stress it was being put through. It was a one-way road running along the top of the town which allowed a wonderful view of the coastline and bay to their right. Treavey couldn't believe he was lucky enough to work in this wonderful place and yet, as well as have the holiday feel and be able to drop down to the beach any time after work, he also had the excitement and adrenaline that any young man would want. For Cornwall, the wages weren't bad either for someone of his young age, who was on the same wages as a police officer in other very dingy city areas further up country. It was only in London where you would receive a little more money because of the expense of living there or the expense of having to commute such long distances.

The two officers travelled down Tower Road past the parish church and towards the harbour. Treavey watched the buildings flash past; mainly guest houses, and family hotels, along with some very small fishermen's cottages, all making the place feel like a little part of heaven. Then swinging left towards the Huers hut but suddenly having to come to a crawl as surfers and families made their way back to their guest houses after the summer day on the beach and in this case, the famous surfing champion beach of Fistral. Yet, whilst people enjoyed the idyllic setting and were busy making their family memories with their small children with buckets and spades, followed by ice cream, there was always the hint of reality in the background that Treavey and his colleagues had to deal with. Somewhere on the top of a cliff nearby, there is a woman standing there who feels she has nothing to lose. Through all this positive feeling and taking in the aura of the wonderful coastline, beaches and sea, there is depression and despair, and it was Treavey and his colleagues who were the only ones who would stand between them and their desperate intention.

Instead of turning left towards Fistral Beach, Sooty continued up towards the Atlantic Hotel, a huge white impressive building which took on the elements on the top of a headland which jutted impressively out into the ocean. Built solidly, it looked as though it had stood there since time began and would have served several generations of Newquay visitors. The sirens were switched off for a silent approach, the single blue light set in the centre of the little car's roof, turned off, and the revs of the car reduced as they knew they were getting near to the woman, and they didn't want to push her into a sudden move they might all regret.

Sooty pulled up near to the Huers Hut where there was a group of five middle-aged adults congregating with concerned expressions. The officers got out of their car and calmly walked towards the group to see what the update was and indeed, they saw, about 20 feet below them, a woman standing precariously on the edge of a ledge above a fall onto jagged rocks. The sea was a broth of churning white foam and powerful green whirlpools which would pick off a human like a toothpick plucking pieces of meat from a cavity. It would drag them into the depths with enough time for the crabs to remove the softer fleshier parts of the lifeless corpse. The eyes first, and then the skin between the thumb and index finger. It would have taken some courage to jump from that ledge, but often people felt it was worth the few seconds of fear to remove the unbearable stresses within their lives and end it all in an instant. But it was so final, and often people who had survived falls were glad they lived, as they had felt regrets as soon as they were falling. It was all so final, and they felt there was always room for one more go at life.

    Treavey saw there was another person talking to her from a little distance off. A woman, in her mid-twenties, and it looked like they had a rapport together. Whilst there was some dialogue, they didn't want to change the mood in case she used it as a reason to jump so they looked on with the group above. Nothing could be heard from where they were standing however, so Sooty asked Treavey to scramble down slowly and talk with the young woman who was negotiating with the girl in distress. Sooty would find out more information about the girl and pass it back to Treavey to help with negotiations, but if he could find out her name and how old she was, they may be able to find out who she was and the reason she had found herself in this situation. That was the first stage in offering any solution to her dangerous predicament.

Treavey carefully made his way towards the good Samaritan who had involved herself in her negotiations by walking further down the road at first and taking a small path to their location. He moved slowly and made sure his radio was turned down, so it didn't break the peace. As he slowly plodded through the yellow gorse flowers and heathers, he could hear with perfect clarity the sound of bumble bees bobbing from one brightly coloured yellow flower to another and then another. The high-pitched rhythmic tweets from the birds darting about the vegetation shot through the calm tranquillity like a laser gun, and something came up into Treavey's mind which he suddenly felt guilty for. "It's a nice day to die."

Usually reserved for motorbike riders who came down to Cornwall in the summer, and who didn't know the roads, full of the zest of being on holiday, it was usually the slowest, being pushed to ride at the speed of the most skilled, who became a cropper. A seasoned traffic cop had said that to Treavey once, at the scene of yet another motor collision they had attended.

Treavey was getting reasonably close to her, but the final part was going to be the tricky bit. The intricate path was narrow and even though he felt quite safe walking along it, he was worried about the reaction of the girl on the ledge if he tried to get too close too quickly. The sea salt from the fine spray filled his nostrils. It was like a thin mist which coated his skin, cooling the baked surface from the sun. It was wonderfully refreshing. He was enjoying the moment and felt awkward doing so, but it didn't stop him from taking a momentary gaze around him. The coastline of Newquay stretched before him.

There was the familiar line of white foam between the crystal deep crimson blues and emerald greens of the sea with darkened areas cast by the clouds above and the sand and cliffs beyond the crashing of the waves on the shore below. And then there was another watercolour palette of blues from the skies beyond producing a stunningly beautiful vista. Treavey checked off the beaches one by one; Great Western, Lusty Glaze, Porth, Whipsiderry, Watergate Beach before he lost sight of any more, all the way to Trevose lighthouse at the furthest point just south of Padstow hidden beyond. The white contrails from aircraft 35,000 feet above on route to the states patterned the sky with streaks of white, as if someone had slashed a knife across the blue painted canvas. He felt awkward as he found himself standing there breathing in the view. He had a job to do after all.

He approached the back of the young woman who had worked herself towards the terrified and desperate victim. Treavey didn't know whether to think of her as a casualty or a victim. A potential casualty if she was to jump into the pounding waves below and there was little they could do until the lifeboat had arrived, and even that would find it difficult to negotiate the angry jagged black rocks. The water was offering a temptation to jump before receding again, exposing the deadly rocks, so any tempted victim was caught and snapped up like a fly unsuspectingly wandering into a Venus fly trap. Or was she a victim of circumstance, of society perhaps. Whatever had brought her up on to these cliffs, Treavey knew if he managed to tell her off them, then it was only a delay to another incident waiting to happen if she didn't receive some sort of long-term help.

He stepped up to the woman who was negotiating and crouched down beside her to get a sense of how the negotiations were going.

"I have a dog too. He'd be really upset if I wasn't here anymore, Jane."

The conversation was at a simplistic level which can often work best. Dogs were an attachment with the person so instilling a feeling of love and loyalty with something such as a dog, could give some time to get a rapport with someone; Treavey was impressed so far. He sat there patiently until the woman he was sitting next to, turned around to him, and said, "Oh hi!"

The sight of her hit him like a bomb shell blast. She was stunningly beautiful. Early 20's, glossy auburn hair, and a tanned freckled face with flakes of sea salt on her skin and she had the most dazzling blue eyes. Oh, those eyes had Treavey quite speechless for a second, before he could pull himself together and reply, "Er, hi!"

That was all he could muster for a moment or two and he knew it sounded a bit lame. She was wearing very feminine floral shorts which exposed some cheek as she crouched. A simple navy-blue vest with no bra underneath, finished her refinery off. Very simple styling. She was dressed for the beach and looked very much like a free spirit.

"Thanks for what you have been doing so far. Appreciated. What's your name?"

"Claire," she replied with a cheerful smile, her teeth gleamed, and her freckles lit up as the sun hit her cheeks and reflecting off the salt. She went on, "I'm not sure how I am getting on to be honest, I don't seem to be making much progress. She's saying she needs help with her mental health, and she keeps having bad thoughts, but she can't get any help."

"Okay, you are doing really well, Claire, if you don't mind, I think you are doing really well for the moment, and it may be better if you are able to continue if you are alright with that. I will cut in if we think it isn't working if that's alright?"

"Yeah, sure, I'll keep trying but I'm not convinced she will listen to anyone right now."

Treavey felt the warmth from the sun hitting his back before the coolness of a wave rushed in the swirling blast of air which almost chilled him. He was still only in his shirt and was a little concerned with when the sun would dip below the headland and cast them into shadow.

Jane was showing no signs of coming back from near the ledge, but Treavey knew things could develop very quickly either way. He glanced over to his left and saw the inflatable lifeboat bobbing 100 metres away. It had managed to get there unseen and allowed the negotiations to continue, but ready to pounce if needed.

And suddenly it happened. Jane straightened her posture and simply stepped off the ledge. She stumbled awkwardly as she fell and plummeted down to the water below. Claire gasped as she hit the water, grazing her left arm off a rock before she disappeared below the water which had swept over her.

There was stunned silence for a moment after the initial shrieks of onlookers leaning on the railing above and Treavey instinctively stood up to move into action, but he realised there simply was nothing he could do to help the situation. The high-pitched whine of the lifeboat outboard engine became louder and louder as the rubber boat with four individuals wearing orange suites on board raced towards the scene below them. The boat seemed to skid to a halt as the front end buried itself into the water and the occupants searched for signs of life at the base of the cliffs. The woman's head came into view with an audible gasp for air before disappearing below once more, her fight to stay on the surface hindered by her broken arm. The lifeboat crew raced into action spinning on a sixpence, white foam jettisoned out from the rear as the front end raised once more and turned to face the location of where Jane had last been spotted, the lead lifeboat woman extending her arm straight out pointing in the direction they needed to travel.

Treavey was holding on to the shoulder of Claire, not only to keep her safe, but to steady himself too as he peered over. Claire's face was ashen. She was in shock at what she'd just experienced. She'd only come to have a walk along the headland after all, and now she was witnessing the most horrible traumatic incident unfolding in front of her.

"I didn't think she'd do it. I didn't think she'd do it." She repeated in disbelief.

The water was angrier than ever, spitting white sputum high into the air and churning like a volcano of molten lava, occasionally giving a hint of possible rescue of its latest victim before dragging her down in a pink glow of salt water and blood.

Treavey's view was blocked by the bow of the boat being thrown between the unforgiving rocks in one last ditched effort, with one of the lifeboat crew, the same woman, fearlessly leaning far over the edge whilst her colleagues kept her within the boat by her legs, and as the boat withdrew, this heroic woman held on to Jane whilst the boat was pulled back to clear water, relieving her of her watery grave to be.

Once clear, there was a struggle as two further crew helped pull the deadweight of a water-logged Jane back into the boat and after an initial pause whilst they stabilised her arm and wrapped her with blankets, turned the boat to head for Newquay harbour. In a flash, they were gone, but a dot on the horizon, and all that was left were the crowd above around the Huer's hut with Sooty next to them, and Claire crouching with Treavey. They watched the dot disappear in silence and then looked at each other.

Claire had a tear rolling down her cheek and Treavey found himself wiping it away with his finger. He felt embarrassed and apologised. "No, no, it's okay. It was just so scary." she replied, "I didn't expect that to happen. How do you do your job?"

Treavey helped her up by the hand and led the way back to the road. "Can I grab your details, Claire? You see, if she…" he hesitated as he realised it was bringing the enormity of the situation to the forefront. "… if she dies, then there will be an inquest. I may need to get a statement from you?"

"Yes, of course." She replied. Treavey stared at the dazzlingly blue eyes of the young woman gleaming in front of him, and her freckles on her bronzed cheeks caught his attention once again. He knew he liked this girl. He liked her a lot and he hadn't felt like this since he had been flirting around with Felicity back in Perranporth, but nothing had gone any further from that, unfortunately, probably because he had chickened out and she had got fed up waiting for him to make a pass at her. This was different though. He couldn't really ask Claire out. She was in a vulnerable state, and he was in a position of authority, and she could be a main witness in a Coroner's court who had just been through an extremely traumatic experience. He would have her phone number and her address but there was nothing he could do with the details unless it was part of the job.

"Can I take a quick statement off you, so we have something now. It would be really useful?" He knew he was being a little cheeky, but he would come across as an efficient and dedicated officer to CID for producing a standby file in case Jane died, but in fact Treavey was going to enjoy every second staying in the presence of Claire, whilst basking in the sun on that cliff edge. And what a place to write it, too.

"Yes, of course, that would be fine. I'm in no rush. Where shall we do it?" She had perked up already which made Treavey feel slightly less guilty for delaying her. She looked as though she was happy to be with Treavey, but he didn't kid himself. It was probably because she wanted to talk about it to get it clear in her head, not because she fancied him. He would make sure he didn't overstep the mark with this one and, after all, an hour now would save a lot of messing about trying to arrange a mutual time for a statement later, if indeed Jane did die, and the evidence will be fresher too. That's how Treavey pacified himself, anyway.

PC Jon Goodman arrived in his panda car to see what the fuss was about. "You're a bit too late Jon, I'm afraid," Sooty pointed out to a very inquisitive Jon who was appearing over a mound of thrift at the top of the cliff.

"Did they save her?" asked an anguished Jon.

"Yes, they did," replied Sooty, "but we don't know what condition she's in, so we'll have to wait. Treavey is going to stay here with Claire and take a statement. Can you take me back to the station so I can get on with my paperwork?"

"Sure, good idea," replied Jon. "I love coming up here to the Huer's hut anyway. Isn't it beautiful looking out from here?" Jon stood rigid with his head back and his hands on his hips, gazing out to sea across the deep blue water and across to the headlands on the other side of Newquay Bay. "You know they used to guide the fishing boats to the shoals of pilchards from here, back in the 14th Century." Jon paused and checked himself, looking around noticing several stragglers listening to him. He smiled with embarrassment and headed for his car with Sooty following.

"Thanks for the history lesson, Jon," Sooty joked.

Treavey made himself comfortable on a grass verge looking out over the cliff and watching a couple of gulls twisting and diving through the air, perilously near to the cliff side whilst squabbling over a piece of food one of them had found, probably something discarded from a tourist rather than a 14th century pilchard. Claire sat closer to Treavey than he expected which he liked but he also felt a little uncomfortable as he could see he was the main attraction to the tourists, sitting there in his white shirt and clip on tie, his black heavy thick trousers and his police cap laid neatly beside him.

He patted his pocket to ensure he had the car keys as he watched Jon and Sooty drive off over the hill and arranged his statement paper using his index book as a firm surface to write on. He noticed Claire flick her hair to the side and brush it around her ear whilst she glanced out to sea watching a fishing boat with a flock of seagulls pestering it as it made its way back to harbour. Treavey caught himself staring as the wind caught her hair and swished it back again across her face. She turned her head directly at Treavey looking him straight in the eye just as the wind filled her auburn hair and flew it up above her head and back over her freckles once more, and she beamed with the brightest of smiles which caused Treavey to blush uncontrollably. He pulled his biro out from his case and took the lid off the end trying to avoid looking at her smooth and perfectly bronzed bare legs lying right next to him. "Right, so it's Claire...?"

"Oh yes, Claire Norris," she waited for Treavey to complete the name on the top of the statement paper and continued, "my date of birth is... 21st February 1970."

Treavey was away and in his flow with the beginning of the statement. "I am the above person and live at the address overleaf," he muttered under his breath. "You see, we don't put your address on the front of the statement because defence solicitors get copies, and we don't want all and sundry knowing your address."

Over the next hour and a half, he completed a very full account of the event that afternoon on that cliff. He had 5 pages finished and suspected there were at least 2 pages there because he enjoyed being in her company so much, but it was a worthwhile exercise too as they had got the evidence right from the scene and at least the job was finished. Treavey knew it was highly unlikely he would see her again unless he bumped into her in the supermarket or similar, but then what were the chances of that, and then what were the chances of her liking him, too? He probably reminded her of an awful event she may never get over, especially if Jane died, so it was more likely she would rather forget him.

Treavey offered Claire a lift home, but she declined and walked off towards the end of the headland, a walk she had intended to do a couple of hours earlier but had been delayed through attempting to save Jane's life. He continued watching her walking away. He pretended he was looking past her at the view but was really enjoying watching her athletic and slight figure skipping over the heather and tufts of grass with her bottom cheeks bouncing in her floral shorts. "If she looks around, then it proves she likes me just a little bit, maybe..."

Much to his delight, she glanced around at him and with a twinkle in her eye, displaying a smile and giving a friendly wave, she spun back around with a spring in her step and continued on her way.

Treavey chose to drive his panda through the town as opposed to taking the small ring road, back to the station. He enjoyed a bit of people watching and he knew he would be in the station for a while when he got back. He wanted to get his papers back to CID so there was some handover available if Jane died during the night as he was off tomorrow and he didn't want any phone calls on his day off.

It was getting on in the shift now, and Treavey was thrilled it had been such an exciting one for his first day and it wasn't even over yet. He made his way to the kitchen to get himself a cup of tea. None of the other officers were there and he had been split from his crew mate, Sooty, so he felt a little bit of a loose end. He stirred his instant coffee in the mug with the hot water and opened the fridge to get some milk. He didn't know the rules of the milk here and it wasn't clear which milk he was able to use yet. There were some with an elaborate home-made locking system on and another in a baby bottle marked, 'Breast Milk.' "Genius!" Treavey thought, as he nodded in respect to the owner of the milk who had thought of that one. It was highly likely it was ordinary milk, but no one was going to risk stealing it in case it was. Unless you like that sort of thing, of course. Treavey chuckled to himself as he slowly made his way back to the report room.

The station was relatively quiet. The main radio set was chirping away with the police channel across Newquay. He could tell by the tone and lack of urgency in their voices there was nothing too exciting going on. He felt content. So much had happened already, and he hoped it would continue that way. He gazed over the walls at the strange faces looking back at him. The wall was covered with photos of suspected criminals with an index card below each, outlining their address and what crimes they were involved in. Usually drugs, burglary, and anti-social behaviour. He smiled as he'd seen something on TV recently where they were talking about a concept at the beginning of the century where they thought they could tell a criminal from the bone structure in their face. Looking at these people, Treavey could understand why they had seriously considered it. They couldn't look more criminal, and remembering some of the previous books of mug shots from many years ago in Perranporth when he was there, a criminal did seem to look very much like a criminal. Case closed, he thought.

Treavey wandered over to the other side of the room and saw a photo of a police night out on the wall. A section of officers he hadn't met yet were photographed mid-celebration at The Sailors night club and yet... they also looked very much like criminals too. Treavey felt he should correct his prejudices on seeing the photo and tried to imagine one of the criminals well-groomed, fresh-faced and with a private education behind them. How may he have turned out? What sort of person would he have been? What would Treavey be doing now if he had been born in an East End London council estate? Who knows, but he realised it was pure lucky circumstances that allowed him to live in such a beautiful area with the comforts he had. Okay, he worked hard for it all too, it wasn't all for free. Some people had it all and didn't do anything with it, and some started with little and worked their way out of their situation. There was no simple answer, he knew that. He wanted to ensure he didn't assume anything with people though. He wanted to try to treat everyone as though they could have been something special even if they weren't.

The radio came alive, and the operator said, "Golf 33, can you attend Bank Street, there's a couple of vagrants, Gary Bond and Laura Neace playing up again."

"Bloody vagrants at it again," Treavey thought before he realised, he'd already broken his new pact to himself.

"His wife's only gone missing, hasn't she?" came a booming voice from a red faced, PC Goodman striding into the report room with some gusto.

"Whose wife?" asked an inquisitive Treavey.

"The Super's wife, the one whose chest you were bouncing on earlier today, Treavey. They've tried to contact her but she's missing, and the house is insecure. It's all looking rather suspicious now."

Treavey was surprised it was still the same day all this had happened. "So, you mean he may have done her in? Seriously?"

"Yeah, who knows mate. She's gone missing and he's in a diabetic coma. All a bit weird really, if he knew to check his bloods then how come he got it so wrong? Gossip around the place has said they haven't been getting on recently. You never know what's going on behind closed doors, mate. You never know."

The two chatted for a few minutes more; Treavey was inquisitive to find out what the plan was and whether the Superintendent was a suspect.

"No, I don't think so, not yet. I was talking to DC Gee, and he said there were too many unanswered questions. They are having a look around the Super's house to see if there are any clues to where she is. There's been some sort of disturbance though."

Was this day ever going to stop surprising him?

Chapter 3
Turning up the heat

Just a couple of days later, Treavey walked from his home where he was renting a room in Lusty Glaze Road. He was fortunate to get it as it was near to where he was brought up and was on the coast road. It afforded him the most beautiful views of the cliffs to the North and of the Atlantic swells. It was another super summer's day and it felt good to be alive. There was a lot of speculation and gossip going on in the station with the Superintendent's wife having gone missing. He was back at work, but his wife hadn't turned up. It was all rather strange, and some were more than suggesting he had murdered her and disposed of the body already, and then tried to induce a coma on himself with his diabetes. Treavey didn't fall for this, however. Why would he have done it in a police station car park where there was a lot of foot traffic about? He hadn't seen the Superintendent since the incident, but it was going to happen soon, and it would be interesting to see his reaction.

This was a day to relax. The sky was a gorgeous deep blue with light fluffy cumulus clouds hanging static above the deep green Barrow Fields which Treavey was crossing with his bag containing a towel and not much else. With the sea to his right, looking its most inviting best, he was marching towards the other side of town to a beach called Fistral, renowned for being the best beach in the capital of the surfing world. Or perhaps just the UK, but the quality of the waves, even when smaller than some overseas locations, were enough to attract the interest of the most respected and experienced surfers. Treavey regularly peered over the steep jagged cliffs towards the golden sands below and listened to the distant shrieks of joy of the children jumping the chilly white frothing waves relentlessly sweeping through from the depths to the shoreline before disappearing into the sand forever. It felt good to be alive. A glance ahead of him revealed the numerous other beaches of choice for him, and the harbour where little sailing boats such as Mirrors, Toppers and Lasers made little progress through the water, but they perfected the idyllic scene before him all the same.

He walked through the town, past Woolworths where he purposefully avoided eye contact with the now familiar faces of Gary and Laura, the vagrants who had been causing trouble a few days before, but who were now dozing with a can of cider slopping next to them. Walking down the road towards the vast beach which stretched for what seemed miles ahead of him, he pondered where he would choose to put his towel and opted to find an area in the sand dunes which protected him from the breeze, and that he felt was slightly out of the way of running children and busy families organising their beach equipment, sandwiches, and beach balls. The sounds of wooden mallets used to beat the windbreak posts into the sand occasionally broke into the background sounds of the sea and screams of delight from the children.

Treavey found what he considered to be the perfect place hidden in the folds of the long grasses whose roots were holding the sand dunes together. It was his perfect oasis, his own little island where he could catch some sun rays and turn his still pale tones hopefully into a gorgeous bronze. This was the look to have in a place like Newquay and was the badge to show you were a local, but it was often difficult to achieve if you had a job such as policing where so much of the time was spent in a car, in an office or sleeping off a night shift. Some sunbathing was required, even if combined with some sleep catch-up if that what was urgently needed.

He settled himself and enjoyed the sense of paradise he was feeling with the heat on his skin, with just enough soft cool breeze gently cooling him to stop him from getting too hot. He closed his eyes and listened to the holiday soundtrack of people having fun, sea, and the occasional crescendo of a screeching cry of a herring gull celebrating the day.

"Hey Treavey! Do you mind if we join you? My friend and I don't want to be disturbed by guys if we sunbathe together on our own. Do you mind?"

Treavey opened his eyes and raised his Oakley sunglasses off the bridge of his nose to see a girl he'd never met before, but then another he most certainly had. "Claire! Oh wow, I mean, yes of course, no problems at all. It's good to see you."

"This is the cop I was talking to you about." Claire said to her friend who she introduced to Treavey as Bronwyn.

The girls settled down behind Treavey so their heads were almost together, but their beautiful slim and already brown sunbathing bodies were in opposite directions to Treavey so he couldn't easily view them. He realised they wished to stay together but still separate from him and he didn't know whether to feel flattered he'd been asked or insulted that he was seen as a safe person to be with who would never chat them up.

He lay there listening to them chatting away. It was calming and he was enjoying this moment. He was with Claire and needed to chat with her, but what about and would she think he was precisely doing the thing she was trying to avoid? He had to say something.

"Hey Claire, did you hear the result of Jane at all? I never got an update."

"Yes, I did," she warmly replied. "She's meant to be doing okay. Physically at least. Who knows what's going through someone's mind to make them jump off a cliff, poor love."

Treavey concurred and chatted about how they rarely got to hear about any results in court, either until the papers published the results or they heard from word of mouth. It may seem crass, but he had moved on from an incident by the following day as there was usually something just as exciting or desperate by then, and sometimes it seemed just too much trouble trying to convince someone in an office you were a police officer over the phone to find out any further details.

Treavey turned over from his back onto his front, so he was facing the girls who were laying on their backs. He perched himself up on his elbows and, "Jesus, they're topless!".

He shuffled uneasily like an embarrassed schoolboy having been caught looking at the underwear models in a Kays Catalogue by his mother.

He adjusted his Oakleys and rested his head on the backs of his hands he'd made a pillow with and lay there slightly uncomfortably, not with the sight he'd just seen, but physically. 'Oh no!' he thought to himself. 'What if they think I'm lying on my stomach for a different reason. Oh know, what should I do?'

Treavey shifted over onto his back again and thought the whole thing was very childish of him and as they were adults, he shouldn't be thinking about it in this way, or perhaps… yes perhaps they were just teasing him, knowing he would feel awkward. But they definitely felt comfortable with him, they'd proven that. Hopefully not too comfortable though. He didn't want to be thought of as a brother figure for them.

Treavey jumped to his feet looking down on them square on and said, "You okay girls, I'm going for a dip, you okay there or fancy coming down too?"

"You go, Claire, I'll look after the stuff, I don't mind." Bronwyn was a heroine in Treavey's mind right now. 'Thank you, thank you, thank you' he muttered ever so quietly, and watched Claire get up and reach for her bikini top. She had the most perfectly slim and tanned body but with the palest of bosoms. She had a body to die for and he knew he would be in heaven if he ever got to be close to her. She didn't seem to mind what Treavey saw, probably because she was quite proud of how she looked. He tried not to gawp at her beautifully formed ski sloped breasts jiggling as she organised her sea blue bikini top before turning around to fasten it. A little too late to hide her modesty at that point.

Treavey and Claire skipped down the sand dunes towards the main beach with Treavey feeling like he was on an awkward first date. Surely, she wouldn't have agreed to follow him to the sea on her own if she didn't like him like that. Or was it that she felt safe because he was a police officer?

Treavey was feeling full of the joys of life and wanted to prove his masculinity and fearless nature so darted off towards the water just a few metres in front. He immediately regretted doing it as he realised, he was not going to be able to bail out if the water proved to be too cold to handle so he was just going to have to dig deep and go for it. Having got up to his waist in freezing cold Atlantic water, and even with a touch of tepid gulf stream to dilute the bitterness, he thought he would go for a dramatic dive under the next wave, knowing full well Claire would be gazing on with full admiration, or so he hoped.

He dived under the water and felt good with his efforts. Straight back and legs and pointed toes like an arrow disappearing under the wave as it rolled over him. He surfaced the other side of the wave for air and realised to his surprise how much brighter the world had become compared to just a few seconds earlier. He looked around him a little confused and the penny dropped. He ploughed his fingers in the water around him and then underneath to try to locate his very expensive Oakley sunglasses, his finesse and grace in the water turning to a lashing panic of limbs breaking up the water's surface in the hope his fingers would glance across the sunglasses but they were gone forever, and probably never to be seen by human eyes again, or perhaps being worn by some lucky tourist the following day once they'd been washed up on shore.

Treavey wasn't in the mood for any more swimming and turned around to see whether Claire had witnessed the entire episode.

"Oh dear," she simply replied with some awkwardness, not knowing what else to say but trying to think of something quickly, "Were they expensive?"

Treavey could almost feel his mother scolding him, "That will teach you to show off to your friends," he could hear her saying, waving her finger at him. There was nowhere he could hide his embarrassment from Claire let alone mourn the loss of his expensive glasses.

"Bugger!" he exclaimed, and that simple word seemed to do the trick. "So, are we going in or what?" Treavey grabbed Claire's hand and pulled her towards the waves, and having been caught in a vice-like grip, all Claire could do was scream and giggle uncontrollably, the same as if she was being mercilessly tickled as she made vain attempts to pull free of his grasp. The situation was recovered as they both fell over a charging wave with more power than its predecessors which threw them over in the most undignified manner.

Claire scraped her hair back which had draped like seaweed across her face, still desperately trying to look feminine and delicate in her manner but it was all lost. They had got to know each other so much better in those last few steps, and things were hopefully going to be different between them now.

Treavey felt a cold shiver as he walked up through the soft sand looking for a subtle landmark of an extra tall tuft of dunes with a sandy pathway leading up to where they had placed their towels with Bronwyn. "Er, Claire…" He paused for a moment trying to find the courage to speak further. He found it almost impossible to force the words out, as if fighting for oxygen, but then, "Are you single?"

"Yes," came the instant reply, almost as if expected. "But I'll be honest with you, I like you and stuff, but I want to have a bit of me time for a moment. It's not been long since I've come out of a relationship, so I want to have some time to myself, you know?"

"I've done exactly what you didn't want, haven't I?" Treavey said with some embarrassment. "You wanted to escape being chatted up and I've just gone and done that, and I interviewed you as a witness. I feel terrible, I'm so sorry."

Claire placed her hand on his arm and smiled, "No really, any other time, but not at the moment, okay?" Her voice ended on a lift as an Australian would speak, which made her statement sound more of a friendly and genuine question.

"Yes, of course, absolutely. It was nice throwing you in the sea anyway. I can take that away with me at least!"

Claire removed her bikini top again and sat next to Bronwyn, which made Treavey feel as though little had changed. She still felt safe with him so that was comforting. The day drew on, and after another couple of swims they parted and headed their separate ways.

Treavey enjoyed the walk back to his home in Lusty Glaze. No taxi was needed, no bus required. It was blissful to think of the day's events whilst breathing in the views around him, and watching the tourists and locals surfing in Towan Beach, then through the Tram Track where the unfortunate youths had fallen to their deaths some years before, and on past Tolcarne Beach where the main road and path was immediately adjacent to a sheer drop down onto the beach below.

He gazed down on the beach huts with alternating-coloured doors neatly placed around the perimeter of the beach, and deck chairs being fought with by users attempting to swiftly put them up with some grace, but inevitably all dignity was lost within seconds and another person would wander over to offer some help.

Treavey had seen it all before over the years. As he walked on with the heat of the day dispersing, he thought about his experience with Claire. He had made a friend, but he wanted more. He also appreciated that she needed some time out, so friends it was going to have to be. For some reason, his experiences with Felicity from his couple of years in Perranporth came flooding back. He'd had the same warm feeling with her, but he'd never made the move and he was ashamed of his lack of courage to ask her out. He had missed out and would regret it forever. Looking back all Felicity's clues were there but he had let them go as he had been frozen with shyness. He had been a coward, and women don't like cowards. For God's sake, she had actually kissed him on his lips before moving away and he still hadn't taken her up on it. He'd felt the same with Claire and without knowing it at the time, had taken the next step of asking her whether she was single. At least he was making progress, even if the reply had been disappointing.

It was his first night shift later that night, so he was going to have a shower, get something to eat and relax until the start of his shift at ten. He'd have four hours before he had to get ready for work. Thinking ahead, he couldn't contemplate how he was going to get through the shift as he felt tired after the day doing next to nothing on Fistral, yet it had taken it out of him. Nervous energy would get him through, perhaps. Strangely it was usually the second night shift which was the killer. If it wasn't a busy night, it could be a struggle to get through. Treavey always tried to get a drink driver or a similar simple offence to deal with just after 2am, as that would keep him motivated with perfect timing for a hand-over or file completed just prior to the end of the shift at 7am, when it was time to go home.

The time came around far too quickly and Treavey dragged himself into the shower to wake himself up. He dressed in his uniform with a padded brown soft leather jacket over the top. He made his usual brown bread sandwiches with strong cheddar cheese and Branston pickle. He had tried other fillings, but they had never hit the mark compared to the tautness of the cheese combined with the tangy sourness of the pickle. He jumped into his BMW he was so proud of. The 318i was his pride and joy. It had a very subtle rubber spoiler on the back and a roof rack for surf boards and simply looked the business. The surfboards were rarely put on the roof but, maybe one day he would get into it a bit more. He felt at work already in his highly polished heavy black boots, his thick black trousers which were far from suitable for a hot summer's day, so he was grateful he was on a cool night shift. He felt like he was on the set of The Bill whilst wearing his leather jacket with his white police shirt and tie underneath. He felt invincible right now, and ready to take on Newquay on a summer evening. He hoped it wasn't going to be a let-down.

The keys were thrown across the table at Treavey and he was up and out of the station as fast as he could, having picked up the breathalyser from the shelf with his radio and ensuring the radio battery was fully charged. He was single crewed which he liked. He could do his own thing and go where he liked. It was nice to mix it sometimes, but there was always someone an officer would prefer not to have to spend a whole shift with. This cut that awkwardness out. Treavey was out on the prowl and determined to get a good arrest tonight. First call, here it comes.

"Golf 31, good evening. Could you make your way to the A3058 somewhere between St Columb Minor and Quintrell Downs? There's a broken-down car causing a bit of an obstruction. We've had a couple of calls now."

It was hardly the start he was hoping for. He sat in the marked police Ford Escort and gazed out of the windscreen for a bit, before he selected first gear, slipped the clutch, and approached the junction just outside of the station. On turning right along Narrowcliff, he flicked the switch for his blue light and another for the two tones. He was on his way and was going to enjoy the drive out to the location at any rate.

It was dark now and the blue was flashing around the buildings on his right-hand side, but to his left there was little apart from the Atlantic Ocean and the depths beyond for the light to be absorbed within, and then the blue mixed with the green of the Barrow Fields, before Treavey negotiating some traffic and heading off along Henver Road out of town past St Columb and out in search of the broken-down car.

A couple of minutes later, he came across the said vehicle, parked badly on the side of a slight left hand bend, this caused cars to break suddenly before negotiating their way around it. It could have been nasty, but now Treavey had arrived he thought with his singular roof beacon guarding the scene, it was like a lighthouse warning surrounding shipping of their potential impending doom. Rather dramatic perhaps but it would stop a nasty secondary collision at any rate.

As Treavey approached the car with his torch, he noticed a shape alongside it but crouched down and in a precarious position. It was a woman who was getting on in years and she wore a long heavy grey coat which he thought was a bit strange for the summer, but the evenings could get quite cool he supposed.

"Hello madam, can I help you? What happened?" He asked her.

She jumped up holding a cat basket in her right hand. "Oh, I'm in a bit of a pickle, officer, I'm terribly sorry."

Treavey asked her for her name.

"Tommy," she replied, looking rather confused.

Had she been drinking? She didn't look anything like a Tommy after all.

"No, I mean, he's Tommy wherever he is, but I'm Sylvia. I need to find him. My car just stopped, and I didn't want anyone to hit it with Tommy in there, so I waited with him out here and, well you know…"

Treavey viewed the empty cat basket and scanned his torch across the tops of the hedges and walked across the road to scan his torch across the fields beyond.

"No dear, Tommy won't be there, he's not that quick."

"I think he could be, Sylvia. A cat could be in Newquay by now. We'll have to get this car moved soon though. Are you a member of the AA or RAC?"

Sylvia was looking frantically around the base of the hedge line and replied, "No dear, he's not a cat. He's a tortoise, and even though he's 60 years old, I doubt he has very good road sense."

"A tortoise?" Treavey exclaimed. "Oh, okay, now that changes everything. I'll stop the traffic and we need to have a really good look."

A careful look along the length of the hedgerows alongside soon located the culprit and the emergency was over. Treavey arranged for recovery to take Sylvia home with Tommy and all was well with the world. Treavey drove back into Newquay to see what was happening on a Thursday night and smiled whilst wondering if the Met police ever had jobs such as these.

Whilst in the town, Treavey decided it was time to have a look at Superintendent Steer's house. He made his way to the road he knew the Super lived on with his wife.

He drove down it and slowly passed taking a good look at the large semi-detached bungalow beyond a small but neat front garden. There was a large pick-up truck in the driveway. He wondered what had happened to his wife. Had he murdered her? He had a feeling the investigation was going to be cranked up soon. She was listed as a missing person by him but how ironic if he was able to have full access into the investigation. He couldn't be suspended. Imagine if he was a victim and his diabetic coma had been an accident after all and not an attempt to take his own life. He wondered if the Superintendent had been interviewed yet. Treavey was happy not to be dealing with this one.

"Golf 31"

A few moments later, Treavey was blue lighting it over to Porth Bay to attend a house fire. On arrival he found a small cottage well ablaze, and a frantic looking young woman outside, screaming uncontrollably. Treavey parked the car on the narrow pavement as he knew the fire brigade were going to be attending and he didn't want to be in their way.

The young girl could have been no more than 16 years old. She was petite in stature and had overly neat chestnut brown hair and a pale oval shaped face which had tears rolling down. Her jeans and baggy T-shirt with a Disney character gave her young age away further. Treavey eventually managed to establish her name was Fiona through her panic. He glanced his eye over the cottage which had smoke billowing from the first-floor window, and he saw a glow of orange emanating from within.

"How many in there, Fiona, anyone?"

"Yes, yes there is. A baby, oh my god little Rose, little Rose is upstairs," her eyes were on stalks, "up there... in that." Terror was ripped across her pale complexion.

With no hesitation Treavey went to push the front door open but it was locked. Why had she run out and locked it? It was a door you had to physically lock with a key so she must have come out of another door perhaps.

"Is there a back door open?"

"No, it's blocked off, we only use this one."

There was no time to argue semantics. He tried to barge the door open with his shoulder, but it was solid, typical of these well-built old fishermen's cottages. He located his heavy Mag lite Torch from his car and swung it at the window watching it shatter into fragments. He stood back waiting for a fireball which never came.

Updating on his radio, Treavey calmly declared, "I'm going to have to go in. No time to waste. There's a baby in there."

He pulled his blue NATO jumper over his mouth and carefully climbed through the shattered window with pieces of dangling frame hanging down. Treavey had just converted it into one large open window instead of 4 smaller ones. He made his way through the neat but cramped lounge area with the wide beam of his torch leading the way. He was glad he had located a fresh set of batteries from the stationary cupboard just a couple of days before. He crawled up the narrow staircase, unnerved by the draft following him up the stairs. He wasn't the only thing which had come through that window. Treavey knew he was on borrowed time because he had added a strong flow of fresh oxygen to the mix to feed the fire raging above him. He decided no matter what, he was not going to turn back now. He had to find the baby. The smoke was thick but clearing at times as it was sucked out of the top windows just as a chimney would.

Clearing the top step, he dashed into a room opposite him which turned out to be the bathroom. He glanced around quickly, but there was no fire there and there was definitely no baby. He was hoping the baby wasn't old enough to be able to crawl under or climb behind something to protect itself. He spun on his heels to find another room to search but hesitated because the enormity of the heat hitting him in his face. A temperature so scorching he could imagine the skin peeling from his face. It was something he had never experienced before. He ran into the bathroom he had just been in, dampened a towel and put it over his head. It was now or never. The door was open to another room where a fire was raging. With every nerve in his body screaming for him to run away, to give up, to realise it was just too late, he ignored them all. Treavey crouched low and moved into the room wrapping the wet towel around his face with just his eyes exposed. He tried to protect his knuckles which had suddenly shown their vulnerability to the heat. The roar of the flames was like the devil himself. Relentlessly spitting and hissing, before groaning and screaming at him. He was sure it was going to suck him into its fiery depths after it had finished playing with him.

He was forced to turn away from the main body of the flames in the far corner and, quite fortunately too, because there in the opposite corner half protected from the main body of heat by the door, was a baby lying in a cot. Without checking whether the little soul was alive or dead, Treavey snatched it up like a ragdoll and ran for the door. He ran as fast as he could, almost missing the top of the stairs and falling down them, but as he got to the bottom of them, he was met with a front door crashing in on top of him, with glass and splinters of wood and the coolest of air which enveloped his scorched face. Oh, how that fresh cool air being sucked in by the devil itself made him feel alive again, and with the holiest of sights which stood before him he realised it was the silhouette of a firefighter standing in the door frame with his arm outstretched towards him. He had made it.

The baby was taken from his arms and disappeared very quickly. Treavey's adrenaline was surging through his veins and the relief made him want to collapse to the ground. He was guided towards an awaiting ambulance by a fire fighter and an oxygen mask slipped over his face. He felt embarrassed with all the fuss. He'd never really been in imminent danger before. He could have run out at any time, right? But he didn't and he hadn't realised that his oxygen levels were very low. He was exhausted and the fire fighter had warned him he was seconds from collapsing. It was true drive and determination, and a will to save the baby which spurred him on.

And then a bit of clarity. The front door was locked. The girl, Fiona, was outside and surely if she'd seen the fire from inside the house… from the bedroom itself maybe, she would surely have picked the baby up and run with it. Why did she leave it there?

"Rose is doing just fine," came the gravelly tones of a huge fire fighter towering above him. "We can confirm there is no one else in there either. You did a good job, officer. Coming from the other side of Newquay, we'd have been too late. Which bedroom did you rescue her from?"

Treavey felt the wave of emotion rush through his body. He hadn't thought about the baby again up to then. Maybe he didn't want to; he'd shut it from his mind. 'It' was now Rose and a 'she.' She was alive, and who knows, she could live to a hundred years old and have many children, grandchildren, and great grandchildren. All down to Treavey. What an incredible thought. He hadn't wanted to name her in his mind until he'd known she was safe.

Treavey pointed to the front top right window. "That one I think."

"Christ, she wouldn't have stood a chance. Even the floor has gone in that room and though there was something which could have been a cot once, it's just a pile of match sticks now."

It suddenly dawned on Treavey, the enormity of the situation. What had just occurred was something he had no idea was going to happen just a few minutes earlier. The rush of adrenaline was wearing off now, and he could feel pain on his face and his knuckles which the paramedics soon confirmed were superficial. Treavey had been in and out in a flash and so not enough time for the heat of the flames to grab him and do its worse on him. He felt exhausted; utterly exhausted in fact. He could relax now, however, if it hadn't been for the rest of the shift to do first, of course.

Something about Fiona bothered him. A nagging belief that something wasn't right, and it made him amble over to her who was now with the ambulance crew with Rose.

"Hi, Fiona. What is your relation to Rose?"

Fiona didn't look around at Treavey. She remained looking at little Rose's face. "I'm just her babysitter. Her parents are out tonight. They are going to kill me."

"Why was the door locked, Fiona. How come you were outside?" Treavey felt for her, but also had a suspicion she was hiding something. She looked ever so guilty, and he wanted answers.

"I was only gone for a second. I went out for a short bit and when I came back…"

"Where did you go at this time?" Treavey asked.

"I know someone who lives up the road. A friend."

"Is he a lad?"

"Yeah. He's a friend, a good friend."

Treavey had the answers he wanted. The parents of Rose had entrusted Fiona with keeping her safe, but Fiona had taken the opportunity to visit a boyfriend up the road. It was incredible, but the stupidity or irresponsibility of some people could be unbelievable, but she was young. Why on earth he hadn't come to the house instead would be established later on, but leaving Rose all alone, for no matter how long, was mind boggling. Treavey made a few notes in his notebook and returned to sit in his car to recover from the ordeal for a moment or two. CID were en route and he would tell them all he knew and hopefully the fire service would eventually be able to explain how it started. He was guessing a small heater with some clothes over it, as the night was quite chilly and after all, they wanted to keep the baby warm and safe after all.

Chapter 4
The knockout punch

A late shift and Treavey was back with Sooty, heading towards the local pub in the High Street. Reports of a fight brewing and Police need to "get here fast as it's going to kick off." The report is nothing more than that, and the call taker was sure it was a genuine call and not one of the drunken idiots wishing to see a bunch of cops pile into a pub.

Within 5 minutes, the panda slewed to a halt outside the 'Pink Diamond' pub and Treavey was out first and at a fast-walking pace, entered the pub knowing that Sooty would be close behind. He made his way into the room to see what the situation was and was quickly interested by a small group who were facing off with each other. It looked like one was outnumbered and was backing off with his arms stretched out in front of him. He was smaller in height and frame and his chances did not look good, so it was a good job Treavey and his colleagues had turned up to turn the tables a little. Treavey checked his back to see Sooty entering through the door having parked the car. Sooty was scanning his eyes around the room to locate Treavey when it happened. Treavey span back around to see one of the larger males going down and the slighter framed man swinging for his life at the others who were hell bent on getting revenge. Treavey launched himself at one of the larger men to pull him away, but he'd turned and went to punch Treavey.

"Police, pack it in, we are Police," Treavey shouted and felt Sooty rushing past him knocking him off balance slightly as he ran at the other larger male. Both Treavey and Sooty were fighting for all their worth whilst trying to grab their radios for back up. It was some moments before everything was calm and they both had their quarry on the sticky wooden floor of the pub. There was confusion as it was still quite crowded and so once they'd managed to cuff their prisoners, they looked around for the other male involved, but he was gone. This had become much more complicated. With no complainant, they only had a public order offence to go by. Treavey went through the law in his mind and settled for the offence of affray. His tutor advised him to know three things off by heart as he could look the others up in a book back at the station, but the three parts of law he needed to know backwards on the street were public order, drink drive offences and his powers of entry. Basically, when he could smash a door down and when it would be frowned upon by a judge.

Sooty was looking concerned at his prisoner. Even he could see he had gone limp and was looking confused, even delirious. His was the one that the other lad had punched so it was likely he was a bit concussed. Sooty called for an ambulance. The colour had drained from Sooty's face. Treavey could tell he was worried especially when he saw him uncuff his prisoner and lay him on the floor telling him to relax and checking to see if he could focus his eyes on his finger, asking him how many he could see.

The man's friend had turned quiet too. All his fight had gone, and he too was concerned about his friend.

"What's happened? Why's he like that, what have you done to him?"

Treavey circulated the description of the man who had left the scene. The one who had originally looked like a victim and probably still was, but the tables had well and truly been turned. Other units turned up, including the ambulance and Treavey took his prisoner to the van and would shortly head on back to the station to book him into custody.

Just as he slammed the van door on him, the man glared at Treavey, "You know who that bastard was. You knew him at school. It's James. James Leverton. You remember him, don't you? That's who you're after."

Treavey turned away in shock. Shit, James Leverton. He was a really decent guy, and wouldn't ever cause any trouble, but when someone is backed into a corner, they can act in one of two ways, and it looked like he came out fighting.

Treavey was distracted by a commotion behind him and saw a stretcher with the man hastily strapped to it barging through the doors of the pub and heading to the back of the ambulance. He had only seen this sort of urgency once before and that was at a road accident. Usually, they liked to stabilise someone before removing them as they couldn't do too much en route to a hospital but when they were losing the patient fast and there was little they could do for him, then it was straight to the operating theatre as soon as possible.

The woman paramedic was jumping in the driver's seat of the ambulance whilst her colleague shut the doors from inside.

"How's he going to be?" Treavey asked, almost knowing the answer already.

She hesitated for a second before turning around to Treavey and replied, "The only fluids this man needs right now is diesel."

She slammed the driver's door, the blue lights were on, sirens on, and they were gone. The scene was back to relative normality apart from Sooty who stood there before Treavey with an ashen face. "I'm fucked."

"What do you mean, you're fucked? You never hurt him." Treavey replied sympathetically.

"You tell that to the family. The last person who touched him was a cop. Death in police contact. I'm fucked."

Treavey put his hand around his shoulder. "Now you listen here. Yes, there'll probably be an inquiry as there has to be for transparency, but everyone knows that this guy called James Leverton did it, and from the looks of it, they guy forced the situation anyway. You'll be okay Sooty. I know you will."

The circus arrived; CID, and even someone from complaints was dragged out of bed but there was little they could do but ensure any CCTV was collected and any potential witnesses found but there were none left at the scene. Of course, the CCTV was facing in a different direction and the quality was only good if you could identify which grey blob was next to which slightly whiter blob. Treavey wrote a statement after initially being considered a suspect too, but it very soon became clear with further independent witnesses that Sooty was going to be alright. No, James Leverton needed to be located, and he needed to be located soon. This could be a manslaughter very soon.

Treavey asked the control room to find the details of James Leverton on the system and fortunately he was known but only on the intel systems from having called the police over a domestic incident he had witnessed. He wasn't known to police in any other way and therefore had a clean record. He drove around to his last known address and spoke to his mother who kindly allowed him into the house.

"Look, Mrs Leverton, I saw what happened and I can say I know it was self-defence. He had his back against the wall, and it was all kicking off. I don't know how it all started so we do need to speak to him as soon as possible."

The woman looked worn out. The worry was eating away at her with the seriousness of the incident which was sinking in. Her entire world seemed to have collapsed on her and Treavey felt a genuine empathy for her.

She looked thoughtful and took her phone out of her pocket and scrolled through it, then put it to her ear. She waited and Treavey waited too, guessing she was phoning her son.

"James, hello James. Are you okay?... right... okay. No, the officer said it looked as though you were defending yourself, but they do need to talk to you. The chap you hit has taken a bad turn... right, yes, I know you didn't… look, I don't think you are in any trouble, especially with this officer, PC…"

"Treave."

"… yes, PC Treave said they need to speak to you tonight… right… oh goodness, where?"

She shut her phone down and placed it back in her back pocket. Treavey looked at the slim woman in her late forties in front of him. Slim with wavey blond hair which fell in front of her eyes. Her face was beginning to show the results of a few decades of smoking, but otherwise he thought she looked relatively young for her age. She looked at him with the saddest of eyes. "He's on the Island."

Treavey knew exactly where that was. Porth Island, a beautiful place where people walked out to from the coast road. A peninsular which jutted out into the ocean and was the most exhilarating place to visit on hot sunny days but more so on stormy winter days. He took the phone number for James and updated the control room with developments and headed out of town towards Porth Beach, past the Mermaid Inn where he used to work as a teenager and just as he began climbing the steep hill on the other side of the valley, he abandoned the police car and began walking the 10-minute walk out to the end of the Island. It's an island because at about half way he had to cross a wooden foot bridge with a raging sea either side of him as it was funnelled within the channel splitting the mainland from the island itself which contained bronze age burial mounds and the defences for a settlement on the island. The cutting for the bridge was created by the miners following an iron ore seam from one side to the other.

Along the sides of the shallow cliffs and the tidal flows were the small harbours where the residents of the stone age, eight thousand years ago, used to fish. Treavey wondered if it had been as idyllic as it had sounded for the miners of the iron age as they sheltered in their round houses from the raging storms or whether the fear of attack to steal their quarry and having to be on constant alert proved too draining. He assumed the protection the island enjoyed was the equivalent protection the United Kingdom had from the marauding French and of course Nazis more recently. And then there was the addition of linear mounds of earth spanning the whole width of the land to give the extra ballistic cover from any potential enemy.

It was relatively dark, yet with sufficient moonlight to light the surrounding vegetation, and, eerily, the drop to the sea below. As he crossed the bridge, he paused to look over the edge. The sea was a boiling caldron, full of energy and excitement. The bubbling and boiling tempest was very much in charge and any victim falling within its folds would have soon been devoured and consumed within its depths, their bones to be spat out at a later date, with only the crabs to pick on any morsels left over. Nothing would survive.

Treavey had always paused at this point when he crossed the bridge in the past, although it was his first visit at night and he found it quite creepy with the shadows which darted about him; some being in his imagination but others he was sure were not. He peered over the side of the hand rail to see the hollow in the rock worn and eroded by spinning pebbles over hundreds or thousands of years to form a bowl in the solid rock about 3 feet in diameter and 30 metres directly below him. This was where his grandfather's whippet dog had fallen or jumped from the handrail nearly a 100 years previously during low tide and by pure chance had landed squarely in the pool, saving the dog's life.

He smiled with the thought of what had happened to his blood relative so long ago in that very spot before continuing to walk to the end of the bridge, and up the steps on the other side. He waited and listened at the top of them but there was nothing but the wind, at first, to hit his senses. He glanced around him and admired the lights from the town of Newquay stretching along the coastline. The ocean between was looking dark, cold, and foreboding. It wasn't a place to be right now, but one glint of light proved there was at least one small fishing boat attempting to make a living out there tonight.

Slowly, he moved on heading for the point most people headed for. The island split into two, like two fingers spanning out from a hand, and between these two fingers there was known to be a point where some had lost their lives. What brought someone up to a beautiful part of the coastline such as this to end their lives? How could it possibly be understood? Treavey shuddered at the thought of being in such despair that the only option was to step off the edge and await whatever happened next. Nobody could tell what it would feel like to drop off the edge of course. Few lived to tell the tale, and no one did from that point at least, but what was it like to die? Did they feel the impact? Was it just a feeling of falling and then it all happened so quickly that everything turned white? No one knew, but what Treavey did know is that the alternative must have seemed utterly deplorable. Oh, to be in the depths of depression and despair to such a level. He prayed he would never visit that place under such circumstances.

And what about James? Hopefully, he had gained some hope from what his mother had told him. Had he had told the truth about being on the island. If he couldn't locate him, would it mean he had already jumped? Did he want to jump, or did he just want some time to himself? Who knew, but Treavey knew he needed to find out very soon if he could, and hopefully he would be alive and well when he did.

He walked steadily up the slight incline of compacted earth, the grass worn away by the continuous stamping of feet from locals and tourists who'd sought wellbeing from that very same spot during the day. It gently steepened to the point at which the island split into two spurs. He was heading to an old burial mound, which would be the point with the best view. The moonlight afforded him the luxury to scan around him, and when he felt it would be too late to alert anyone for them to quickly hide, he would shine his torch around him to mimic Trevose lighthouse some 15 or so miles further up the coast and very visible with its broad beam of light.

He stopped and listened, before climbing the mound to get a better look around him. He could find James up there and wouldn't want to spook him into running which could be fatal. Oh, what to do, but standing there with only the darkness and the breeze flowing through the spongy grass as company wasn't going to achieve much, so he started walking slowly again, and stood still on the top, like hundreds of thousands of people had done over the centuries. The view was spectacular.

There was a gentle swell rolling in. The smooth and unbroken waves approached the coastline rocks like a stalking panther, with less of a crashing against them as with many other days and nights but more caressing them, this time, as if rolling themselves around the rocks to hug them as they disappeared under the wave before being exposed once more for the next wave to do the same. Every six waves or so would be larger than the rest. This would result in the swell showing its displeasure with the obstruction in front of it.

It was hypnotic, and for a moment in time, Treavey forgot why he was there. He flicked his Maglite torch on and scanned it about him but there was nothing in view. Maybe James was already at the bottom of the cliff between the two spurs, or maybe he was already on his way home. He heard a distant thump. A rapid thumping which became louder every few seconds and the relative peace was shattered by the sound of what he now knew was the police helicopter above him.

Treavey's ribs were vibrating with the clatter reverberating through the air. The awesome power which hovered above him and was now scanning its immense torchlight around the coastline made the hairs on the back of his neck rise. He felt part of an incredibly powerful and exciting being, a group of people, an organisation which could call on unlimited resources to do good, to search for, and to protect the vulnerable and to expose the guilty. It was a feeling he never got bored of and hoped he never would. It was always a reminder of how incredible being a police officer was, and far from being bored in a sleepy county Force as many from city Forces believed, the isolation and limited available back-up often made life far more exciting.

Treavey pressed the radio head to his ear to hear what the helicopter observer was saying. It was believed there was a heat source on the other headland to the one Treavey was on and so he made his way down to the base of the burial mound and headed towards the location.

The rockface he was climbing up was far more rugged and steep than the first. He felt protected by the helicopter hovering above him, guiding him and making sure he was clear of all danger. The observer spoke to him… "A bit further on and then swing around to the right. He's behind the rock in front of you. Be careful though. There's quite a drop below him. We are backing off a little as I think we are agitating him."

Treavey gingerly negotiated the rock and saw the foot of someone sitting there. He followed his impulse of slumping down beside the man and looking out to sea and up the coast towards the lighthouse. "You good?" Treavey asked.

"Been better. Is that thing for me?"

"Yes, it is. We were concerned you may do something silly. You aren't, are you?"

"I've no intention to, no. But I have had better days to be honest with you."

Treavey sat in silence, then turned to face James. "Look. I won't beat about the bush, the guy is in a bad way, but I saw what happened. But because of that, you can understand why it has to be fully investigated with nothing taken for granted. I don't know what led up to it so that needs to be looked into. I don't want you to tell me anything now either. Leave that for when you have a solicitor and you are being formally interviewed, but don't worry too much, James. At the end of the day, if you had no choice, you had no choice."

They sat in more silence gazing at the dark ocean stretching out in front of them. "Funny, isn't it?" James said rather unexpectedly. "If this hadn't happened, we wouldn't be here looking at this incredible scene. I've lived here all my life and have missed this all this time. It's incredible, isn't it?"

The two made their way back towards the police car, firstly stopping at a granite seat at the top of the steps which led down to the bridge. "My great grandfather put that there," Treavey commented. I always have to sit on it for a few seconds when I'm here. You have to follow the tradition now, right?"

They both played their shortened version of musical chairs before laughing like children and headed across the bridge and back to the car. It was a solemn journey back to the police station where Treavey booked James into custody. It was always nice to tidy a job up before the end of the shift and he felt it had gone as well as it could having considered the circumstances. He headed back to the report room where he bumped into Sooty.

"You okay buddy?" Treavey asked him, apprehensively.

"Yeah sure. I can't change things now and I'm not sure I could have at the time either."

"Mate," Treavey said in a comforting tone. "It was just bad luck for you I had chosen the other guy. If I'd gone after yours first, I would have been the one facing all this shit, and I made that clear in my statement."

"Cheers, Treavey. Appreciated. Nice to know people have your back," Sooty replied with some relief.

Attempting to change the subject, Treavey asked, "Any news on the Superintendent?"

"Which one," Sooty asked, his mind still elsewhere. "Oh, you mean Superintendent Steer? No, I mean if he's innocent he's in a worse position than me cos everyone is suspecting him of murdering his wife. Poor guy if he's innocent. I heard he's been suspended whilst the investigation goes on, but the reason's disguised as 'welfare' reasons, I think."

Treavey sat down and pushed his seat back to allow him to rest his feet on the table. "I thought it was a little weird he'd have full access to the file he could well be the main suspect for."

"We have to remember," Sooty interrupted, "there's nothing to say he's done anything except he had a suspicious episode where he coincidently nearly died and would have died if it hadn't been for you saving him, and the fact his wife has gone missing, isn't going in his favour."

"But that's it, isn't it," replied Treavey. "He has a diabetic episode, and his wife has left him, probably sunning herself with a man half her age on a Jamaican island somewhere."

"Precisely that," Sooty leaned back casually against the wall with his arms crossed, "Tricky to investigate, especially if nothing turns up. I wouldn't like the investigation. I understand she's still just registered as missing, but DC Gee hinted to me, they were going through his house with a fine-tooth comb on the pretext it was to find out where she's disappeared to, but he has access to Steer's bank accounts and phone records now. How could Steer refuse to give the details to CID? There's nothing much private for him anymore."

Treavey got up and walked over to his skippet to see if anyone had given him any paperwork to do, or if there were any messages. He had learned early on in Perranporth to not prioritise things in his skippet as urgent and non-urgent work as the non-urgent work inevitably never got done. He tried to have a, 'when it comes in, it goes out' philosophy instead. He noted a scruffy piece of paper on the top of his usual folder. He picked it up and read it. It said, 'Can you visit Supt Steer's house on Saturday. He'd like to see you and thank you for what you did in saving his life. Can you report back to me when you're done?' There was a telephone number written on the bottom and it was signed by DC Gee.

That was a surprise for Treavey and in any other circumstances he would have felt happy to do so, and he still would, but the shine of the happy reunion was rather taken away somewhat by the fact the Supt was technically being investigated for murder. That point couldn't be avoided. He would be entering his house and wouldn't be sure if he'd murdered his wife there or not. Was he going to broach the white elephant in the room? It was an uncomfortable situation, but he would just own it. He decided he would contact him and agree to meet him for a coffee. He couldn't help thinking he could be resented by Steer if it had been a suicide attempt, but maybe he felt he had to invite Treavey for Tea and medals to keep the pretence up. Who knew?

The rest of the shift went without any more drama. He wrote his arrest statement and ensured the hand-over for CID was the best it could be at four in the morning. He'd heard that working at this time of night was the equivalent of being drunk, and it could feel like it sometimes. He wanted this to be right. He knew the nine to five jury would be pawing over his paperwork looking for something to criticise, and he didn't want to give them the satisfaction. Right. Back home, a day off and then a visit to Superintendent Steer.

Chapter 5

Tea and medals

Having parked his panda car further down the road to the house, so as not to bring attention to the neighbours, the walk up the driveway belonging to Superintendent Steer was a somewhat foreboding one for Treavey. Perhaps he had psyched himself up more than he should have. He squeezed past the black immaculate looking Mercedes, whilst having a quick glance in the front of it but there was little to see. He took his time walking up the stone steps to the large Victorian semi-detached house whilst taking in the impressiveness of the large wooden door in front of him before ringing the surprisingly conventional doorbell for such a lavish house.

He waited but there was no sign of anyone opening the door and yet Treavey was sure he had come at the pre-arranged time. He rang the bell again and having waited a further amount of time, he contemplated taking this opportunity as an excuse to leave. What else could he do except the last time he had seen him he was unconscious in his car so maybe he was again, but in his house, or maybe he had timed it so Treavey would discover his body. He stood there and looked around at the neighbourhood around him. No one was mowing lawns or walking their dogs. There was no one to ask if they'd seen him. He quickly walked back to the Mercedes and felt the temperature of the oil sump at the front of the car. This would cool more slowly than the exhaust pipe which many officers would go for in preference to see if the car had recently been driven. The car sump was cold, so Treavey stood up again but hesitated. Whether to go back to the station or whether to look further and the copper in him told him to stop being so bloody stupid and to get to the bottom of the mystery.

He put his hand over the top of the rear gate and unlatched it allowing himself into the garden. As he walked through into it, he saw Supt Steer in a pair of tattered white shorts and nothing much else but a pair of Walkman earphones over his ears. He was holding a pair of secateurs in his hand and fortunately caught sight of Treavey before it all got even more awkward.

"Hello dear boy. My saviour. Thanks for coming, goodness, is that the time, I'm so sorry."

Treavey quickly relaxed in his company as they chatted about the garden and the events of what had happened. He was surprised at the candidness of him explaining what had happened between him and his wife. As he listened, and now holding a cup of coffee in his hands, Treavey scanned the garden which was very well kept including some perfectly pruned rose bushes and a small vegetable patch.

"I know about the rumours," he openly admitted, fully addressing the elephant in the room. "I thought we were alright between my wife, Lisa, and me. We'd been married for 15 years, and everything was okay, or so I thought, but she had been acting a bit strangely recently."

Treavey was feeling uneasy with the detailed manner in which the Superintendent was discussing his personal life, and it was as if he was treating him as an equal, not a Superintendent talking to a police constable where he would have been expected to speak when he was spoken to and then with "Yes, Sir" or "No, Sir". He thought it best to comment as little as possible and to just listen instead. It was as if his boss was finally managing to get something off his chest with someone who had been so close to him and had kept him alive. Maybe he felt he could trust Treavey, that he had little to lose now.

"Then suddenly she'd left. Without warning. I mean not a word, Treavey. Not a clue. I've searched this house high and low and so have our colleagues..." he looked into the middle distance, "and they don't seem to have found anything of any help either."

Treavey observed a deep sadness which had fallen over his boss's face as he described his loss. Without warning, and instinctively, Treavey found himself asking, "Did you love her?"

"Yes, I did. I was besotted with Lisa. I thought she was my soul mate, but perhaps I'd just taken her for granted, always thinking she would be there... but to leave no sign? Not even a note." He gazed out to the end of his garden towards his vegetable plot. "I was getting very depressed because she'd gone missing for the week without a word, and I completely misjudged my eating. That's where you came in and ended up saving my life. I can't thank you enough Treavey but wish it was under happier circumstances to come back to."

The vegetable patch next to the small wooden garden shed looked freshly dug and Treavey found himself wishing he had Xray eyes. What if she was down there?

What if all this was an act? What if he despised his wife and wanted rid of her without having to split his wealth in half through a divorce. But then he wouldn't bury her in his own garden, would he? That would be ridiculous, or is he thinking it's hiding her in plain sight?

Treavey left the house feeling more confused than ever. He so desperately wanted to believe him and hoped she turned up having had a few weeks away with her new lover before seeing sense. He thought if it were all true, that his Superintendent would have every right to be livid with his wife for dumping him in this situation and making him prime suspect for her murder. How could she do that to him. In fact, why would she do that to him? The more plausible reason for her unexplained disappearance would have to be that she was dead, surely. Treavey felt a little dirty, thinking he may have been taken in by the Super's manipulative ways which attracted Treavey's empathy. Had he been that naive? He was going to see DC Gee on Monday and give a full debrief.

He was thrust out of the daydreams with the control room requesting him to attend a suspicious male having appeared from a rear garden of an elderly person's residence. Reported by neighbours in an area where there had been several burglaries over the past few weeks, Treavey knew this was his chance to bag himself a burglar if everything went to plan.

He approached the area as quietly as he could with low revs, no sirens, and he kept his blue light off. He had learned that 'slowly does it' was often the best way to creep up on someone and arrest them before they knew you were there. Before closing in to the location he had last been seen, Treavey confirmed that Dave the dog handler with Finchy his German Shepherd dog was en route, but they were coming over from Perranporth which would take them 20 minutes or so.

The panda car ticked over as he almost glided along the leafy residential road with well-kept large bungalows either side of him. He counted off the house numbers and established the suspect would probably be coming towards him so he slowed, further squinting his eyes to see as far along the road as he could. "There, there he is!"

The man slowed. A slim man in his early twenties with a small backpack. He turned and quickened his pace at first before breaking into a run, and then a sprint away from the panda car.

"Victor, I've got a runner, Tamarisk Road, heading towards town."

He didn't wait for a reply but accelerated his car to where the man had darted into someone else's garden and disappeared. Treavey was out of the car and sprinting too. "Male white, medium build and height, about," he was gasping for breath, "... about 22 years old, blue T-shirt, jeans and a dark backpack." That was all they were going to get. Treavey was spending the rest of his energy on catching his offender. He could solve a dozen burglaries and losing him now would be unimaginable.

The man was fast, and able to skip across low walls and garden ponds with some ease, showing a degree of athleticism which Treavey was not too happy to see, as he was wearing police boots and heavy thick trousers himself, along with numerous bits hanging off his belt, swinging and clanking about. He was keeping up with the man, however, probably because of the man's unhealthy life of drugs and poor diet. They ran at full pelt across a perfectly manicured lawn towards a wooden panelled fence which they both cleared easily before smashing into a pond on the other side, stepping on netting for protecting the fish who no doubt had the shock of their lives before heading off down the side of another house where they came to a locked gate. Treavey had him.

The burglar had other ideas however, as he rushed Treavey who still managed to grab the man's back pack as he wriggled his way past him. The man flicked around the corner of the house and straight into the door into the house itself. Treavey followed through the kitchen where he saw an elderly couple having lunch at table for two. They casually watched the burglar run straight past them followed by Treavey who couldn't resist a "Afternoon," as he sprinted past. The comical aspect of the incident was obvious, with little explanation being required when seeing a young man being chased through the kitchen by a uniformed officer.

Out through the front door and down the front path onto another road. Treavey hadn't a clue where he was in relation to where he had started off, but he was relatively content he wasn't going to lose this man now. The distance was being maintained and it would surely only be time before Dave or other officers located them both.

"Ulalia Road, Ulalia Road," he shouted over the radio as they ran past the junction road signs which finally allowed Treavey to identify his location. Treavey was getting concerned as this guy seemed to have great motivation to keep on running and find energy out of somewhere and it was the first time, he began to doubt his own fitness. Was he going to lose this chase? Was he going to lose the first chase in his career? He wouldn't allow it. He had to find some extra energy from somewhere.

"Stop, police, stop you little shit." He said in some desperation. It was no good. Nothing was working and his frustration was showing through, but something did come into his mind he'd heard from an officer talking to his section in the canteen once. Many had laughed about what he had said but he had insisted it had worked every time for him. So Treavey thought he'd give it a try. He found his last breath to fill his lungs and whilst running at full pelt still, said in as calmly and controlled words as he possibly could muster, "I'm caaaatttccccchhhhhhhing youuuuuuuu."

The man threw his arms up in despair and came to a crumpled stop, bending over forward with his hands on his knees and gasping to fill his lungs with air. He too had been digging around for the last bit of oxygen he could from the bottom of his lungs as the more he sucked breath in, the less oxygen he could find. "Okay, okay, I give up man. You got me."

Treavey had used the last breath he had for the all or nothing trick of psyching the man out, and it had worked. He would have loved to have thanked that officer in the canteen those few years ago, but he didn't have a clue who he was. His fool-proof method, when used with enough conviction, had bagged him his quarry and he would feel like a king returning to the station with this burglar in his custody. This is what Treavey had joined up for. This was real policing, and he was loving every moment of it. There was no other job like it.

Treavey helped his sweaty burglar into the rear of the newly arrived police van before slamming the door shut. He had nothing on him as far as stolen items were concerned and no actual evidence that he was a burglar yet, so he asked Dave to meet him at the beginning of the track where he had first seen the man. Dave and Treavey had known each other for a while and had done a few good jobs together when Treavey had been stationed in Perranporth. Dave covered a large area of Cornwall so he would often be in demand. There was a discussion between the two officers which went a bit like this… "So, Dave, I saw him here at first. He saw my car at the end of the road there and darted off down here out of sight for a moment until I could get down here to give chase on foot through the gardens here."

Dave was sorting the line out with an exceedingly excited Finchy, a beautiful German Shepherd dog with a glistening auburn and blonde coat at the end of his lead which he was reeling out. Dave was in his forties but apart from moaning about the usual aches and creaks, was relatively fit. He swept his wispy blond hair to the side, "Yeah, Treavey mate, if he's disposed of any stolen property around here, then I reckon he'll find it. We'll give it a go, eh boy?". He proudly glanced down at his dog whose head had now disappeared inside a bush, and so patted his rump instead.

Treavey waited for the magic to happen. For Finchy to make off at full pace across the garden where he'd seen his arrestee run, but Finchy was taking more time than usual to start the track. Dave was looking a little confused and hesitant. It seems the usual impeccable link between the two was not making the contact it should. "I don't understand… come on Finchy."

Finchy was too busy being distracted with his head in a bush, and once Dave finally gave him a yank, Finchy barked and refused to budge. He stayed put and nothing was moving him. Dave tried again but Finchy was having none of it.

Dave bent down to investigate the bush where Finchy was still staring at and barking and immediately pulled out a pillow case being weighed down by its contents. "Medals." he claimed with delight. "Good boy, Finchy, why did I even doubt you?"

When Treavey attended the house of a very elderly lady nearby to get the medals identified by her, he felt the most enormous relief. On the wall was a wonderful oil painting print of a Lancaster bomber. "My husband," she said through her tears of relief, "he was the tail gunner of a Lancaster bomber in the war. He died just 5 years ago. A wonderful man, he would have entertained you for hours with his adventures."

Treavey sat next to her with the medals carefully laid on his lap ensuring they were not touched for any potential fingerprints, but he was quite certain of the conviction as the pillowcase in the main bedroom was confirmed missing. Same colour and pattern. He sat looking into the glistening tearful eyes of the lady whose face was bronzed with valleys of wrinkles which told their own decades of experiences with joy and grief. What she must have seen, and what adventures she had had.

She smiled and chuckled, "He would always tell this story about the Lancaster, and I'd always tell him off, but I end up telling the same story now he's gone. I think he'd tick me off for being so tough on him now!"

"Oh, yes?" Treavey enquired with enthusiasm.

"Well, he said that the documentaries never mentioned the toilet arrangements, and sometimes he could be up there for 8 hours. In the tail gunner position it was cramped so he had to pull all his necessities down for a number two and very carefully position the turret so he could throw it out. Often it was almost frozen so less dangerous if you see what I mean? God knows if there was an unsuspecting cyclist or farmer beneath at the time." She laughed heartily as if it were the first time, she had told the story, but Treavey knew it was probably because she was remembering her dear husband. She looked lonely. Casting his eyes around the house, she clearly doted on her husband's memory.

"Do you get out much?" He asked her, whilst carefully rolling the medals up in the same pillow case having been positively identified.

"Not too much dear. I prefer to stay and watch television here or listen to the wireless. I get awfully bored with all the old people in the day centre. Although most of them are probably younger than me!" She roared with laughter again and slapped her knees as she rocked back and forth.

She must have been wearing the same style clothes as she would have worn in the 1950's. He thought it rather strange that elderly people wore the same style as in their youth. They didn't just decide to wear knee length brown skirts with cardigans and a grey perm when they got to a certain age. They, of course, had always been dressed like that, with the grey hair as an exception but the style was the same.

She saw him to her front door. Just before he stepped onto her door step to leave, the lady faced him head on and held both his arms by the elbow and looked him directly in the eyes. "Thank you, young man. I am so grateful; I cannot tell you how much. I look at those medals and think what my dear Ernie had to do to get those medals. He defied all the odds. He didn't win those medals you see, he earned them and losing them would have broken my heart."

Before getting into his panda car, he initially waited for the blast of heat to leave where it had been sat in the hot sun and he observed a teenager wandering along the road in front of him, very much minding his own business. He wore a baggy T-shirt with a motif of some sort and jeans with white trainers. 'That's the fashion for us when we are elderly,' Treavey thought despondently. 'How dull when compared to the smart elderly gents in their suits, shirts and ties and donning a smart trilby hat.

Treavey was pleased he was able to tick off another part of the job having taken a quick statement of identification. Now he needed to do the search of the suspect's house to see if he had any other stolen goods there from previous burglaries.

The accommodation was not as nice when compared to the victim's house. It was a flat at the end of an alleyway, initially quite difficult to locate and Treavey had spent ten minutes going around in circles until he finally got out of the car and searched on foot. He made his way up some exceedingly dirty concrete steps to the door which had some chisel marks and dents from a crow bar. Possibly an opposition drug dealer or maybe it was the police. It looked like the landlord had given up replacing the door and was just patching it up as best as he could with all the repeated forced entries.

Treavey looked up the face of the building to the 3 stories above and rang the doorbell to flat 3B. No answer, so he rang the other two bells, and one occupant buzzed him into the building. Treavey smelled the musty corridor and walked up the stained and threadbare carpet up the stairs to the flat and knocked loudly on the door. He held the search form tight in his hands to hand to the occupant. A gaunt looking woman in her mid-twenties but looking more like a young teenager, answered the door. There was little attempt to make herself presentable apart from some chipped bright red nail varnish, but her greasy dark bob attracted the attention more. She was painfully skinny and relatively petite. Her Charlie Brown t-shirt hung off her, limply, having little more support around her shoulders than a coat hanger. "Yeah, what?"

Treavey coaxed himself into the flat and felt his boots sticking to the floor in the bedsit which was dark and foreboding and stunk of filth. There was little natural light, and any broken bulb was considered a luxury to replace. A stickiness on the carpet was often found in suspect's houses such as this. It was a feeling of satisfaction he had as he knew they may get away with their offences most of the time, receive light sentences in court if arrested and charged and generally they may make people's lives a misery, but look at the environment they lived in. They didn't get away with it really. No one lived a happy life off the spoils of the, often devastated, victims. They lived in pure squalor most of the time because of their lack of self-discipline and their selfishness. That was their punishment in Treavey's mind. That's where they paid for their crimes and that got Treavey through the day hoping there was at least some justice in the world, even if it was indirect.

It was obvious there was little in the flat of any worth and so anything stolen must have soon been sold off for drugs at a fraction of their true value. The girl, named Angela, looked frightened. "Don't worry, love, I'll be in and out in a minute."

"When is he back? Do you need to release him?" She had a bleak tone to her voice. There was no smile or laugh to follow her comment. She was scared.

"What's the problem?" Treavey asked her, not expecting too much of a reply. Questions to people who follow a life of crime normally received a blunt retort.

"Oh, nothing. I just like it when he's not here." She adjusted her tone to an even more serious one, leaning forward and grabbing Treavey's forearm. "Don't for god's sake tell him I said that, will you?"

"No, of course I won't." Treavey replied quickly. "Come on now, tell me what the problem is. Does he hurt you?"

"No," she almost shouted. "No, he's not like that, but he checks where I go. He times me when I am gone and questions me when I've been gone for too long."

Treavey sat her down and had a chat with her. What she thought wasn't too serious and was just 'what he was like' he quickly recognised as controlling behaviour and domestic abuse. It was time to try to give this young lady a way out, and to give her the confidence and protection to make that decision and to seek help for any drug addiction she may have.

"Do you have somewhere else you can go? A friend or a family member?"

"Yes, my Mum always wanted me to leave him. She hates the way he talks to me so she'd have me, but who wants to move back with their mother?"

"Do you have any friends at all?"

"I used to, but they seem to have disappeared. I think they got fed up with him."

Treavey got up sharply and turned to face Angela who was somewhat startled at his unexpected reaction. "Okay, here goes. You either stay here in this utter shit pit, excuse my language, and no offence intended, or you can take hold of your life with the right support, and I can take you to your mother's house so you can regroup and get your life in order. I will report this abusive situation you have here and give you a log number so that if he comes and follows you, we, the police, will know the situation exactly. Living with your mum for a little bit, in a clean house, being fed, and having clean laundry is a small price to pay whilst you reset your life, then go and get a job and leave this utter loser to his own miserable life. It's your decision, but it may just be the most important one you've ever had to make."

To his astonishment, Treavey was in the panda car with bags of clothes and belongings driving Angela to her mother's house. There was a cryptic note left on the table for the boyfriend's return which told him not to come looking. Treavey had signed the letter too, explaining that he was not wanted, and police would look upon any attempts to contact her as wishing to cause trouble and there would be firm action as a result.

On the journey, he advised her to talk to a solicitor about an injunction or to at least see if one was achievable at that stage. Her boyfriend may just leave her alone, but it was, perhaps, unlikely. The log number would stop a lot of explaining to officers attending any incident. Treavey knew she would be safer with her mum. She just had to maintain her stance to give herself a chance of starting a new life.

Treavey pulled the car up to the front door of her mother's house. It was a respectable looking mid-terraced house, with a clean and tidy frontage and a front door which showed no signs of previous forced entries as Angela's had done. He opened his driver's door and got out and looked at Angela's gaunt looking face as she quickly glanced at him with a smile like a summer's day shining across at him.

"Here goes then," she said and opened the rear door to pull some of her bags out, as did Treavey.

"Hang on, just a moment," she said and disappeared into the car again. Treavey dipped his head to see what she was doing and could see the strap of a little white bra as she was reaching up and over her head, and he quickly straightened up and glanced around him to see if anyone was watching.

Angela got out of the car again and collected her bags. Once she'd appeared around the back of the police car, he noticed she was wearing a slightly creased but far more appealing autumn silk blouse top, far more appealing and suiting to her than the Charlie Brown one she had been wearing. She stroked her somewhat greasy fringe to the side of her face and smiled again, but this time more nervously.

"You, okay?" he asked more in a comforting tone than an enquiring one.

"Yes. Come on then, what's there to lose?"

Some twenty minutes later, Treavey was driving back to the station for a cup of tea. He felt happy with the work so far on his shift. He had caught a persistent burglar who was preying on the vulnerable elderly in the area, and he had the double success of not only giving a controlled and bullied young woman a fresh start but had been the cause of moving her away from the burglar boyfriend. He was going to be mad with Treavey, but he didn't care a jot. A wry smile spread across his face as he allowed another motorist to take precedence out of a junction in front of him. Treavey gave him a small salute and grinned. It had been a good shift. A great shift in fact.

He'd almost forgotten the fact he had a hand-over to do with the burglar he had in custody but at least he would have something to show for the fact he had been delayed. On getting back to the station he skipped up the steps which led to the CID office and feeling very much like an imposter in the office of desks and piled up paperwork, looked at all the officers in there until one caught his eye.

One CID officer glanced up at him and looked as if he had immediately regretted what he had done. The more experienced officers had turned their desks, so they weren't facing those coming into the room. Fewer jobs and awkward questions, or maybe purely coincidence.

"The guy brought in for custody? Tom Clarke? He's mine and I wondered, as he's suspected to have been involved in all the burglaries recently, if you'd be interested?"

The CID officer put a good effort on looking keen. "How long has he been in?"

Treavey had a pang of guilt as he confessed his detainee had been in custody for nearly 4 hours already. He'd got caught up in the moment and he thought perhaps he should have at least tipped off CID before he had gone to do the Section 18 search on the flat. He sheepishly apologised and the CID officer looked displeased until he found that Treavey had completed the search and not only located the stolen property but had also got it identified along with obtaining the statements to prove it. The officer was more than forgiving after finding this out and happily took the job off Treavey as he felt there would be a good opportunity to build his TIC (taken into consideration) record and boost his reputation with his DS.

Treavey was very happy to not only get the arrest and follow the job through on a practical aspect, but now he had managed to delegate the paperwork to a specialist in their field so he knew they should get the best out of it and it would help him towards getting a good reputation as a thief taker.

It was nearly time for home, and he'd handed the car keys over to the next shift having refuelled it as it only had a quarter of a tank in it. An extra pain in the backside but it wasn't worth the grief from the following shift if he didn't.

The clock ticked on the hour and Treavey made his way to the locker room. There was an older officer, Mike Bassett putting his civilian coat on next to his own locker and Treavey smiled as he hears him repeat his mantra, "Testicles, spectacles, wallet and watch." The officer pats himself down and says, "Right. Home now." He did it every time and Treavey couldn't get it out of his head.

Chapter 6
Sun, sea and sinister endings

10.30pm and Treavey had had to leave the briefing early to attend what looked like a concern for welfare on one of the beaches nearby. It appeared there was someone at the water's edge and it struck the informant odd as they were just standing there fully clothed and yet they were allowing the water to lap around their heels, and they hadn't moved in over 10 minutes. The informant was standing at the top of the steps which lead to Lusty Glaze Beach looking down at the tide half way out.

Treavey knew the area well. He had lifeguarded the beach some years earlier and he was currently renting a small flat in the same road. He had been brought up as a child nearby too, at the Glendorgal Hotel which his parents had once owned. They had moved on by now, but he still loved the area. He parked the panda in the car park at the top of the 133 steps which led down to the beach. The informant was an older woman whose loosely tied up grey locks reminded him of his old history teacher. She was waiting for him with a small scruffy brown terrier dog getting impatient and standing off some distance and barking at its owner.

"Hello, I'm glad you've come," she said warmly in a well-spoken voice, "I'm getting a bit concerned. It's very odd behaviour. I don't know what they are up to, but I don't really know what to think, really."

Treavey peered over the edge of the cliff and scanned the area from the cliff below, along the slipway which he'd swept of sand every morning before the day had begun when he was working there, past the lifeguard hut where he'd hired out surfboards, and the ice cream kiosk and beach shop on the left. Then his eyes adjusted further to scan the sandy beach which looked dark and foreboding, and quite intimidating at this time of night. The light was gone completely, and it was only the silhouette of a person on the shoreline which broke the natural lines of the cliffs, beach, and sea shore. They stood pillar like, jutting out like an abandoned lighthouse. The waves were reasonably small but were rushing up the legs of the person to their waist, sometimes causing them to stumble back slightly, before regaining their composure and taking a step forward again.

Treavey noticed a small clump of what looked like belongings piled neatly on the beach behind them, or was it just a pile of seaweed? What he did know, is he would have to get down there quickly to start talking to the person. He knew it was only a matter of time before they saw some sense and returned to the sanctuary of the beach or decided to walk out into the black cold water and never turn back.

"Have they taken your details yet?" he asked the woman who confirmed the call takers had, so he was happy he didn't have to take his pocket notebook and torch out to do so.

He said his goodbyes to her and started running down the steps. They weren't lit, but he had sprinted up and down them hundreds of times whilst being brought up in the area and working the summers there. As far as he could remember he had never walked up the steps, only jumping them two at a time until three quarters of the way up when he was forced to take them one by one as his heart would be pounding out of his chest.

It was strange to do this for the first time at night, so he thought at first, but then corrected himself as he remembered walking back from Sailor's night club at 1.30am at low tide with friends and taking a skinny dip before running up the steps to cook up some pasta and tuna to soak up the beer.

As he got to the bottom, he had to lose sight of the person at the shore line for a second or two and dreaded rounding the corner to find they had gone already, but there they were, standing as they had been for so long without ever looking back. It was almost as if they were in a trance as he skipped down the slipway onto the soft sand. It was such a different sensation than he was used to, normally walked on in bare feet or flip flops at most. In heavy police boots it was altogether a different experience. He felt he was walking in quicksand until he got to the damper, firmer sand where the tide had washed it clean and continued to do so twice a day. Only with higher spring tides did the soft sand at the very top get a cleaning, and sometimes the currents would shift thousands of tonnes either exposing the foundations of the sea wall or filling it so high you could almost step off the top of the wall onto the beach. The power of the sea was incredible.

His eyes were strained against the bleakness of the night to take in as much detail of the person as he could. Should he rush them? Should he stand back and catch their attention? Should he take his boots off first, but then if they turn back and walk towards him, he'd have his boots to put back on. Should he walk in next to them? He decided on doing what took the least effort and that was to stand at the edge and call out to them, but first he stared at them to see what clues he could pick up from behind. Anything about them at all to help, or did he even know them?

He studied the slim statue like figure with a dark coat and jeans which were completely soaked. The coat hung just below the person's bottom, and the long brown hair hung straight and lifeless. There was the glint of silver from a hair grip which caught the moonlight but there was nothing more.

Treavey called out softly, "Hello, are you okay?"

The girl stepped forward without looking back and working on instinct, Treavey shouted as loudly as he could. "Just stop there, I'll be mightily pissed off if I have to get wet, but you will not be drowning tonight, do you understand?!

The girl stopped in her tracks and glanced back at him.

"Look, you know I can't let you do anything like that tonight. There is always another way, you know, of getting through your pain, but this isn't the time. We seriously need to talk, and I need to listen, and then we can see what can be done to help you."

It was another fifteen minutes before Treavey had managed to get her back onto dry land, and he was particularly pleased he hadn't had to get his boots wet either. That would have been an uncomfortable drive back to the station if his trousers had been soaked, or even worse if he'd had to struggle with the girl in the water.

The girl slowly walked up the steps to the car park with Treavey behind her and he put her in the police car with the heater switched on. He asked her several questions to confirm who she was but there was little forthcoming. He noticed a tattoo on her right hand near her thumb of a black broken heart which he thought strange. He informed the police controller who had been getting concerned with the lack of radio reception down on the beach and no updates. He asked for a check on the system for people living in Cornwall with black broken hearts tattooed on their hands. It was extremely distinctive but had someone put it into the system yet? Whenever someone was arrested, they had every detail noted from them, but some officers skipped a few details to get on with their interview more quickly and something could be missed. If she'd never been in custody, then of course, they wouldn't be recorded anyway.

"That was easy," the controller said with some satisfaction. "We believe you have Sarah Norris there, of 15 Mitchell Avenue, Newquay. Standby... right," ...tapping could be heard over the radio, "she drives a red Vauxhall Cavalier B25 NPA.

That was a good amount of information which could stop a lot of waiting around trying to establish her identity and even though he wanted to help her, he'd far prefer to go hunting for a drink driver or attending pub fights.

He took his torch from the car and scanned the car park which was nothing more than a field with a bit of asphalt at the entrance and some gravel which made up a driveway to the bottom of the field. "Bingo," Treavey said under his breath because there in his torch light was a red Vauxhall Cavalier and, "Yes," the registration was the same.

    Sarah hadn't offered any keys, and he was not able to search her properly as he'd have to wait for a female officer who was not currently available and the clump of clothes on the beach had been a rock after all.

    He strode over to the car and shone his torch into the car but nothing. The doors were locked. He walked around to the rear of the car and pushed the boot catch and the boot lid pinged open. He shone his torch into it and wham!

    Treavey fell back onto his backside in shock. He scuffed his hands on the gravel which felt like a cheese grater whilst he scrambled to crab backwards with his hands and feet before some sanity came back over him. "Jesus, I mean, fucking Jesus."

    He composed himself for a second or two and nervously glanced back at his police car but there was no movement from it. He could see the interior light was still on how he had left it, and he could see the silhouette of Sarah sitting still in the car.

    Treavey stood up straight and approached the darkened opened boot again and shone his torch inside. He stood with his jaw dropping and slowly moved his hand to his radio clip on his shirt.

    "Victor. It's G32, receiving?"
    "Go ahead, G32."
    A pause as Treavey collected his thoughts.

"Victor from G32, I've found a body in the boot of the concern for welfare's car."

Another pause.

"Er, right G32. We'll get CID down to you and some back up. Any obvious cause of death at the moment?"

"No, no idea, but they are as stiff as a board. An ambulance will not be required. It'll be tricky getting the body out. I'm not attempting CPR because of that."

Treavey realised this last sentence sounded a bit strange, but he knew they got the point and any piss taking could occur later. At this time, it looked as though he had a murder victim and the murderer in his care. He made an effort to walk confidently back to the police car where he could see Sarah staring at him and who must have seen the whole discovery.

Treavey was trying to give the impression that this was all in a day's work for him and he wasn't intimidated by the whole process, but inside he was screaming like an excited school child. Every sinew in his body was telling him he had a body in his boot, and he had to run, run, run as the murderer was sitting in his car. One thing he did know was he wasn't going to get into the car with her.

"Hey Sarah," Treavey said without being entirely sure of what he was going to say next, "The er, that er," Get a grip Treavey for God's sake, "That body in your car had something to do with you being on the beach, I take it?"

He remembered he needed to get everything right and darted in with a caution before Sarah had any chance to reply. He didn't want to screw it up at this point, and the caution had changed very recently so he was going to have to recite the new one with the old one still in his head. It was as if he was a brand-new officer all over again.

Under pressure, he managed to get it out neatly, "But first Sarah, I have to tell you, you do not have to say anything, but it may harm your defence if you do not mention something which you later rely on in court and anything you do say may be given in evidence."

There, done. He was happy and he knew that anything Sarah may volunteer now may be used as evidence in a court of law and he could say that with a clear conscience.

"Oh, and you are under arrest for suspicion of murder, okay? The caution still stands."

Even though technically all fine he'd wished he could have neatly arrested her and then cautioned her but under the circumstances he wasn't going to beat himself up over it.

Sarah stared ahead through the windscreen, "I am free of her now. She was a bitch and I'm glad it's over with. Even though I'm going to prison I am freer now than I've ever been with her."

Treavey wrote her reply in his pocket notebook hoping there was going to be a full confession but nothing else came from her. She remained staring straight ahead. He felt some empathy for her but didn't know why. Maybe, it was just a feeling. Maybe, he was just being naive. Maybe, she was not in control of her actions, but all these things weren't for him to judge. This was for the criminal justice system to look at and hopefully sort out, but Treavey knew he had done his bit for the night.

CID arrived at the scene and arranged for Sarah to be booked in to custody on behalf of Treavey as they wanted him to point out where she was on the beach and what exactly had happened. Treavey noticed it was DC Gee walking towards him. It made him feel happy as he got on with Adam Gee since his involvement with Superintendent Steer and the suspicions over his wife's disappearance. This may be an opportunity to get to know him better and to learn a bit more 'off the record' with what was happening with the investigation.

"Adam, good to see you mate."

"Hi, Treavey. Always where the trouble is, aren't you? It's just the murder and an armed robbery you are involved with now? I'm starting to get suspicious!" He laughed in his hearty gravelly chesty laugh and took a cigarette paper out to roll some tobacco. Treavey could already tell he liked this man. He was incredibly experienced as a detective constable, and he had an aura about him, and he had no pretentiousness. He spoke to the most senior and junior officer in the same welcoming and warm manner however experienced they were. Treavey felt completely relaxed in his presence. He felt that one of the reasons may have been because Adam had a mutual respect for Treavey. Adam respected a worker. There were too many shirkers in the station, but Treavey knew Adam wasn't one of them and vice versa. Treavey realised more effort could be spent trying to avoid a job, than to just get on with it and get it done. It was what he was employed to do, after all. Some officers spent their whole time trying to get rid of jobs or avoiding them entirely. They were always 'backing up', where as they should be attending the job as everyone was and if they were the first ones there, they should be the officer running the job, not backing up. There were stories of officers attending an incident and driving past others who were parked on the side of the road, 'backing up.' They didn't have a very good name after that.

DC Gee rolled his cigarette and chortled, before farting like an extended fog horn and laughing hysterically. He found it immensely funny which Treavey found contagious, and they both found themselves at one of the most serious crime scenes they could be at, but acting like two twelve-year-old children.

Adam's expression suddenly turned very stern. "Right Treavey, down to business. I have SOCO coming to sort the car out before we have a full lift on that car. These Special Constables turning up have kindly volunteered to look after the scene for us. I'd grab your jacket mate; I need you back to the beach to point out where she was. It would be good to see if she disposed of a weapon down there."

For a second time that night, Treavey skipped down the steps to the beach, but this time the temperature had cooled somewhat so he had wisely taken his jacket with him. A reversible jacket with black on one side and reflective yellow on the other. It was a clever design and one of the first Forces to have such a thing. He wore his navy-blue NATO woollen jumper which he felt was very 'The Bill' like and just the smell of the wool made him feel ten feet taller.

"Don't say I never take you on a romantic walk on the beach by moonlight now, will you Adam," he joked whilst looking for the same rock he had seen from above which was now his marker post.

"I've had better dates!" Adam chuckled. "So, you say about here, and this is the rock you thought were a pile of clothes then?" We need to get a dog here so we should only walk where we know you and her have previously been. If she's been anywhere else to get rid of evidence, the dog will hopefully find it. We don't even know how the woman's been killed yet. A knife, strangulation, or a blunt object? Who knows but we should have that answer when SOCO get here."

Adam carefully lifted the rock and unsurprisingly for him, found nothing underneath. Life was never that simple. They stood on the cold beach looking at the glimpses of the moonlight reflecting off the clouds and the surface of the sea. The sea lapped on the shore as if taking a rest. Maybe the lull before the storm but both officers felt at peace. They had a taste of what Sarah may have experienced with a mind full of confusion but down here in the dark at a time when no one visited the beach was an opportunity for some clarity but with a hint of creepiness thrown in. The towering, gloomy cathedral of cliffs was a dominant feature. The herring gulls were tucked up in its crevices which formed shapes like huge pained and screaming faces in the gloom. The sand was dark, or black even in areas protected from any reflection of light. There was no joy here at this time in this place. It would be another twelve hours before any families were experiencing the joys of its warmth and soft sands, along with leaping over the waves and screaming with joy, not torment as was running through Sarah's mind in that very place just a couple of hours earlier.

With nothing of interest found the two returned once more to the car park where they saw the scenes of crime officers donned in their white paper suits examining the boot of the car with the body still in situ. The occasional lighting flash from a camera would light up the surrounding field and hedges. Both officers waited patiently by their police car, Sarah had been removed some time before and Treavey passed the time with one of the special constables who were standing at the gate. They had put barrier tape at the entrance to prevent anyone else contaminating the scene. A police dog was sniffing the hedges nearby.

"This should be sorted for the beach opening time, won't it?" Treavey enquired.

Adam answered whilst rolling another cigarette. "No, we'll be getting the search team in here to do a fingertip. Over the hedges near the cliffs and around this whole car park in case she's thrown something somewhere. Recovering a weapon would be nice but we don't know what we are looking for yet. This area won't be open until past midday, if not later."

"NORRIS!" Treavey shouted, which startled Adam causing him to almost drop his rollup.

"Yes, that's her name, what's the problem Treavey?"

"It could be a coincidence, but there can't be too many Norris's about. Her name was Sarah Norris, right?"

"Right." Adam was beginning to look a little less interested in Treavey's revelation. "Is that it?"

Treavey composed himself. "It's just that I went to a jumper on the cliffs near the huers hut across the other side of Newquay and the member of public who stopped to help her was called Claire Norris."

"Okay, so what?" Adam had turned towards Treavey awaiting his revelation.

"Oh, nothing really, but I could nip around there even though it's quite late to see if it's a close relative. I don't think she'd mind as she didn't seem to mind me seeing her half naked after all."

Adam replied after some considerable thought, "I don't think I want to know about the half-naked bit but if you think it's worth an inquiry to get some background on this Sarah girl, and discover who the body in the boot could be, then it's worth you taking a look."

Just five minutes later Treavey was heading to Claire's address which he'd recovered from his pocket notebook. Even though he'd written it on the statement at the time it was very good practice to write everyone's details you'd had contact with in your notebook as well, as you never knew when you may need them again.

He approached the main door to the several flats contained behind it and fortunately, it was unlocked. The smell was musty but not unpleasant as he made his way up the concrete steps towards the flat. Before knocking on the door, he checked the time.

'Bloody hell, it's 1.30am. She could be really pissed off and if she'd had any attraction towards me, it could soon be forgotten, especially as she won't be looking her best and women really hate being disturbed not looking their best.'

If it were anyone else, he'd be knocking on the door too, so just to get on with it. Who knew whether there was another person involved who was in danger, or dead, even. He wrapped his knuckles on the door and pressed the doorbell a couple of times. He waited a few moments before popping open the letterbox and in a slightly raised voice but not enough to wake the whole block of flats, said, "It's the police, Claire. It's Treavey. Can I have a word please?"

He would usually add, 'nothing to worry about' but that may not be the case here.

The door opened a crack and then the chain was removed and pulled open. Treavey walked in to a very sleepy Claire who was dressed in some powder pink cotton pyjamas which were delicate enough to show her form off. It reminded him of when he first saw her with her floral shorts which hugged her perfectly formed buttocks which had caught his attention a little bit more than it should have.

She made her way into the lounge area and spun herself around, slumping down on the settee in one slick move before raising her knees together and pushing both her feet to the side.

"You could have just asked for a date, Treavey," she joked. Her dazzling blue eyes were shining as bright as the day she met him on Fistral Beach and Treavey affording himself a seductive memory of her jumping around in just her bikini bottoms. He caught himself momentarily staring at her cleavage before shaking himself out of his trance and reminding himself he was there for a particularly serious job to do.

He sat back on the soft armchair which he instantly regretted as he felt himself disappearing in the folds of the cushions. He felt like a small child in the headmaster's office and spent the next few seconds attempting to recover himself from the situation by pulling himself up and sitting himself on the edge of the chair.

"Claire. Firstly, I'm so sorry for disturbing you at this time of night. I thought about leaving it until the morning, but I think it's too important. Is Sarah Norris a relative of yours?"

The look of fatigue on Claire's face turned in an instance, "Shit," Claire rose up bolt upright. "Shit, shit, shit. She's killed her, hasn't she?"

Treavey blurted out, "Killed who?"

"She's bloody well killed her. No, no, no! My poor Sarah, my poor little sister. Tell me she's not dead."

Treavey thought it best to just say what he knew as it was getting a little confusing.

"Sarah isn't dead, but we suspect she has been involved in the killing of someone, another woman. I was sent to a report of a woman standing in the sea, a concern for welfare, and it turned out to be Sarah. I did some checks, and her car was in the carpark. I searched the boot of the car, and there was the body of a woman in there."

"Oh, thank Christ," Claire stood up and paced up and down the room. She looked relieved, then confused, and made several attempts at asking a question but stopped herself. Then, "The dead woman. Oh my God. You mean… Oh. Her name is probably Sitara Cian. She was a bitch. She was so controlling and made my sister's life hell.

Sarah was a shadow of her former self since she met her. They were living together, and that woman was all sweetness and light on the outside, but she had an infatuation with my sister and would never have let her go. Sarah had told me she'd tried to leave several times. It looks like Sarah has found her way out and got herself into a whole lot of different shit now. Oh no, silly girl."

Treavey sat in silence taking in what he was hearing, watching Claire walking from one side of the lounge to the other, before disappearing into the kitchen and walking back out again.

Claire spurted out her words, "I can't believe it. She must have been desperate. Was it self-defence? She's a lovely girl, Sitara was awful to her, I mean she would shower her in wonderful compliments, say how incredible she was, how clever she was and then she would go into these out-of-control rages with her accusing her of being a bully, a narcissist and on more than one occasion accusing her of being racist when it didn't all go her way."

"Racist?" Treavey enquired.

"Yes, I wouldn't have known about it at all because Sarah was too frightened to tell me about it. Sarah confided in a friend of hers. She has a Jordanian friend who looked at her messages and raised the alarm with her immediately and asked if she could speak to me so I could support her too. Thank God for her friend Amoora. She is a saint, and she gave her the confidence to act. Too much confidence perhaps."

Claire sat down again, but this time was sitting on the edge of the sofa with her forearms on her legs. "If Sitara saying, 'poor me, poor me, I'm sick, I'm ill,' didn't work, which we never did confirm her cancer scare, she'd go on the attack to get her way instead. Sarah was trying to get away from her, but Sitara would claw her back by using pity, aggression or would insinuate she'd have to spread it around that Sarah was racist and that's why she'd left her. Sarah felt trapped because her reputation was important to her and for her work in this town. She always said, 'Who would believe me, a white girl against a Pakistani Muslim woman saying she's a victim of racism. I've no chance.' The poor girl felt she was completely trapped until Amoora arrived on the scene. She was a blessing because she realised Sarah was being abused by Sitara."

Treavey sat there in silence for a second before fumbling for his note book in his trouser back pocket. It was in a leather pouch and gave off a wonderful aroma of leather when he opened it. He started writing the details he'd recovered so far with his biro which refused to work at first, but having drawn the nib along the rubber sole of his boot the ink began to flow freely.

He paused before asking, "How long were they together for?"

"About two years, I'd say." Claire estimated then shook her head in despair. "Poor Sarah, my dear sister, can I see her?"

"Not at the moment Claire, I'm sorry. You know, forensics and stuff and the station are not set up for visitors either. She will probably be allowed a phone call though. Are your parents about?"

"No. No parents. Both dead. They are both dead."

Treavey decided it wasn't the time to ask any more. "I'm so sorry to hear that, Claire."

Having obtained Sarah's and Sitara's address along with a few other details such as establishing there was no local next of kin for Sitara, Treavey moved towards the door. Claire followed him and stood there whilst Treavey turned around to face her and put his hands on each of Claire's arms.

"I'll tell you whatever I can, you know. Sorry this had to happen."

Claire looked as if she was going to give Treavey a hug but caught herself. "The worst part about this Treavey, is that all the bullshit that woman was spreading about my Sarah, they'll think it's all true now, won't they?"

"Does it matter what they think Claire? Does it really matter what some people in Newquay think at the end of the day? It's very easy to believe one account, especially if it's from a person they like, but they don't always see the real person. Infatuation is a dangerous thing if not handled well. It becomes a drive which takes over them, and they will do anything to either get that person back and continue to abuse them or to destroy them if they do leave. Those who think those things, it's probably not even their fault. They are probably decent people but have just believed one person's word. I bet they didn't know Sarah, did they?"

"Oh god no." Claire replied with a hint of a smile beginning to break. "Sitara's friends liked her because she always helped them out and like I said before, she was an angel on the surface. Just don't get on the wrong side of her, and I suspect some of them knew that, so it was simpler to stay on her side."

Treavey left Claire having told her that CID would be in touch later. He would hand the address of Sarah and Sitara over to CID, but they were probably already at her address from having already booked Sarah into custody.

Treavey asked for radio talk-through with Adam and passed the address. He growled back, almost like a drunken sailor, but Adam was drunk on happiness, not alcohol. He didn't need alcohol. Just his tobacco.

"Thanks, G32, that's good work. I'll pass it on to the DS as she's not saying anything right now and she's got a door key on her so that makes that easy, obliged."

Having been satisfied with his work so far tonight but knowing he had a long statement to write, he thought he would make some time to drive past Superintendent Steer's house for good measure. He didn't know why but he was just drawn to it. He wondered what had gone on in that house. So many questions. Was his Superintendent lying to him when he said he didn't know what had happened to her? They were cranking up the missing persons reports on her and making them more public. Of course, you'd have the suspicions circulating about him and much speculation. Those anti police brigade was already publicly crying,' police cover up.' There was nothing he was going to achieve by driving by, but he did so anyway. It was 3.00am and all was in darkness, apart from a security light in his rear garden shining up above the bush lined fence. Treavey told himself off for imagining his boss burying the corpse of his wife or digging it up to move it. It was far more likely to be a fox which had wandered in, to feed on tit bits left around the dustbins.

He drove off once the light switched off and noted to himself to record the event and time in his pocket notebook later. You just never knew what could be important later.

Turning into the police station car park, Treavey noticed Adam heading towards the front door of the station from his own car.

"Hey Adam. Quite a night huh?" Treavey shouted from his open window as he parked up.

"Yes, Treavey," Adam replied, not breaking his pace towards the door but he turned to face him as he slipped his security tag into the side panel and pulled the heavy metal door open. "It's all going off tonight. Some information about the Superintendent has come in too. Don't for God's sake say anything, Treavey," he looked around him as if he was just about to pass a secret code to a foreign agent, "The neighbour's come up trumps, we hope. Can't say anything more at the moment, mate."

"You can't do that to me, Adam," Treavey protested. "Come on, give us a clue. What have they said?"

Adam tapped his finger against his nose, grinned and paced off into the station. Treavey made a vain attempt to catch up, having locked his police car but the door swung back behind Adam, and he was gone. Treavey was left to fish around for his own tag to follow.

He made his way to the report room and pulled some slips of statement paper from the neat stacks of wire trays, each with a separate form for a different task. A front page of headed paper, and a few copies of continuation paper. He sat down and took his pen out from his shirt pocket, pulled the cap off and held his hands aloft as if just about to conduct an orchestra. 'Right,' he thought, 'I am police constable Mike Treave from the Devon and Cornwall Constabulary, currently stationed at Newquay Police Station...' It was going to take a while, but he may just be finished by home time.

Chapter 7
Love on the Island

Another simply gorgeous day and Treavey had decided to take a walk to Porth Beach before his late turn at the station. There was no need for shoes from where he lived in Lusty Glaze Road and the only clothing was a pair of blue surf shorts and a simple white t-shirt. His tan was coming on well, despite the regular night shifts. As he started along the road from his flat, which made up part of the coastal footpath, he began to appreciate the career he had begun. He thought of all those officers who were working in inner cities who may just have a small park to walk in, or maybe the only respite they had was a coffee shop somewhere. He breathed in the warm air, feeling the soft caress of the Cornish breeze coming off the sea. There was a slight saltiness which, whenever he smelt it, it reminded him of home; of Cornwall and it was an instant memory which he was recharging again.

The road came to a sudden stop and a path led on across the top of a lush green field with the odd wild rabbit grazing in the distance on some dandelion and fresh shoots of grass. They were far too timid to jump and bounce towards him to see who the stranger was crossing their territory. As a teenager, he would wait for his friend who had a lurcher dog to come to his window and they'd sneak out in the night to go lamping. He could never do that now, and he even felt uncomfortable at the time, but the rabbits they caught went to good use for food for the dogs and meat for his friends. Treavey hadn't told his parents at the time so could hardly turn up on the kitchen table with a brace of rabbit to cook without some searching questions.

The path worn into the grass where many walkers had etched their proof they'd been there with their feet, wound its way down the hill to a more substantial path at the top of Porth Beach. Some steep concrete steps with a rusty handrail invited the walker onto the beach at low tide but led to a swirling cauldron of broth of greens, blues and white at high tide. Treavey chose to continue down the rustic earth and rock path with the original field continuing beside him but above head height to his right. On his left, a thick continuous bramble bush which supplied cover for many a garden bird. The chirps of small sparrows could be heard from within but were rarely seen. They had a different world in there. A world of tracks through the branches towards their roosting areas within and communal meeting places for the other birds, such as robins, and blue tits. Starlings would rather roost somewhere with hundreds, if not thousands of their namesake in what were like cities of roosts compared to the towns and village communities the garden birds preferred. All were well protected, the starlings by their numbers, the smaller birds by the thorns which entwined the bird villages of bramble bushes.

Treavey exchanged some pleasantries with some passer-by before continuing to the bottom of the path where it met the road. A skip down a couple of concrete steps and he was feeling the hot sand under his feet and between his toes. This was a pleasure he would never get sick of. He began to walk across the soft sand, winding his way around the territories of families who had set their boundaries with blankets or towels, some with windbreaks, and others with surfboards. Holiday makers of all shapes, colours and sizes relaxed their stresses away under the baking sun, smothered in sun lotion and smelling of coconut oil. Treavey instantly recognised the most blissful feeling of all when he sighted a couple who had just returned from the chilly sea in their swimsuits and flopped down on their towels letting the sun dry their glistening bodies naturally. The salt water sparkled as their stomachs rose and fell as they breathed heavily from the run up the beach. They would taste the salt on their lips whilst a shiver travelled down their spines followed by an instant blast of warmth which would hug them like a loving parent. There was no other feeling like it.

"Treavey!" came a familiar voice. It was Claire.

The two chatted for a moment or two. Claire was on her own and was wearing pink flip flops, a short summery floral skirt over, he presumed, her bikini bottoms and a pink bikini top. She flicked her fringe from her gorgeous blue eyes, Treavey had fallen so much in love with, along with her perfect white teeth with a smile which he instantly relaxed with.

"Hey, I'm just going for a walk on the island to clear my mind. Did you... want to join me?"

"Sure, why not?!" Claire replied enthusiastically and they both started walking towards the Mermaid Inn steps which was like the gatehouse to the beach entrance on the opposite side. As they made their way towards it, they both glanced over to their left at the Island which lay in wait for them. A river entered the far side of the beach near the Mermaid so crossing that for a more direct path would have meant negotiating a current and sometimes thigh high water, so the Mermaid Inn entrance meant a calmer and dryer adventure.

The island rose out of Porth Bay like the spine of an athlete pushing up from a powerful press up. Every sinew of muscle was etched into the earth and rock, the shoulders seemed flexed, and the spine narrowed towards to waist where the landmass joined the coastal road once more to some form of normality.

"You seem deep in thought, Treavey," Claire commented.

"Sorry, I just love this place, and you've made this day that little bit better."

Claire giggled and an awkward silence came over them for a second before Treavey recovered the situation, "I come here often, it's the most incredible place. Do you come here often?"

Claire giggled again, joking with Treavey, "Do I come here often? Is that the best you can do?"

They both laughed and chatted as they climbed the few steps on to the pavement to the coast road and walked towards the island with the fast-flowing river between them and the beach.

"I've watched a few rescues because of this fresh water, Claire. Sounds strange but when fresh water in a current such as this river joins the sea which is obviously salt, it doesn't mix very well, and can form two layers running in different directions, so if someone is swimming in it, they can get into trouble. It causes a rip tide and then people are just swept away."

He glanced across to Claire for some confirmation he wasn't boring her too much. It didn't look like he was, so he continued.

"I remember one of those yellow Wessex rescue helicopters coming to this very spot, as a small child. I watched from over there, where I've just come from. The diver was lowered after a while of hovering, and he put a man in the sling, and they started to raise it up but what turned out to be a very dead body fell out of the sling and onto the diver. Can you imagine that?"

"Jesus Treavey, how old were you? That must have been nasty to watch."

"Oh, about ten, I think. Maybe twelve. I would have just run out to watch the helicopter like everyone else and then I would have gone home afterwards as if nothing had happened. We got used to watching rescues around here."

They walked through the metal gate from the road onto the path which led to the island where Treavey had located James Leverton, the man who had been involved in the pub fight. How different it looked at this time of the day; so inviting and welcoming with a vast green and lush view stretching ahead to the rocky mounds in the distance. Treavey stopped noticing the scenery around him as he enjoyed the company of Claire more. He thought back to Felicity and how he had messed up so badly with her as a potential girlfriend by not reading the signals but if he was honest with himself, he had ignored her signals entirely. Claire had been freely topless with Treavey on Fistral beach, a moment he had re-lived in his mind many times, but had it been because she'd merely felt safe with him? Was she going to be horrified and embarrassed if Treavey made a move on her? And now there was the small matter of whether it was appropriate to have a relationship with her if she was a potential witness, being the sister of a murder suspect. Was she considered vulnerable as her sister had been arrested for murder and Treavey had been directly involved by being the person who'd arrested her. It was getting complicated.

Contemplating his disastrous love life so far, Treavey glanced over to the river down to the side and saw a peculiar sight of a young seagull rolling in a shallow part of the water where the river widened. He'd never seen this before and pointed it out to Claire. Younger herring gulls were grey and mottled, and this one had learned quickly by managing to wash itself in the shallows of the freshwater stream running down the beach towards the sea edge. Its colleagues standing around him were ignoring his antics but instead were dipping their heads under the water to do the best they could. Even in a flock of gulls there were individuals with their own characters.

"Treavey, you know that copper's wife who went missing?"

"Er, yes," Treavey replied suspiciously, already thinking about vetting any answer he would give.

"Have they arrested him yet? The gossip in town is all about it being a cover up. I mean, it has to be him, right?"

"Not right, no Claire. There's nothing to suspect him of it apart from it being his wife but I can say that all avenues are being investigated, okay?"

He felt he'd been abrupt and could see that Claire had got the message not to speculate any further. She had witnessed Treavey's personal side, and his professional side and she'd just found out she'd probably just crossed the line.

Treavey broke the awkward silence. "It is strange though, I grant you. His wife, Lisa, has been reported missing as you'll have noticed in the press and there's no hint of her, and yet nothing to raise suspicion against the Superintendent either. I'm not giving anything away because I know as much as you. CID don't exactly share what they know to us minions on response. He thought back to what Adam had told him at the station about the neighbours being particularly useful. Best that was kept to himself.

They both began to walk over the wooden footbridge which led to the Island itself and stopped halfway to look over the edge at the sand far below with a trickle of water. Treavey felt obliged to tell Claire about his grandfather's dog which fell over the edge but survived. This time there was no water below them apart from the circular rockpool which was refilled with fresh salt water every high tide, and which shared the history of catching his grandfather's dog, Gyp, within its grasp, and thus saving its life.

They enjoyed the view, looking one way out to sea, with a series of boulders and another smaller island with breeding seabirds keeping watch some 100 metres away, and then they turned to view the other side, watching where the channel, blasted out by the iron miners, led out towards Porth Beach itself and the families having fun beyond.

Treavey was feeling relaxed and took the chance of a quick look at Claire standing closely next to him. She glanced up, catching him out, flicking her eyes up at his and smiling beautifully. He noticed the sun was shining off her hair which fell over her forehead. He was falling for her, but he was undecided on what to do. He wanted to go further with her, but he knew it could be looked down on by his peers. He turned around and grabbed her hand as he did so, encouraging her further, up the steps and past his grandfather's granite bench. He'd show that to her on the way back, but he was enjoying pulling her up the path listening to her giggling as he did so.

They crossed the 'bouncy grass' as Treavey used to describe it when he was younger. He would run across it and feel like he was on the moon with it being so spongy, which forced him to run slowly taking large, slow strides. It was when he was with his parents in the past, his father now dead, but his mother still in Newquay flooding back the memories for him.

It was whilst they were enjoying each other's company Claire stopped in her tracks and her eyes settled on something in the distance. Treavey could feel it was serious and he followed her gaze to a man standing on the edge of the cliff which looked out across Whipsiderry Beach and up towards Watergate Bay.

"Not another one," she quietly whispered. "I don't want another one."

They approached the figure carefully who didn't look back, but remained looking out to sea, standing motionless. It was a stout figure with grey wispy hair which fluttered in the breeze, the only part of him moving. His arms held straight down by his sides. He wore a blazer and some faded jeans. Even from the back he looked sad.

Treavey approached a few metres off to the side and assumed a similar position as the man before glancing over to him as if he'd done so casually for a friendly conversation.

"Mr Steer? Oh, Superintendent Steer, it's you."

It had taken him aback. Treavey was caught off guard and struggled to gather his composure. The Superintendent looked across before smiling at him. "Oh hello, Treavey, I'm just enjoying the view. Everything okay with you? Who are you with? Who's this delightful young lady?"

Treavey joined him before walking back towards Claire and introduced him to her. He wasn't convinced the Superintendent was just taking in the view, but maybe he had been. Maybe he was enjoying the solitude before Treavey and Claire had disrupted it so abruptly.

The three of them walked towards the end of the Island where the lush soft grasses met the sudden drop onto black, knife edged splinters of rock, all of them breaking the ice by commenting on the wonderful view and how fortunate they were to be living and working in such a beautiful area. Treavey approached the elephant in the room.

"How are you Sir?" Treavey felt he needed to show the level of respect he would as if he were at work. It may not encourage such a relaxed reply but would have risked him coming across as a cocky young PC just out of his probation.

"I'm a bit out of sorts to be honest with you. I have no idea where my wife, Lisa has gone. I don't even know if I want her back anymore because I am angry with her now. Why would she have just left me with no notice like this? Why make me look like a suspect in everyone's eyes? Does she hate me that much?"

With every word, Treavey couldn't help himself wonder if what he was being told was the frustrated words of an abandoned husband or the jealous words of an evil killer? Maybe he had been visiting her when Treavey and Claire had come across him. Was this where he had disposed of the body?

"What brings you here though? Just out for a walk?" Treavey asked hoping he wasn't being as transparent as he sounded.

Superintendent Steer took his blazer off, hooking his finger through the collar loop and casually slung it over his shoulder. "We used to walk here when we first met. It's a lovely place, and helps clear the mind, don't you think?"

"I thought you were thinking of jumping for a moment." Treavey found himself directly coming out with.

Superintendent Steer glanced across at him, surprised at Treavey's candour. "Oh no, no chance of that. I want to find out what has happened to Lisa. Yes, it goes through your mind, I can't deny that. It's a horrible place I am in, at the moment. Everything is in suspension, even me, you could say. I am suspended from work, or on compassionate leave as they put it officially, but I know what everyone is thinking, but no, I wouldn't do that; not yet anyway!" He laughed with a hint of embarrassment as if he had regretted saying it.

"I hope you don't mind me asking. What do you think has really happened?" Treavey was in for a penny, in for a pound. At least he would know what he'd told CID, and it sounded as though he was grateful to just be talking to someone."

"Look, Treavey," he replied, as if getting ready for a difficult conversation. "I think I have a link with you, with you saving my life and all that. I can tell you I didn't suspect a thing, but many men are in the dark when it comes to what their partners are up to. I think she's just upped and left. I think she's found someone else and had the opportunity to disappear. No children, no parents here either. No reason to stay."

"Do you think she's safe?"

"Is she alive, you mean? Oh yes, I've no doubts about that. With all respect to her, she was an older woman than the usual type abducted and murdered by strangers and usually it's done in such haste the body is found relatively quickly. There are no signs, there has been no major arguments between us, and she hasn't been depressed as far as I know so I can't see any reason why she would just disappear, unless..." he looked across towards Newquay across the golden beaches towards the harbour in the distance, "... unless she had got utterly bored with me and found some excitement elsewhere. I can't blame her, I suppose. She'd got to know a woman in town recently and I'd assumed they'd just hit it off, but she was quite young. An Asian looking woman. Unusual in Newquay."

"Asian?" Claire pricked her ears up. "Do you know her name?"

"Talusa or something," he replied. "She must have mentioned her once so I can't remember. Maybe she went off with her, I don't know."

"Could it have been Sitara?" Claire suggested.

"Yes, it could have been. Talusa, Sitara. Maybe, maybe not. Who knows? It wasn't a name I'd heard before."

Having returned to the road, they parted company with Treavey and Claire deciding to have a drink in the Mermaid Inn. They collected two glasses of Coke and took them to a table outside at the back on a picnic table. They looked at each other in silence for a few seconds.

"Wow!" Treavey exclaimed.

"Yes, wow," Claire admitted. "It has to be the same person, doesn't it?"

"We can't jump to conclusions but it's worth noting. It's sort of a similar name but doesn't even start with the same letter. It only has three letters in common in fact. But there aren't many Asians or South Asians in Newquay. You sort of notice these things." He sipped his Coke, put it down, then picked it up for a larger gulp. "And even if it is the same person, it's Sitara who's dead, she wasn't the murderer, your sister…" He faded away.

"I know. My sister is." Claire ended the sentence for him. The mood turned solemn, and they both awkwardly turned away from each other to stare across the beach. Claire looked devastated. She had forgotten the stress for the morning, and it had now come rushing back to her. Treavey felt guilty for bringing it up. He knew he had ruined the atmosphere. They didn't mention it again.

Treavey was on patrol in his panda car just a little later that afternoon. He loved driving in afternoons such as this, with the sun shining and everyone in a good mood and yet there was always a chance that something exciting was about to happen. He waited for the radio to call his call sign, but it just babbled on about someone making a complaint about their neighbour. Neighbourly disputes were a nightmare as often it involved one bully and the other desperately trying to have a normal life. The bully was usually someone who shouted and got what they demanded from society without lifting a finger themselves, and the poor suffering neighbour was having to deal with the other parking on their land, damaging their fence or creating unnecessary noise late at night. Treavey had told himself never to get a solicitor involved in these cases and one poor victim had racked up £30,000 in solicitors' bills and the neighbour simply changed his tactic and hassled them in another way instead. Treavey had sworn that if he ever had a noisy neighbour himself, as it would inevitably be in the early hours of the morning when he was trying to get some sleep for an early turn, he would make sure he put his own stereo on loud for 6.00am as loud as possible next to the wall of his neighbour who wouldn't have a job to get up to for sure.

With his future neighbourly dispute tactic sorted, the rest of the afternoon was uneventful, so he decided to go back to the station for an early meal break. Sooty was there, the officer he first met at the scene of the armed robbery, so he had a catch up to see what he had been up to. Treavey munched his cheese and pickle in granary bread sandwiches he enjoyed so much and had a cup of coffee. As was usual, just as Sooty was getting on his soap box about the lack of support police were receiving from the courts, the police radio called out for any unit to attend a report of a domestic incident occurring at a house in Mount Wise. Without hesitation, the remaining sandwich was pushed into his mouth and Treavey was on his way out to his car, half choking on the remains.

As he slammed the door behind him and headed for his panda parked reversed in to the parking spot and ready to go, he heard Sooty behind him. "I'll come too, mate."

Sooty headed for his own car, and with Treavey putting his foot to the floor, both police cars roared out of the station like an old-fashioned formula one race start and headed into the town with blue lights flashing and sirens nee-nauwing.

Only seven minutes later the two cars arrived at their destination and Treavey was the first out of his car, walking up to the front door of the house. An elderly woman neighbour caught his eye and beckoned him over to them.

"Excuse me, Officer. I called you. I'm really concerned about the children in there. There are three of them, they are young, and I rarely see them but when I do, the poor little mites are filthy, and they look malnourished. They look as though they could do with a good bath and some food. My nephew knows the older one in school and says the family are known as 'the stinkies.'

Oh, and the language by the parents. It could make your ears bleed."

Treavey noted she'd already given her details to the police control room, and he had a good feeling about her information being accurate. She had a motherly look about her and a concerned tone to her voice. Sooty was already wrapping his knuckles on the front door of the flat into a semi-detached local authority house. The address was the bottom floor of what used to be a two-storey house.

Sooty was shouting through the letter box but getting no answer but there was obviously someone in there as voices could be heard. A moment later the door cracked open slightly with a chain clinking in the gap and a very gaunt looking middle-aged woman with filthy long dark straggly hair peered through the gap.

"Wayne! It's the cops. Am I letting them in?"

"Yes, you are," replied Sooty in a stern voice without any hesitation.

The woman didn't budge however, even when a voice boomed out from behind her. "Tell them they can fuck right off. We don't want any filthy pigs in here."

"I suspect we'll be the cleanest things in there," Sooty replied under his breath but not quietly enough.

"Cheeky sod," the woman replied. "No, you lot can fuck off. There are no problems in here. Get lost."

Sooty stepped back as the door slammed in his face and he nonchalantly turned to Treavey. Treavey had been talking to the neighbour to get more information from her and had made his decision.

"Sooty, we have to go in. That lady has been telling me there's been a woman screaming in there and the children have been crying. She said it was like Armageddon in there, the children have gone silent without warning and she's frightened that something sinister has gone on in there."

Sooty agreed. "Now the neighbour has told us, we can hardly ignore it. We've got a power of entry. Think it's the children's act or something, anyway I don't care what it is, we've got to go in to check those children are safe, agree?"

"Agreed," replied Treavey. "Let's do it."

Treavey approached the door this time. Maybe with Sooty being the bad cop, he could be the good cop. He banged on the door and asked the lady to come to the door again. "We need to come in for a chat, just to see if the children are safe, that's all. We won't be long."

There was no reply. Treavey looked around him to see there was a bit of a gathering of neighbours congregating. He knew he had to be confident and get it right as it could get very awkward if they thought the police were hassling the couple and started taunting the police, but he hadn't had trouble on this estate before.

He needn't have worried. The residents were very much on side of the police. They were fed up with the family and their antisocial behaviour, shouting in the street, arguing with each other, and fighting amongst themselves.

Treavey shouted through the letterbox once more, "We are going to have to force the door if you don't let us in. We have concerns with the children. Let us in now or we will break the door in, do you understand. I am not bluffing."

"The kids are fine, thank you very much. We look after our kids. Fuck off why don't you?"

Treavey was losing patience. "Strangely enough, we can't just take your word for it. We'll come in, in 2 minutes, so it's up to you whether you prefer to do it the civilised way or with a broken door to fix."

Sooty and Treavey counted the two minutes leaving the last 10 seconds to count out loud. They were committed. Their bluff had been called.

'Bang' and the door went in with the use of the 20kg 'red key' which was a weighted battering ram kept in every station for just these moments. It was a bit of overkill to be honest, as the door flew open over 90 degrees slamming against the wall behind it and immediately jamming. Treavey was the first in, as he liked to be, to show he wasn't intimidated, only to be met with the couple backing off into the lounge shouting, "Okay, okay, there's no need for that. You'll scare our babies."

Sooty stayed in the lounge whilst Treavey searched the flat for the children. The flat smelt horribly and on opening the door to the bedroom, he was hit by the stench of ammonia. It was a scene out of Oliver Twist. The depravity which lay before him was staggering. The results of little or no care, bone idleness, selfishness, anger and perhaps a little evil. Or was it? He knew it was a complicated situation, but he didn't feel like giving the parents much sympathy at this stage. Were they criminals or did they need help? What was their upbringing like? Will the police be smashing the doors down of these little mites in 15 years' time.

There were two younger girls with an older boy sharing only two bunks in the tiny room. The bunks had filthy mattresses with no sheets, the quilts were scrunched up on the floor and had been discarded weeks earlier by the looks of them. The smaller little girl, who must have been no older than two years old, was sitting on the stained and torn carpet exposing the floorboards beneath. She had the largest of deep hazel eyes staring at Treavey underneath a frame of matted blonde hair. Her mouth was held open in shock and wander, her red cheeks prominent and her bare arms coming from her dirty vest held out to her side as if she were unsure whether to crawl away to safety or to risk feeling some warmth and contact and risk being picked up by the stranger who had entered the room. Raw red marks framed the nappy which was clinging to her waist and hadn't been changed for some time. The middle child of approximately four years old was at the end of the bottom bunk holding a plastic toy from a cereal box, and the oldest child, a little boy of seven was lying on the top bunk with a tear rolling down his cheek, too frightened to cry audibly.

Treavey spoke with soft words of comfort, and the children visually relaxed a little and continued playing with whatever they had found around their prison cell. Treavey couldn't stand the smell any longer so reached across to open the window, but he already knew it would have minimal effect on the stench which lay within. He returned to the lounge and stood with Sooty who was taking some notes in his pocket notebook.

"Sooty." Treavey interrupted.

"Yes mate?" Sooty replied, not taking his pen off his pocket notebook. "I'm just grabbing their details. I've got Angela Johns here and Andy Simmons, right? I've called for the Sergeant to examine the door and bring the station camera to photograph the damage. It's been smashed open a few times in its life I see, but I suspect your landlord will have trouble repairing it this time. The frame is completely buckled."

"Mate, you need to come and have a look." Treavey watched the couple who were looking decidedly nervous, the woman of whom, a skeleton of a woman with thinning greasy black hair and saggy undefinable tattoos on her arms stood up and approached Treavey with some haste.

"Leave my babies alone," she screeched at the top of her voice. "I've done nothing wrong, leave my babies alone, I look after them."

Treavey put his arms up to prevent her from coming closer. "You need to stop there. Those babies of yours are in a disgusting state. They are filthy and you've decided to shove any money you've had up your veins instead of giving them the life they deserve. You've decided that, no one else has."

Treavey was fuming and could feel he'd lost it completely. Sooty looked agog but remained rooted to the spot, watching. The male partner, Andy, sat motionless watching the show developing before him. He was the mouse of the family. It was clear Angela was very much the person in charge.

"I can't afford anything, can I?" she protested.

Treavey hadn't finished. You can't afford some elbow grease then? You can't afford some water and some basic cleaning product to wash their bedding or their clothes? You can't afford to change their nappies or even use terry's nappies so you can reuse them? Instead, you leave them in their mess, so they get sore? Seriously?"

There were tears rolling down the woman's face. She showed her frustration by slumping her body like a child, "humph." she replied. "I can't help it. I don't know what to do, I don't know where to start. Don't take my babies away, please."

Sooty walked out to see the children for himself and Treavey remained with the couple. "Look, we must have someone come and look at their condition and welfare. I don't know what will happen, but you've got a drug habit you need to sort out before anything comes close to changing around here. You are at a junction now. You decide to sort your miserable lives out now, or you carry on like this until you've lost everything, including your life. Only you can decide that."

"Andy and I just have a little smack now and then. We need it but I promise you on my kids' lives we don't do too much of it. We couldn't afford it anyway. We always know what we are doing, never spaced out, don't we Andy? I mean, those kids are safe with us. No harm can come to them."

Sooty returned to the lounge area again and Treavey waited to hear what he had to say.

"That is criminal in there. You should be ashamed of yourselves. I'm calling the Inspector out so we can decide the next step, but it will involve social services. Are they involved already?

Angela slumped back onto the sofa again. "Yes. We did have a social worker, anyway but I can't remember her name... I can't remember."

Whilst Sooty went out of the room to speak to the inspector on the radio, Treavey stood in silence, looking around the room at the filth and he doubted it had ever been cleaned since they had moved in. The floor was a thinning carpet matted in dirt. Patches of browns made up the tapestry of hair, dust, and dirt. There were piles of video boxes, and laundry which hadn't quite made it back to the bedrooms again, and several ash trays utilised out of any receptacle they could find at arm's reach at the time. The sofa showed a history of spilt liquids, and looked stained and worn. Treavey was not going to be sitting down. The whole place would have sent a petri dish wild. Even the air felt dirty. He hated this part of this job, breathing in the dust produced from God knows where. There on the ledges around the electric fire on the floor were several cups with blue and white mould in the bottoms of half-drunk discarded cups of coffee. He wouldn't be accepting a coffee here today either. Sooty returned.

"Right, we are going to get social services out to have a look but if there is any delay, we will have to take you all the police station so we can wait there. You will be voluntary attenders for now unless you don't want to be, of course. You do understand we can't leave these children like this and kept in this environment, don't you?"

"How long are they going to be?" Andy asked.

Sooty propped himself against the edge of an armchair, checking his back so he could see he wasn't going to fall back and make a fool of himself. "Who knows? We'll give it half an hour to see if we get an answer but otherwise, we'll have to take the children into safety ourselves with you guys and that paperwork will have to be sorted out then."

Andy stood up and began walking towards the kitchen. Treavey kept an eye on him in case he was making an attempt to run but could see everything without moving himself. Andy shouted, "Any of you two want a cup of coffee or tea?"

As quick as a flash, Treavey blurted out, "Well that's very kind of you, Andy. I've just had one, but my colleague was just telling me how thirsty he was."

Sooty looked at Treavey in horror. "What, no. No, don't worry about me, I'm fine, really."

"No bother really," Andy shouted back. "I've got some clean cups around here somewhere or I can rinse this one out." Andy clanked about in the sink, and a cup being rinsed under the tap could be heard.

"No really, Andy, I don't want a coffee thanks, thanks anyway." Sooty glared at Treavey who was beaming from ear to ear trying to restrain a laugh which was bubbling away and ready to erupt from his stomach. Sooty shook his head and was failing to see the funny side. Treavey, however, was enjoying the moment with relish.

Treavey took the opportunity to have some fresh air whilst they waited for some more instructions from the Inspector who was currently calling social services to decide the next stage. He wandered around to the back garden and gazed across the long grass and faded plastic sand pit which had long since witnessed its last play. The sun was blazing down, and as he walked around the garden, Treavey felt the sweat begin to trickle down his forehead. This was miserable now. He didn't want to drink the water in the flat, but he didn't have any on him either and it was going to be some time before this job was over. How he wished he could forward time.

"Officer!" A muffled voice came from the opposite side of the garden. Treavey wandered over to get closer to a shifty looking elderly man with a bald head and deeply wrinkled face which gave his years of smoking and poor diet away. He estimated he was in his eighties, yet he was quite a sprightly man, peering over the top of the panel fence.

"Yes Sir. How can I help you?" Treavey replied. He suspected it was going to be a comment about how things had changed and that criminals just got away with it nowadays, or that he was once caught scrumping and got a clip around the ear and when he'd gone home and told his parents, he got another one from them. He had heard this story so many times before.

"I suspect there's something around the side of that shed, officer. You didn't hear it from me, but they are often coming out here and so I look through the fence here, through this knot in the wood which has fallen out. The man especially, Andy I think, goes there all the time. I've been dying to find out what it is."

Without any delay, Treavey traipsed over to the side of the shed and initially felt disappointed as it looked like whatever had been there was there no longer. He knelt down on his haunches and began prodding about where he could reach under the shed in the gap between the wall and the shed. He could feel a bit of plastic so withdrew his hand and quickly put his leather glove on to avoid contaminating any fingerprints there may be. He was back where he had been a minute later and gave it a tug and was relieved to see it come out quite easily and was surprisingly clean for where it had been stored. It was a Tesco's plastic bag with a weighty object in it. He glanced over at the old man who had gone out of view, but he was looking through the hole in the fence as Treavey could see the movement from behind. He reached inside the bag and pulled out two large blocks of what looked like heroin. He was no expert so would have to have it tested but it was a yellowy brown substance, and it was more likely that than anything else, especially in the rear garden of these two.

"Hey, Sir?" Treavey called out to a blank fence.

The elderly man popped his head back over the top and replied, "Oh, hello officer, have you found anything?" as if he were showing little interest to the proceedings.

"Only what you've already seen," Treavey replied knowingly. "Would you be prepared to give me a statement on what you've seen? I need to link them to the bag, you see."

The man's wrinkles tightened up even further. "Not a chance, I'm afraid. I'm not a snitch."

Treavey nodded, half expecting the answer, and couldn't resist a "Not on paper, anyway sir," before walking back towards the flat with the carrier bag swinging in his hand. It was worth asking the neighbour, but he didn't blame him for not wanting to get involved. He would send the bag and packaging to forensics who would hopefully find some carelessly left fingerprints by

Adam and, or Angela. Otherwise, they may say the bag had been there for years from the previous tenants. Unlikely though, as the bag looked so knew but there would be sufficient doubt. How he had found the bag would be a mystery to them, however.

Having put the bag with the drugs safely in the police car, he returned to the flat to speak to Sooty who was looking very bored, by now.

Sooty pulled Treavey aside and said "Mate, I've just checked the children who don't seem in any immediate danger, and they aren't looking too thin however the baby has a nasty nappy rash which needs being looked at by medics, so I've called the ambulance to have a good look at all of them. I've ventured into that hell hole of a kitchen and strangely enough," Sooty turned to a sarcastic tone, "... I haven't been able to locate any vegetables anywhere. The freezer is empty, there's a couple of baby food jars out of date some months ago, and the only evidence of food I can find is half a loaf of white bread and several empty crisp packets. Poor little sods. What chance do they really have in life. Fast forward and how many of these three will be taking drugs to get over the trauma of their Mum and Dad?"

Treavey took a breath, "Sooty, I think I can short cut a few things. If we don't have enough for neglect or cruelty, which we probably do have, we certainly have enough for Peewits."

"Peewits? How come you think we have enough for possession with intent to supply?" Sooty exclaimed with surprise, but with some inquisitiveness too. He wanted to know more.

Treavey explained what had happened and Sooty slapped him on the arm. "Well done buddy, nice one. You'd better do the honours then and I'll arrange another unit to help with the kids and a van for those two. Best try to keep them separate now so they can't confer and cook up a story between them."

"What do you think will happen to the children, Sooty? They'll be okay, won't they? I don't want them separated and in care homes if possible. They aren't good places."

"You've got to be joking, right? The parents will get done. No doubt Adam will cough the possession to leave his missus to look after the kids, and at least the kids will have a full MOT and a meal at the station whilst the authorities check them over. They only separate the kids as a last resort now, and the abuse hasn't been severe enough to take the kids off their mother. It's the luck of the gods it wasn't you or me being born into a hell hole like these poor buggers."

Chapter 8

Cash not in transit

The weather across Newquay was not looking as charming as it had been recently. Treavey had arranged to meet Claire in town at a cafe in that afternoon. It was drizzly outside, and the beaches were empty apart from the odd dog walker who was hunched in their coat with the hood pulled up around their faces to protect them from the elements. They were enjoying a little time together sipping their coffee. He was confident enough to feel comfortable with keeping his stare on Claire's enticingly deep blue eyes. He could see she was relaxed with him but there was something holding him back, still.

"Claire, I need to confront the elephant in the room."

Claire smiled and acted as if she were offended. "I didn't know I was fat," she replied.

"No, no, you have a perfect body, believe me, but you know, I need to put my cards on the table and tell you, my predicament."

Claire could see things were serious suddenly and shuffled on her chair as if finding a more comfortable position. She took a sip of her coffee and kept her eyes on Treavey, staring right into his eyes.

"You aren't making this easy for me," Treavey said. "Look, I don't think I'm wrong when I say I think we quite like each other, right? Am I right?"

Claire didn't say anything for a few uncomfortable few seconds; and then… "You wouldn't be wrong, Treavey. Yes, I do like you. I like you like crazy." She placed her elbows on the table, placed her chin in the cups of her hands and smiled at him.

It was Treavey's turn to be silent. He was quite taken aback and thought carefully about his next move. "Look, I'm really glad to hear you say that, and I can't wait to kiss you, I mean really kiss you, but there's a problem."

"My sister, right?" Claire blurted out.

"Yes. You could be considered vulnerable, and it could be thought that I'm taking advantage of you."

"By all means," Claire replied, her eyes fluttering and a smile which showed off a naughtiness which sent a feeling of excitement rushing through Treavey's body. "Yes officer, if you really need to take down my particulars. I'm at your mercy!" She held out her hand to him across the table.

Treavey laughed nervously and took her hand in his, a motion he felt was so natural. He loved the feeling he had with her right now and just gazing into her face, analysing her freckles and a sudden dimple which surfaced from nowhere.

"Are you purposefully not making this easy for me?" Treavey replied hesitantly.

Claire pulled his hand closer to her, and her foot touched his, under the table. "Look, Treavey, I'm a member of public who happens to be related to a girl who in my mind is a victim, but, yes, she's been arrested for murder. I can't help that, but I'm not vulnerable. I'm not falling apart. I will hope that justice will be kind to her because that bitch deserved everything coming to her."

"Not sure if my bosses will see it like that though."

"Look," Claire said, "we don't have to advertise it yet, if you don't want. We can keep it under wraps until this is over, but we aren't doing anything wrong. Surely loads of cops have relationships with people they meet during their work?"

"Yes, there are," Treavey replied, feeling more relaxed, "but it very much depends on the circumstances. If you were a witness to something like before, you know the suicidal person on the cliff by the Huers for example, then that wouldn't be a problem I guess, but now they may consider your head is elsewhere and you may just need comfort and I'm sliding in to take advantage of you."

Claire's tone changed from flirty to a somewhat more serious tone. "Look, I'm a grown woman. I am not a wilting flower. We liked each other when I met you up on that cliff. I saw you looking at my legs like that when I was wearing those shorts. I'm glad I was wearing those then."

"What do you mean?"

"I saw you staring at me, Treavey, you looked like an awkward school boy with your hand caught in the cookie jar. I knew I had you then. You do realise I had to persuade Bronwyn to join us on the beach and go topless with you. I wanted to tease you to see how you'd react with two beach chicks! I wouldn't have done that with just anyone. I wasn't sure I was getting enough attention from you, so I stood up and put my bikini top on in front of you. I would have normally done it lying down or turned away from you."

Treavey was relieved to find he hadn't been imagining all this. He fancied her from the very beginning, and it turns out she fancied him too, and not only that but she was making a play for him. He felt relieved that his instincts were good after all, following his dire performance with Felicity in Perranporth at his last station. Maybe, he should have been more open with Felicity when there was a similar feeling. He'd missed his chance, and he knew it, but perhaps it was for the best. He would most likely not be sitting here with Claire otherwise.

"Look Treavey..." Claire said as if about to make an announcement. "Let's just play it by ear. Step by step. There's no harm in it. It would be a travesty to ignore what we have in front of us and anyway, I want to snog that face of yours. It's my right as a public citizen and you are my public servant."

Treavey felt a shiver run through his body. He was excited and felt ever so safe with her but there was a nagging issue he couldn't wipe from his mind completely. Was he trying to ignore the obvious? Was it going to end in a disciplinary investigation against him later? Was he just taken over by him being so keen on her and perhaps she was more involved in the murder that her sister was involved in after all? Was he being naive?

The conversation changed to a lighter tone. "You live down in Lusty Glaze, don't you?" Claire enquired whilst running her finger along the grain in the wooden table in front of her.

"Yes, that's right. My parents ran the hotel down there. The Glendorgal. It used to be my father's parents' house. When his parents died, he turned it into a hotel."

"Oh my God," Claire exclaimed. "I heard about your dad. I was a waitress down there when I was 16."

"I was quite young when they had it, and as I got older, I went to London for a year working with the disabled to 'cut the apron strings' so I would have more chance of getting into the police. If I had said I was living at home, they'd have sent me out for some life experience, so I did a voluntary year in Hornsey in London. Just where Keith Blakelock was stationed. You know that poor PC who was murdered in the riots. Just down the road in fact."

"I remember," Claire replied, "During the Tottenham riots. The poor man. He had his head severed, didn't he? The bastards."

Both looked thoughtfully out of the window taking in the terrible impact that the murder had had. "Anyway, I reckon I knew of your dad. Was he Nigel?"

"Yes, that's right. He was older than most dads of kids my age. He had me when he was sixty. He used to be a spitfire pilot in the war. He died after having a stroke when he was just 79 unfortunately. I was 18, but I guess I grew up with the knowledge I probably wasn't going to have him for as long as other kids had their Dads around."

Claire decided to break the atmosphere. "I remember something really funny about your dad. The staff down there always spoke about him. He was funny, and very clever."

"Oh, yes?" Treavey looked on with interest.

"Yeah. They said he had this really posh lady come into the restaurant. She marched in as if she owned the place and ordered a cream tea. When they served her, they said they already knew she was trouble. She had massive diamond rings and a necklace more suited to an evening out, but she was trying to make a statement. Anyway," she grabbed Treavey's hand across the table and smiled at him, "When it came to paying the bill, she kicked off. I mean really kicked off. She was shouting so everyone would hear, 'I'm not paying this, it's far too expensive.' They ran through the bill, but she wasn't having it. She demanded to see the manager, so the waitress told her she would get the owner, but your dad was already on his way towards her table."

Treavey leaned forward with a smile as he knew he probably would be enjoying the next bit. He enjoyed hearing about him as he missed him and learning new things about him renewed his memories about him and even added to them.

"So, he comes up to the table, right, and asks her what the problem is, and she makes the mistake of thinking he was just the manager and begins berating him about the price of the cream tea, which to be honest I think was a pretty reasonable price. It wasn't a Woolworths Cafe after all. Your Dad says, "Madam, you are not just paying for the scones, the jam, cream, and tea, but also the incredible view of the coastline, the Renoirs on the walls, the marble fireplaces, and the general atmosphere. It's the experience you are paying for."

She keeps on moaning and the whole restaurant is looking on at the performance and your dad loses patience with her and says, "Madam, please just pay what you can afford."

She went apoplectic saying she had never been so insulted, and she wouldn't be coming back again and your dad..." Claire composed herself to prepare herself for the next bit she was going to enjoy and was doing all she could do to hold back her laughter. "...Your Dad says, "Well Madam, if that's a promise, you can have it for free."

Claire burst into laughter, quickly followed by Treavey. Treavey loved the fact he had heard something about his father he hadn't known before. He revelled in the fact his father was popular in the hotel, but he already knew he was extremely professional, and he respected people whoever they were and from whatever class they were from.

Claire was on a roll, enjoying some memories of her working in the hotel as a teenager. She remembered another story she had heard about the infamous father of Treavey. "Then there was the time when one of the waiters, Simon, came in late to start his shift and he crept past your dad who was sat in a huge leather chair reading a newspaper, and he stopped and felt guilty as he respected your dad. So he goes back to your dad, to give him credit, and say's to this large newspaper with your dad's legs appearing from below it, "Sir, I'm sorry I was a little bit late today." He replies, and I kid you not, your dad lowers the newspaper and appears over it and over his glasses and with perfect timing says, "My dear boy, you flatter yourself if you believe you were even missed."

Treavey let out a burst of laughter and forgot himself for a moment and glanced over his shoulder to see if anyone had noticed, which they had. An elderly couple looked on disapprovingly for causing a scene and went back to staring into the middle distance between them, continuing to say nothing to each other. They seemed to be going through the motions of being married but hating every part of it, or maybe they were just bored of each other.

They both left the coffee shop and made their way into town along the main street. The weather wasn't changing from the depressing dark cloud and fine mizzle. The two of them risked walking hand in hand, Treavey being nervous that anyone from the police station should see him. He was confused and he wasn't comfortable so he pulled away from her hand as naturally as he could, making it look as though he was interested in something in John Menzies' shop window. Just at the point Treavey had turned around to face Claire again the relative peace of the high street was broken by a noise. An automated voice. 'Cash in transit van being attacked. Call the police! Cash in transit van being attacked, Call the police!'

The noise was coming from a security van outside the Barclay's bank in front of them. There was a guard tugging on a large black container with a balaclava clad figure tugging just as hard on the other end with another thief beating the security guard around his helmet with a metal bar.

"Leave it, Treavey. Don't get involved," Claire pleaded but Treavey had already made up his mind and was heading towards the disturbance.

He broke into a trot taking in the scene looking for other suspects before fully committing himself to the two. He was looking for other weapons other than the metal bar. The two robbers had not noticed him approaching at first. Other passers-by were looking on, holding their children behind them for some protection and partly frozen to the spot. The van was continuing to sound the audible warning and request to call the police. Treavey spontaneously ran to the group of three who were making no progress between them as one battered the security guard who was holding tightly onto the container which must have had the money in it and the third robber pulling as hard as he might to try to snatch it off him.

"Police, stand where you are!" Treavey shouted in his unexpectedly booming voice. It was a sense of freedom to shout as loudly as he could in the middle of the high street and with such authority behind his demands. He hoped the shock and awe of the booming voice would break the stalemate. The man tugging the box gave up his grasp and ran towards Treavey making a detour from crashing into him at the last second to run past him. Treavey made a vain attempt to stop him by pushing his leg out to trip him up but a light skip and the man, still with his balaclava on, was up and over his leg before disappearing through the crowd. Treavey was going to get at least one offender, so he launched himself at the man who was holding the stick, but the robber was already on his feet running away up the street and fortunately away from where he knew Claire was standing.

Treavey was after him shouting, "Stop Police," whilst sprinting after him. It was only now he was taking in that the robber was a strong athletic looking man who was still wearing his black balaclava. Treavey's quarry sprinted around a right-hand bend onto Fore Street with Treavey hot on his tail. He would leave the van and the security guard to other people to sort out, but Treavey was desperate to get this man, so it was worth the risk. He couldn't possibly return without him. He simply had to catch him, and it was out of the question to do otherwise. He wasn't going to walk past such a crime in progress any time soon. He could hear a racing engine behind him which comforted him. Maybe it was someone coming to give him assistance. The car tailed him as he continued to run after the robber along the road.

The robber ran without slowing, darting from the pavement to the road to avoid colliding with any of the startled pedestrians staring in shock as he ran towards them, before darting back onto the pavement again. Treavey knew that this was the time to use his secret weapon, as he was making no headway on closing the gap. He took a lungful of air and calmly boomed, "I'm caaaaaaatching you!" The man threw his arms up in despair and pulled up like a stallion with an injury at Ascot. It was abrupt which caught Treavey by surprise who practically fell into the man pushing him towards a shop window. He slammed into it making Treavey wince, half expecting it to shatter but fortunately it held. Both men fell to the floor but before he landed on the pavement, Treavey had whipped off the balaclava revealing a young pasty-faced teenager. Not what he had expected at all. The metal bar rolled along the pavement and under a nearby parked car. Treavey was panting as much as the youth and was ecstatic he had caught up with him. He knew his reputation would be boosted massively within the station. This was a big one. He was comfortable that the young man was not going to escape. He had him well under control lying him on his front with his arm behind his back. "It's over mate. You can't do anything now. Just chill out, okay."

Treavey felt a tap on his shoulder. He wondered if the other man had come back for a second and a pang of adrenaline rushed through his body. Maybe it was the car driver who had been following so closely behind him, but it was an old man with his walking stick. "Well done son, well done, good on you," he declared, with a smile on his withered face reaching from ear to ear. He was in his late 70's if not older and his crooked teeth showed decades of life experiences, and every wrinkle was as animated as the other. He doffed his flat cap before continuing on his way, "Yes, very impressive son, well done to you," and he could be heard chuckling as he disappeared through the crowd.

Treavey looked around to see where the car driver had gone but there was no sign. A small crowd had gathered around him, one of whom caught his eye before he disappeared into the melee again. 'Hang on, was that Superintendent steer, and did he have his arm around a woman? Surely not.' Treavey thought it couldn't be. He wouldn't be so blasé about it, or could it have been his sister, or another relative perhaps? He noticed the man was visibly shocked to see Treavey, but could it actually be his wife, Lisa, who had been reported missing? Unfortunately, he hadn't got a good enough look at her. It looked like he was shocked to see Treavey but then why did he slink away. It was all very strange.

He noticed Claire pushing through the bustling holiday crowd. She wore a pained expression on her face. "Oh my God, Treavey, are you okay? I was worried about that car following you."

"Yeah, I need to thank him if I can. I mean, I think he was there to cover for me in case I got into trouble as he was sticking at my pace."

Claire crouched down beside him and said, "No, Treavey, he may have been keeping an eye on you, but he was waiting to pick your little friend up. He was the getaway driver. He soon sped off when he realised you had him pinned to the ground."

"Oh, blimey, he could have run me over then," Treavey acknowledged without taking his eyes off his prey he'd captured in front of him.

"Yes, he was choosing his moment but there were too many other people in the way luckily," Claire said whilst placing her arm around his shoulders having understood the danger Treavey had been in.

Treavey's blood ran cold. He knew he had been incredibly lucky to get away with his life. "What about the other guy who was attacking the guard, I take it he's got away, Claire?" Treavey asked with some resignation.

"Yes, I think so. He ran from you and was out of here as quick as he could. He didn't want to stick around for any more" Claire replied. "I don't know, Treavey, we go out for a coffee, and you have to get yourself involved in an armed robbery!" Claire chuckled whilst patting his back.

"Yes, I'm sorry about that. I couldn't really ignore it though."

"Don't be silly," Claire cut in, "I haven't had so much fun in a long time!" She laughed and gave him a peck on the cheek before feeling awkward realising Treavey was still holding down his prisoner who had now accepted his fate.

A little while later, the suspect was led to the police van and taken away and Treavey said his goodbyes to Claire and headed towards the station on foot to begin his statement. He was beginning to get a name for himself around the station as a thief taker, and this was most definitely going to add to that reputation.

Before he did though, he took a detour and headed towards Superintendent Steer's house. He couldn't leave it there. How could he make it an off the cuff visit? Was it his wife who'd gone missing that he'd seen him with?

Surely, he wouldn't be in town with her if it had been. Someone would have recognised her so it must have been someone else, but he looked like they were close, as if they were partners. They had their arms around each other, after all. On arrival at his Superintendents house, he walked up the steps to his front door and rang the doorbell.

The door opened and his Superintendent opened the door and stood before him. His face was like a big pink beacon with silver wispy hair on top, stout in stature, but standing straight and proud. "Hello Treavey, how are you dear chap?" He was looking happy and relaxed.

"Hello Sir, just checking on how things are with you. Everything okay?"

"Yes, yes, as far as they can be. I can't really do much about her going off and leaving me, now, can I? No, I'm determined to carry on with my life. Many have had to do so in my position."

"So..." Treavey searched for the words to ask him. "...so, was that not you with Lisa in town I saw you with then?" He thought he would just come straight out with it.

"Good God no. I wasn't with anyone. It must have been someone standing close next to me when I was seeing what the fuss was about. Clever work there Treavey, but I didn't want to get in the way. You seemed to have everything in hand."

Treavey was certain she and he were very much together, and he was cursing himself he didn't get a better look at her to compare with a photo of Lisa he'd seen on the press releases. He'd have had his mind put at ease if he'd found out it had been his sister or someone close in the family, but he found this suspicious. Maybe he had mistaken the woman for being with him. Maybe it had just looked like it. There had been quite a lot of pushing and shoving by people.

The two men wandered into the kitchen and the Superintendent made them both a cup of coffee. They stood in the kitchen staring out of the window gazing over the garden. That ground dug up by the shed was starting to show signs of the grass growing on top now. Treavey wondered if it was feeding off a particularly rich fertiliser beneath. He could only assume that CID was satisfied his missing wife wasn't buried there.

"I haven't murdered her, Treavey. I know some people think I have, but you have to believe me, I could never do that to her... or anyone," he awkwardly laughed at what he had just said.

"Of course, you haven't, Sir." Treavey replied more convincingly than he may be had felt. "It's a bit of a mystery, that's all. I wonder where she's gone, but she'll turn up, I'm sure. One way or another." Treavey looked at him wondering if he was speaking to a murderer. "One way or another Sir." He repeated for extra emphasis.

The Superintendent placed his mug down on the draining board. Treavey noticed a large kitchen knife laying there in the drying rack. The Superintendent picked it up and held it in a manner which made Treavey take a quick glance for the door, but the knife was carefully placed into a draw and slammed shut.

"Right, well, there's not a lot I can do to establish where she is now. I just have to wait for her to contact me, or the police or God forbid, someone to find a body. But it won't be because of me I can assure you."

Treavey was surprised he spoke so candidly about it. He wasn't a grieving husband pleading for him to find his wife so they could return to normality. Who the hell was that woman he was with and what was their relationship? Was it his new girlfriend or one he'd had for some time which was the reason he'd 'got rid' of his wife? Time would tell, he was sure of it.

Treavey returned to the station and climbed the stairs to the familiar hallway leading towards the CID offices. "Hey Adam, how are you mate?" he shouted as he saw Adam Gee making a coffee in the office. The rest of the office was empty of officers. "Where is everyone?" he asked him.

"Johnny is doing an interview for some crappy assault and the other two are out on enquiries. Hey Treavey, I hear you've been playing superman again. That cape of yours must be wearing out, no?"

Treavey smirked. "Yeah, well, you can't really ignore it when it's happening in front of you. Hey, any update on the missing Superintendent's wife? I am sure I saw him with a woman in town, and they seemed close. I wondered if it was his wife for a minute, you know the missing Lisa."

"No chance," Adam replied. "He wouldn't walk through town with his wife on his arm in broad daylight. People would notice. It's quite a public story now. Wonder who it was though."

"I went around there to ask him." Treavey replied.

"You what? You just went around and asked him if he was out with his highly suspected murdered wife?"

"Pretty much. It sort of came into the conversation when I went around for a welfare check. He trusts me because the last time I had had any form of contact was when I was beating on his chest and kissing him."

Adam poured the kettle of hot water into his mug and stirred it with a stained looking teaspoon before adding the spoon into a half glass of dirty water with several others. "What did he say?"

"He said he wasn't with anyone. I'm not so sure. I mean it was pretty tight with people close to each other pushing and shoving but they looked very close and comfortable with each other. He said he hadn't murdered her. Straight out like that. No messing. He said, 'I haven't murdered her Treavey.'"

Adam went over to his desk and sat down heavily on his chair which slopped his coffee over the side onto the desk. "Oh, shit and bloody hell."

Treavey grabbed a tissue from a nearby box and sauntered over to help dab up the mess. "I just don't know what to think, Adam. I mean, I hope he hasn't as I quite like the man, but he doesn't seem to be very upset by the whole thing."

"I agree. I thought the same. He's acting as if she's popped out to the shops and will be back in a moment. Anyway, do you know that other murderer you arrested the other night over at Lusty Glaze? Sarah Norris."

Treavey pricked his ears up. He'd just spent the day with her sister, Claire, after all and he was hoping beyond anything it would be good news. By some miracle, he was hoping she wasn't involved after all.

"She coughed the lot. Said she'd poisoned her girlfriend over time because she hated her so much and wanted rid cos she was being controlled and bullied by her. There's nothing much more that can be done on it. The post mortem results will come back in a couple of days. There's been a bit of a backlog so they are delayed, but by the sounds of it, we will have to wait for the toxicology results as it's doubtful they'll find any wounds inflicted on the body now."

Treavey sat down at the desk opposite Adam. "Gutted. I'm a little gutted for her. She felt she had no choice I guess."

"We all have a choice, Treavey." Adam replied as he took another slurp of coffee and kicked back his chair placing his feet on his desk. "Ever fancy CID, Treavey? Reckon you'd enjoy it."

Treavey was already on a thought which he was processing. "No mate, I prefer fast cars and maybe guns one day. On the firearms department one day, I hope. I'll leave CID to you egg heads. Did you interview that woman called Amoora? You know, the one who tipped off Sarah's sister, Claire about how she was concerned for her in the toxic relationship with Sitara. She was the one who realised how controlling Sitara was and how Sarah wanted out but felt she couldn't leave Sitara."

Adam looked disinterested. "Yeah, we got a bit of background. Her statement may hold a bit of mitigating circumstances for her, but the Judge isn't likely to see it that way. She had a choice at the end of the day and there's no evidence to show Sitara was violent, and yet someone's lost their life, therefore someone has to pay."

Treavey's shoulders slumped as he stood up and he headed for the report room where he knew he had a long statement to get on with. He needed to get this right. He wasn't in much of a mood for it. He was probably going to have to give up the love of his life because she was involved in a major investigation. Her sister was the main suspect, and it wouldn't look good with him being involved with her emotionally, let alone sexually. He slumped himself down on a chair and threw the statement paper he had grabbed on the table. His whole life was crumbling around his ears. He really liked Claire and now he knew she liked him too, but everything was telling him it wasn't right to carry on and he could get into serious trouble if he did. Maybe he should speak to Sgt Fox about it, he trusted him, but what if he reacted badly. What if he thought he had committed disciplinary offences already. He decided that he was going to tell Claire it was over. Over before it had even begun.

Chapter 9
Pot and pursuits

Night shift had begun and Treavey was keen to have an exciting shift. He couldn't wait to do some 'sharking'. This involved him patrolling the area waiting to pick up some prey; the prey being criminals like hardened drug dealers, disqualified drivers, drink drivers or even, anyone without car insurance. It didn't have to be the crime of the century, anything would do, just so he felt he had earned his money. He decided to head out towards an industrial estate area where he was told some drug dealers tended to meet up before heading off to deliver their hoard of illicit drugs, and the night shift was the time to do it away from prying eyes.

He was excited. There was an underlying nagging feeling that he knew it was still unlikely he would find anything tonight but the fact the possibility was always there was usually sufficient to get him through the night. As he approached the industrial estate just a few miles out of town, he had no expectations. He would turn into the dark and ghostly entrance which was in sharp contrast with to the otherwise teaming with energy location in the daytime. He would have a casual look around for people up to no good skulking in the shadows, before probably heading back into town to prepare for the night clubs turning out.

He rolled his Panda car into the industrial estate and coasted with the engine off and his window open taking in the sounds around him. It was almost silent apart from a distant alarm from a car. He jump-started the car whilst it was still moving by dipping the clutch and putting it in second gear before releasing the clutch again and the engine roared into life once more.

He reached the end of the road and swung it around before heading towards the exit. He stopped. Something didn't feel right. It was almost too quiet. There were no cats, no foxes, even, which was very strange.

Treavey reversed back to a side turning and steered the front of the car into it. He noticed a set of headlights switch on ahead of him. He stopped his car; the engine purring and he contemplated what he was going to do next. 'Don't be silly, Treavey,' he thought. 'It was just as likely going to be an innocent motorist. Nothing unusual around here. A business owner working late perhaps.'

The car was initially stationary, but this changed instantly as Treavey saw the lights rise momentarily as the car accelerated towards him before the car regained its level and the lights got bigger and bigger. It was almost as if he had frozen in the headlights but just for a moment. His policing brain kicked in and he flicked the headlights on to full beam to attempt to get some sort of description of the driver. The driver was dipping his head looking away from him, seemingly avoiding eye contact with Treavey. He was wearing a baseball cap which obscured his identity even further. The car was by in a flash, but Treavey reacted instantly, planting his foot on the accelerator, before dipping the clutch and waiting for the car to gain traction, yanking the steering to the right, and pulling the handbrake hard. The Panda slewed around a perfect 180 degrees and with spinning front wheels, was hot in pursuit of the disturbed vehicle.

Treavey had some catching up to do but he now knew the driver was trying to evade him by the looks of the back end swinging wildly as it negotiated the junction and headed out in to the main road towards Newquay.

"Golf 31, I've got a fail to stop. I need backup. Heading from St Columb Major towards Newquay. Can you inform other units, traffic, dog units and air support if available?"

The control room operator was quick on the reply expertly organising the requests but almost routinely informed him the helicopter was in Exeter and some distance off. He wasn't going to be able to rely on that. He was just about able to catch up and keep up with the car which he identified as a black Audi 80, and he shouted out the registration number into his mic and the control room operator began running through the registration to establish some further details. He sincerely hoped he could keep up with it as the Audi 80 was more powerful than his own car and it was only his skill and knowledge of the roads that meant he was able to keep him in the game, but for how long?

Treavey was on the edge of his own and his car's ability as it swung violently up a side junction off the main road and headed towards the coast. He could hear other units organising themselves on the radio so he knew he would get some help soon, but he was particularly looking out for the traffic call sign, and it soon came.

"Tango 32, we are making our way towards."

Treavey was ecstatic. He knew that Tango 32 were driving the new Sierra Cosworth, and it went like a rocket. Sometimes literally as the last one they had burst into flames and was written off, but he knew if they joined the pursuit, it would be over very soon as it was built like a rally car, and nothing could shake it off. He also heard that his friend 'Sooty' was making his way towards on the coast road so would probably get there first.

Treavey negotiated through the narrow and very dark lanes, relying totally on his headlights, and hoping with each tight bend he would still have the Audi within his sights. It was kicking a lot of dust up with its tyres which was quite comforting in a way as he knew he was still on the right track. It would get thicker in consistency telling him he was getting closer, then as he rounded a bend onto a straight the dust would thin as the Audi had made good progress before him and gained some distance. It had felt like a long time since he'd called for assistance, but a pursuit was something everyone wanted to get involved in and officers would have thrown down their mugs of tea and biros to be a part of it and would soon be with him. No one wanted to be late to the party, so he had visions of everyone making their way at breakneck speed towards him.

Treavey couldn't see how many people were in the car. He knew he had this pretty much under control as the Audi was failing to shake him off, as long as he didn't get to a dual carriageway, but that was in the other direction and some distance off. He was straining at the windows to see if anything was being discarded such as packets of drugs, but it didn't seem so.

The Audi rear brake lights illuminated sharply, and the rear end of the car raised substantially as the driver misjudged a particular corner and the front offside corner glanced off a Cornish hedge, something which doesn't give easily, as it is constructed with stone and earth. Treavey hoped the tyre would be punctured but he also almost hoped it would continue until the backup arrived as he didn't fancy dealing with a potential car full of runners on his own.

There were a few lefts and rights, but Treavey was able to update the control room with the general direction being west towards the coast. He was keeping an eye on his direction by looking at where the exceedingly bright moon was in relation to him to ensure he didn't get disoriented.

He heard Sooty's voice coming through the airwaves, "I'm ahead of them control, I'm going to fend them off."

The cars were reaching incredible speeds with the uncut vegetation flicking off the door mirrors of the cars causing grass, twigs and even the odd branch to fly off and bounce off his windscreen. Treavey would dodge all he could and even made sure his distance between was sufficient to cause less damage if an extra-large branch came flying his way. Soon the dust thinned, and the view became clearer. The car was planting its backside low on the road as he saw it accelerating away in front of him and become smaller.

'Damned these straight roads,' Treavey thought, as he was wondering whether his prey was going to get away from him after all. 'But what about T32, and Sooty. Where the fuck is Sooty?'

What looked like a tornado happened in front of him in the distance. "What the... what the fuck is that?" Treavey exclaimed, craning his neck forward towards the windscreen as if the extra few centimetres would give him a better view. He braked gently at first and then, on seeing the debris in the air, dust, glass, plastic trim, more glass, and the reflective blue stripe of a patrol car spinning and twisting erratically in the air. Treavey knew something horrible had happened and slammed his brakes on hard, in fact as hard as he could. His face was of shock and terror at the same time. It was impossible to make out the flashes of black and then white metal panels. It dawned on him. Sooty had arrived and the two cars had collided at speed. This was a big one. This was terrifying. Surely no one could survive that.

The tornado died leaving the stillness of the destruction left behind. Debris from both the police car and the Audi was scattered across the road, up the hedges and across the junction where they had met. As Treavey drew his car to a stop, he could see the glinting of the glass and exposed silver metal flickering in the moon light. The police car was some distance off having collided into the front nearside of the Audi and spinning both cars off in different directions. Treavey could only imagine what Sooty had experienced as he jumped out of his car grabbing his radio mouthpiece and shouted for assistance. His sprint slowed to a halt as he got up to the caved in driving seat area. The police car looked like the motionless hulk of a slain dragon, steaming, and broken with no life.

"Ambulance on route to you Golf 31."

The words rang around his head but made little sense to Treavey as he put his hand on the door sill and bent down to see what condition Sooty was in. He looked unresponsive and collapsed forward against his steering wheel. In the gloom he could see a black liquid running down from his hairline on the side of his forehead which Treavey took for blood. Treavey put his fingers on where he believed his carotid artery was to look for a pulse. He felt nothing. "Shit, Sooty, are you alive?"

"Now if I wasn't, how the fuck am I going to answer you Treavey mate?" Sooty sat up and wiped his forehead smudging the liquid across it making it look far worse than it had.

"Jesus, Sooty, you scared the living daylights out of me. Jesus, you bloody well stopped the pursuit, I'll give you that. Thank fuck. I think I heard an ambulance is on its way mate. Stand by and don't move, okay?"

"I'm comfortable here for a moment Treavey, just a little tired. Make sure those bastards don't get away."

Treavey updated the radio operator on Sooty's condition and trotted back to the Audi which resembled it having been through a mincing machine. There was one male in the back looking dazed but otherwise, he was okay. He rubbed his head and unexpectedly told Treavey, "Those two bastards have just run off that way, towards Mawgan Porth. I told them to just bloody stop for Christ's sake and now look what's happened."

A car pulled up behind him, it was the Cosworth traffic car, and if it could pant it would have been. It had been put through its paces. The engine was pinking with the heat it had generated and it smelt of brake dust and clutch. Treavey pointed in the direction of Mawgan Porth, and the Cosworth accelerated off with its blue lights illuminating the surrounding hedges and bushes like an alien mothership taking off over the horizon, but wisely the occupants turned the lights off as they didn't wish to warn the criminals, they were hot on their heels.

It was a few moments later when the ambulance arrived and its two crew checked on Sooty and the passenger in the Audi. The car wasn't stolen, much to Treavey's surprise, but the driver was wanted for several serious offences in the Midlands which gave him the reason for him not wishing to stick around for a chat with Treavey.

The fire service turned up soon after and began lifting bonnets and cutting battery cables along with setting up lights on tripods to illuminate the scene. They couldn't rely on the moon for too long with some cloud cover approaching. They were looking a little busy around Sooty. A paramedic waved them over to him and the fire fighters began getting their cutting equipment out of the truck. Purely routine as they would have been concerned for his spine in a collision such as that but nine times out of ten casualties would be absolutely fine if they had survived the crash.

Dave, the dog handler, arrived with Finchy. "Hey Dave, good to see you, mate, two of them went this direction, we think. The Cosworth has gone looking for them, but no one has walked further than that point so I suggest that's a good place to start a track."

Dave was already taking the harness out and putting it on his Dog Finchy. He was a stunning chestnut colour with black swathes across his gleaming coat. He was a proud dog, and it was almost like he knew he was the most handsome dog the unit had. He always attracted a lot of attention because of it.

They were off on a long line. Dave was pacing at speed, his shoulders sloping back behind his hips as he attempted to stop Finchy from pulling too hard. No wonder dog handlers' backs were fit for nothing at the end of their careers. Treavey ran over to Sooty.

"You good mate? I'm going to follow Dave with the dog. You going to be okay?"

"Me, yes mate... they are making a fuss about nothing, I'm good mate. Go get them. We have to have them in the bin for this trouble otherwise it's cost us this car for nothing."

Treavey sprinted after Dave who had made good progress up the hill and was disappearing over a hedge and heading inland away from the coastline. Treavey followed, a little cautious in case Finchy got spooked by him and doubled back. That would be seriously uncomfortable.

"Control, I'm following the dog handler to give him a hand and report his position, Golf 32?"

The control room operator confirmed and tapping could be heard over the radio as she updated the incident log.

It always surprised Treavey how fast the dog handlers moved. There was no messing with them. They wanted a criminal at the end of the track, and they had to go faster than the person they were after to catch them up. They had half a chance with criminals who had made off unexpectantly as in a crash or a 'star burst' when the occupants of a car ran off in different directions. It meant they were unlikely to be near a waiting car. They may try to lay low and call for a taxi, so Treavey ensured the control room operation informed 'Taxi watch' making sure they were informed if anyone called for a taxi in the area.

The field was being lit by the moon but there were areas where it fell into almost complete darkness as a cloud drifted in front of it. The ground was hard but uneven and it would be easy to twist an ankle. The clinking of the leads and buckles were his main source of direction, but before long, Treavey had made up sufficient ground to be in talking distance.

"It's Treavey, Dave. I'm behind you mate."

"No bother, mate. Good to have you back there. Come on Finchy lad, do your bit."

The track led across some paths along the edge of the fields. He wondered if they were on an official footpath, but he had no idea where they were leading. Treavey updated the control room, mainly with the direction being Easterly as there were few other landmarks to go by, until he came across a farm entrance with the name plate of Fords Farm on it. Finchy turned sharp left and headed directly for the main farm house and sniffed enthusiastically around the bottom of the door.

'That had to be it,' Treavey thought and carefully tried the door handle which opened surprisingly easily. He stepped in looking back at Dave who just shrugged his shoulders and smiled as if to say, 'This is your job now, mate. I've done mine.' Treavey turned and tip toed along the hallway listening with the senses of a bat with. Had the offenders sought refuge in this house and the occupants may be in danger or as he believed, this was the offender's house. He would go for the former which simplified his powers of entry with the nine to five jury the next day. That would sort the criticism out. He knew he would be outnumbered but would be counting on the element of surprise if he were to suddenly come across them.

He slowly walked up the stairs, as if every step was a potential landmine. He felt completely out of his comfort zone however he was now committed. He could hardly go back to Dave and say he'd turned back half way up the stairs because he was scared.

He approached the landing and gazed around. Two doors were open, and one closed. He checked the two open doorways as quietly as he could and then approached the closed door. He pulled the handle down as gently as if he were defusing a bomb, and then applied a little pressure to nudge the door open. It stuck for a second but then opened with a crack and then a creak as it swung open by six inches or so. There was silence so he opened the door wider and peered around the door. Treavey's eyes were, by now, well accustomed to the dim light and he could see there was a double bed in front of him. He saw there was a duvet on the bed covering two human forms and their heads were at the top of the bed sleeping soundly. Without being too blunt about it, Treavey realised he had just broken into a sleeping farmer and farmer's wife's house, and they were none the wiser for it, at the moment at least.

Treavey about turned as quietly as he could, but with a heartbeat feeling like it was going to bring the walls in on top of him, he carefully started walking down the stairs but by half way down was breaking into a run and heading towards the front door which couldn't come quick enough. The front door seemed a million miles away and the hairs on the back of his neck raised with a shiver of cold running down his spine as if an ice cube had been slipped down the back of his shirt. The next moment, however, he was out into the fresh air again, but Dave was gone.

On scanning around the area, he could hear a noise to his left and confirmed from the radio that Dave was on another track. Maybe the offenders had gone to the front door to shake them off the track or maybe to think about going inside the farmhouse in order to hide from their pursuers. Finchy was dragging Dave away from the farm house, having double tracked on himself slightly and darting off to the right behind the building instead. Treavey was relieved to get out of the building unseen. It had been a very close things and if they had woken up with him peering through their bedroom door, not only would he have not liked to see their reaction, but it may have taken them some considerable time to get over the incident, and Christ knows what the complaint would have been like. It would have taken some explaining however reasonable it had felt to him at the time.

Treavey was hot on Dave's trail after only a few seconds, being relieved he had caught up with him just in time. He would never have found him otherwise. It was darker than he could imagine it with the moon hidden behind a large cloud and showing no signs of returning any time soon. It made his own sense seem even more precise. He could hear the crunching of the gravel under his boots, and the occasional owl hoot in the distance. That same shiver returned down his neck and spine, and he had to shake himself out of his sudden feeling of been so exposed. He was a Police officer for God's sake. It isn't expected or accepted that he should fear the dark and the unknowns beyond its mysterious depths. He glanced around him as he followed Dave and Finchy and imagined the area in daylight. It felt so much more welcoming already if he let his imagination take over. He wouldn't feel a spec of fear if he were here in the daylight so why now it was dark?

His daydreaming, if it could be called that, was suddenly shaken as an explosion of sound erupted from just in front of him. He stopped to assess what had just happened, his reactions on a hair trigger as he strained his eyes to see what had happened through the gloom. The silhouettes of Dave and Finchy in front didn't alter their course seemingly with no alarm to what had just occurred. What he now understood was panicked squawking and flapping got fainter with every flap of the wings and the pheasant was gone, his slumber on his nest disturbed for the night.

Onwards they trod but not for long. They were confronted by a huge barn which towered above them, made from metal corrugated sides and a vast metal sliding door which was firmly closed. Finchy's nose planted at the gap. He had huge gasps of air rushing through his nose passages, as he sniffed the scent and there was no hesitation; Finchy barked at the gap of the door and stood back and continued to bark. Dave was in like a shot pulling the sliding door apart enough to allow him and his dog egress. Treavey raised an eyebrow. There was no challenge or waiting for a reply; no time for that, just straight in and running on the trust between man and beast to get him to the target as soon as possible.

There was an incredible stench of cannabis in the barn and as they continued through it, they could see a bright light coming from around the cracks in the door in front. Finchy walked straight to the door and Dave pushed it open. There before all, in the brightest of lights was the largest cannabis plantation either of them had ever seen, and there in the middle of it were two figures vainly trying to hide themselves amongst the leaves. The suspects had led them straight to their hoard of cannabis and to themselves for good measure. Dave glanced back at Treavey in disbelief and shrugged his shoulders. They both gazed around them to take in the scene and the stench which filled their nostrils. Finchy sneezed and shook his head. Dave threw him his toy and Finchy tossed it about enthusiastically. He had done all this for his reward, and he deserved it. A barn full of cannabis and two in custody for failing to stop at the very least, was a fair deal for a bit of time with his favourite toy.

The two gave no fight and almost seemed relieved it was all over. It was soon confirmed they were attached to the property so once a sample of the cannabis was recovered and returned to the police station, and the rest was destroyed, they'd have a tough time denying it was theirs or that they didn't know about it.

"I thought they were flying the police helicopter over roofs at night with their heat seeking equipment to pick up the heat lamps to find this stuff in attics and barns like this, Dave," Treavey was surprised this had been so brazen and how no one visiting the farm had smelt the stench.

"Yeah, but they've got enough to do in Devon before coming all the way down here. Did you find anyone in the farmhouse, Treavey?"

"Yes, mate. I guess I'll have to go back there and lift them. They must have known about this."

One of the suspects broke into the conversation. "They don't know anything. Gormless farmers, they are. I rent the barn off them, and they stay well out the way. They never come in here. We told them it was for storage."

"Fair enough," Treavey replied, "We can talk to them later if necessary. Let sleeping dogs lie for now. We've got enough on our plates, and they aren't going anywhere if they own and run this farm."

Some moments later, and with the barn being guarded for the night by a couple of Special Constables who volunteered for the job, Treavey and Dave, and of course Finchy, managed to get a lift back to their cars from the Newquay station van driver. Treavey was in a good mood. It wasn't often a result like that came to them and it was a great team effort. He was going to tease Sooty about his stopping technique, but he managed to get the job done at least, even though it had destroyed a perfectly serviceable panda car.

He wasn't surprised to see the collision site cordoned off with police barrier tape. The council had put a diversion in. There had been a devastating collision but fortunately they had got away with it. Sooty would have run after the offenders with him if he had been able to, but he'd have to wait for the traffic Sergeant to go through the police accident forms. He could see that Sooty was no longer there. Sergeant Olly Tayler from Bodmin Traffic was on scene with another officer, clipboard in hand, and strangely enough the collision investigator had turned up with his van.

"A bit overkill, isn't it?" Treavey called out to Sergeant Tayler. Are they gunning for Sooty, are they? You know, complaints?"

The Sergeant glanced up at Treavey. His face was sullen. The officer with him stepped back, turned around, and moved away. The Sergeant moved towards Treavey, dropping his clipboard to his side, his other hand out in front towards Treavey, open flat, almost like a priest. 'What was this about?' Treavey thought. 'This wasn't funny anymore.'

"Treavey, Dave." Treavey looked to his side and Dave was looking ashen next to him.

"Is he injured? Is Sooty okay? Tell me Sarge." Treavey demanded.

Sergeant Tayler took his hat off as in telling a member of public their relative had been killed in a road accident. 'Surely not. No, Sooty was fine. He was willing Treavey on to catch the runners. He was fine.'

The Sergeant stood close in front of Treavey and put his hand on his shoulder. "Mate, I'm sorry. It was an aortic rupture. They think his artery opened like a zip and he bled out in seconds. If there had been an emergency team here ready to operate, they still wouldn't have been able to save him. He died in seconds, mate. He knew nothing about it."

Treavey didn't reply. He was in shock and dazed. He could hear murmuring in the background as Dave was talking with the Sergeant, but Treavey was stumbling back by now and lent against the front wing of Sooty's car to steady himself. The world was spinning around him. 'Pull yourself together,' he told himself, but he felt tears welling up, and he knew he was about to lose control. A wave of nausea enveloped him and so he turned towards the hedge with the stench of differential oil from the axle completing the urge to vomit and threw up at the base of it. He had just spoken to Sooty a few moments earlier just a few feet from where he was being sick. He couldn't stand the acrid sweet smell of the differential oil which always signified a hard collision for the axle to be compromised. That oil was well hidden, and it would have taken a considerable impact to rupture it.

Treavey straightened up and fanned his face. He felt sweaty when before the sweat on his face cooling in the breeze had made him feel chilly. He touched the car and ran his fingers around the metal panels following the contours until he got to the rear and followed it around to his driver's door where he had lent in to talk to him. The roof had been cut off when they had been recovering him from the car to not stress his spine in case he had suffered an injury without knowing it, but all for no reason now. Treavey peered into the car where his friend had been moments before. He touched the seat. It felt silly to do so, but it was where he had been sitting and would not long have been cooled from his body heat. The car smelt like death. There was dried blood on the steering wheel and his police paperwork was scattered over the entire front seats and in the footwells.

Treavey had heard about the aortic rupture. It would have to be confirmed, of course, but it happened particularly when there was a vicious side impact. The huge artery ran from the heart to the rest of the body and is 2cm wide. It was quite robust with an impact from front to back but had space to swing from side to side and if sufficient enough in a side impact in a car, it could tear. Sometimes it would initially tear just enough to bleed a little and Sooty would not have noticed it at this stage. He probably did not feel any pain from it but before long it could bulge and then open, and as the Sergeant said, like a zip down the full length and deposit an enormous amount of blood into the chest cavity in seconds. Sooty would have dropped like a stone or would have just closed his eyes and fallen asleep if he had been on a stretcher.

Treavey walked over to Sergeant Tayler. "Sarge. Sooty's driver's door was dented but the main collision was straight ahead on the front end, no?"

The Sergeant beckoned him up the road between where the main front end collision with the Audi had taken place and the resultant position of the panda car. "See there Treavey. If you bend down to the road level, you can see the marks from the panda. They are faint but they lead from the collision with the Audi, they spin almost 360 degrees and his driver's side hits that hedge hard. Side on. I mean, it will have been hard. I would not be surprised if he's hit his head as well. We will have to wait for the post mortem for that." The Sergeant checked himself. "I'm sorry. You don't need to know that right now. I'm so sorry mate. I'm so, so sorry."

Sergeant Tayler offered to arrange a lift for Treavey, but Treavey knew it would be a deep inconvenience to lose another traffic car to taxi him to the station and he felt okay to drive anyway so he said his goodbyes to Dave and having taken one last look at the scene where he had last seen his friend alive, he began the drive back to Newquay Station. He wasn't much in the mood for anything else tonight. There was an obvious gloom over the airwaves. Word had spread and the seriousness of the job he had been involved in suddenly became ever so apparent. It was going to take a long time to get over this, if ever.

He opened his driver's side window to feel the gentle onshore breeze from the Atlantic. The ocean looked calm as in showing some respect. The moon was back out from behind the clouds as if to show its respects for a good man lost from this earth. Treavey treated it, almost as a journey of memorial as he knew he was driving along the same route which Sooty had taken from the other direction. The man had received those fatal injuries whilst his blue lights where lit and sirens were still sounding, and he had got his man, too.

Sooty had ensured there were two in custody and there were substantial offences to put to them too, but Treavey had lost his friend and the finality of it was sinking in. Another blast of cool air rushed into the car relieving Treavey of the sweaty hot flush which had come over him. He was concerned he was going to faint as he felt clammy and nauseous. The relief from the fresh air soon faded and Treavey was forced to pull over to the side of the road in what looked to be the middle of nowhere. He flicked the ignition off and jumped out of his car and ran to the grass bank where he leaned over and threw up into the darkness for the second time that night. He remained cramped over with his hands on his knees, feeling miserable before summoning the strength to straighten up and with his hands on his hips, look to see what was around him.

He was on the coast road between Porth and Watergate. It followed the cliff line sandwiched between an aggressive steep drop on one side and RAF St Mawgan airfield where the Nimrod Russian submarine hunters were based, on the other. The silhouette of the airfield looked ghostly at night, and on turning his attention towards the sky, he was taken aback by the depth of it, put into perspective by the diamonds of bright, bright, glinting stars of varying depths which, quite simply, took his breath away. He wanted to spread his arms and leave this world. He'd found his space in heaven on that verge, the utter beauty, the peace, the serenity, it was as if he were being reminded that he was but a spec in this massive universe of which he played a pitiful part in trying to make it easier for others to live. Suddenly this earth felt like a pea in an aircraft carrier. He was insignificant and just a few feet over to his right was the edge to the cliffs towering above the waves crashing against the cliffs below where he could end it so easily. So, then what was the point in doing that? Treavey strained his eyes to view around him, but then the scent of the hedgerow flowers hit him filling his nostrils. Life felt good again. He would make the most of it. He believed he now had the strength to help others and support his colleagues instead of revelling in his self-pity.

He had felt a euphoria, and it was as if he had cleansed his body of the negativity and evil which had bestowed him by him throwing up, and he had felt an epiphany but not a religious one. This was far bigger, yes as crazy as it sounded, this universe was so vast, it felt like no one would miss him if he jumped off those cliffs. So, it was as if he had nothing to lose, but to go hell for leather from now on. He was going to go for the things he wanted to achieve. He would be fearless with defending those who were unable to fend for themselves. He felt all powerful. There was nothing to lose.

Chapter 10
A fine day for a funeral

"She's been remanded? I guess that's normal, Claire. I'm sorry to hear it but you can see why. They don't know if she's a danger to others now so must play it safe."

Treavey was attempting to pacify Claire who was visibly upset about her sister being remanded for the murder of her girlfriend.

"I know, Treavey, but it's still a shock. My sister is in prison. I never thought that would ever be possible. She is so kind natured. I just don't understand it. It so fucking unfair, she felt trapped by that bully Sitara. I mean, we'd never have known about that part if it hadn't been for Amoora, who she'd confided in."

Treavey placed his hand on her forearm. They were standing in the kitchen and Claire was making them both a cup of tea. "Amoora? Oh yes, the Jordanian woman, wasn't she? I know Adam took a statement from her so it will go down as a lot off mitigating evidence but if she wasn't in imminent danger then Sarah is going to have a hard time winning over the jury, Claire. We must be realistic about that."

Claire poured the hot water into the two cups, placed the kettle down but stayed motionless as if in deep thought. Then, "you said that Sarah had said she had poisoned her, right? She doesn't know about poisons. I mean, how ridiculous. Are you sure she meant to kill her or just make her ill?"

"I don't know Claire, but I know it will all come out in court. Just make sure she has a good barrister. You want to make sure she gets the best help she can. Kick up a fuss if you aren't happy with the one she has.

Treavey made his way back to the station and nipped up to the CID office to speak to DC Adam Gee to catch up with things.

"Hey Adam, you good?"

"Yes mate, I'm good but bloody busy and I'm struggling to keep up. I can't afford to get anything wrong, so I do far too many hours. Take Steers wife for example. She's still missing, and I keep racking my brain to see if I've missed something. Is she buried under our noses or is she on a beach in Mallorca at this very moment?"

Treavey was surprised how candid Adam was being and he felt flattered he was trusted, it felt nice.

"Oh yes," Adam shouted as if startled, taking Treavey by surprise.

"What?" Treavey replied keenly. All cops liked a bit of gossip; the more speculation the better, because then they had something to pull apart and find the truth from.

"She was strangled."

"What? Who was strangled? Lisa? Steer's wife?"

"No. Well, she may be, I don't know yet, but I was talking about Sitara. She was strangled. So why did Sarah say she had poisoned her. What's that all about? I could do without time wasters you know. Why didn't she just say that? Surely, she knows we would find out the corpse had been strangled and not poisoned."

Treavey was stunned into silence. "But wait, so she was strangled?"

"For fuck's sake, Treavey, are you being dense or something? Yes, Sitara was strangled by her lover Sarah, not poisoned."

"Was there poison found in her system?" Treavey asked, trying to find some answers.

"No idea," Adam replied. "The toxicology has gone off and will take a couple of weeks to come through."

"So, she may not have murdered her. Will she still be remanded?"

Adam looked at Treavey and rolled his eyes. "Look, Treavey, I know you have a thing for her sister, but for fuck's sake, get your copper brain back on your shoulders. She was found with a fucking murdered corpse in the boot of her car, and she was trying to kill herself on that beach. What do you think?"

Treavey felt foolish. "Fair point, Adam. You're right." Treavey could tell Adam was stressed and thought it best to leave him to it.

It had started to rain, and the wind was getting up. There was a squall coming through and Treavey took the panda car out to see what jobs were going to come in. He enjoyed working in harsh weather. He loved the fact there was rarely any paperwork which he despised. He loved feeling the elements and getting out into them to help people who were distressed. He thought that was the best bit about policing.

It was late evening and the tourists had disappeared back to their bed and breakfasts and hotels to seek some sustenance and shelter. The clouds were menacingly grey and fat with rain. The wind was warm but strong, almost as if a tropical storm was scrambling across the Atlantic to devour the Cornish inhabitants within its reach and looking at the impending doom laying just off the coast, Treavey knew it was more than possible that it would.

He drove his panda car to the Killacourt, an area of greenery used for relaxation and recreation with wonderful views of the harbour and Towan Beach just below. He watched and waited for the front to hit and when it did, it was as if someone had flicked a switch. The flags had been limp with the occasional flutter but now were horizontal and the poles were bending with the strain, there were already a couple of house sale signs flipping end over end across the grass and he could hear something repeatedly slamming as he sat in his car with his window cracked open slightly, to get the sense of the impending storm around him. He could even smell it as it grew in ferocity. A smell of warm sand, a musty smell and it was strong. He shuffled into his seat with some excitement. He already had his waterproof trousers on in expectation, but he felt cosy in his car in the meantime which protected him, but he knew it wouldn't last for long before the first job came in. Either a roof flying off into the street or a tree down blocking the road. He couldn't wait. Weather related police work could be exhilarating and best of all, rarely included any paperwork.

"Golf 32, can you attend Towan Beach. There has been a rock fall and there are persons reported trapped."

"From Golf 32, en route." Treavey was out of his car and running down towards the beach below him. There was excellent access via some steps from the Killacourt where he was parked and before he knew it, he was skipping down the steep concrete steps to the bottom, where he could quickly see two young hippy, surfer types scrabbling earnestly at a mound of rocks, earth and some sort of material.

Treavey was on top of them immediately and could see that a small landslip, probably from the sudden heavy rain bringing it down, and it looked as if it had collapsed onto a tent of some sort. It was a small slip but from the exclamations coming from the two young men, they were homeless people sheltering side by side with a young girl between them inside the tent when the slip had fallen on them. By pure chance they were able to scramble free, but the girl had taken the brunt of it and was buried beneath. They had managed to pull the debris aside, but the tent material was tight against her face which gave the appearance of an Egyptian Mummy.

Treavey pulled out his trusted knife. All his colleagues owned expensive Leatherman knives, but he had a cheap version with no identifiable make on it, but it had served him well over his few short years. He frequently boasted it had defused many a bomb when he had been sent to suspicious packages. He would carry out a check through the control room to see if there were any specific threats to the location and even now, he would carefully cut the bag open to have a look at the contents. All these suspicious packages with a £2.99 knife he had picked up at the market, but now it was cutting the tough tent material which was stopping the young girl breathing. Her face and chest were quickly revealed and Treavey went to work, pulling her arms free ensuring there was no weight on her chest. He had already shouted to control room to send an ambulance and he was pushing on her chest attempting to push some life back into her.

She was pale and, quite frankly, dead looking. She was a rather large lady in her early 20's. Treavey had exposed her chest by cutting her bra off to get better compression and he was counting the timing of his compressions to himself. He felt bad that this woman's dignity was being revealed to all, and where she would normally have been mortified exposing herself to her friends like that, this was a lifesaving situation and very necessary. He had chosen not to carry out mouth to mouth. This wasn't a huge issue as he knew sufficient air should be reaching her lungs by carrying out the chest compressions. She had vomited and it smelt strongly of cheese, her last meal, which made him retch slightly but he carried on all the same. Her body was slippery as he continued with his rhythmic pushes on her sternum as the rain beat down hard, and it had dawned on him the wind was becoming even more ferocious.

The paramedics arrived but asked Treavey to carry on with what he was doing which felt good as it meant he was doing it right. Police officers would often wish to get a CPR under their belt, but they also knew they were very unlikely to work unless the person had stopped breathing only very recently. He had learned that the patient had 20% less chance of survival for every minute not breathing so there should be no delay.

One of the paramedics placed a plastic airway tube in her throat and attached it to oxygen then begun massaging a clear bag to push some oxygen into her lungs. Treavey didn't want to let on, but he was exhausted. The paramedics had done all they could and with the help of some firefighters who released her legs, she was out and away.

Treavey sat there in the dirt on his own for a moment with the rain streaming down his face. Her friends had gone with her in the ambulance, and it was just him there now, taking a beating from the weather but it didn't encourage him to run for shelter. He couldn't move. He was simply exhausted as every ounce of strength had been drained from him. He tried to get up, but he staggered to the side, and he opted to sit down in the spoil from the land slip again. He was a dead weight. He glanced around him as he felt embarrassed and didn't want people to notice his plight but fortunately there was no one around. They had run for shelter long ago, so he sat there taking in the view before him gulping lungs full of oxygen from the storm.

He took deep breaths of fresh, salty, cool air and studied the grey waves coming in from the Atlantic which had picked up and were climbing to a huge peak before crashing down into a turbulent white foam before losing their energy and submitting to the sand lying in wait ahead. The clouds were dark and angry, moving at speed inland and dropping a huge weight of rain down on him. He was past the point of getting wet and was enjoying the liberated feeling of it all. The warm rain lashed down on his face. He had done his best for the young girl, but he feared it wouldn't be enough. He would find out later. He dreaded the headlines of, 'Homeless person killed in rock fall,' as to a parent it would haunt them that their beloved Annie, or Kirsty was 'just a homeless person.' It was unbearable to think of, and how unfortunate had she been? She had been lying between the two other young men seeking shelter from the oncoming storm and yet the men had not only survived, but they had also walked free without injury. How could she have been so unlucky?

Eventually, Treavey managed to summon enough energy to pull himself up on his feet, and with a quick scan around to ensure no one was able to see him, he limped like an old man along the promenade of the beach to reach the same steps he had run down. The return trip for him was quite different with every step feeling like the end of a route march. He was amazed how exhausted he felt. He managed to walk up the gradual incline back up to his car and slumped into his front seat, resting for a moment. He breathed deeply. He'd heard about CPR being tiring and the reason why people should only do it for a short time before swapping with someone else as the technique could falter with fatigue. He was proud the paramedics had asked him to carry on as this meant they considered the quality of CPR he was giving was of a suitable standard. It didn't seem so tiring in the first aid training room however, but this had brought it down to earth for him. He smiled. He had realised he could now tick the second CPR box off. The first time with Superintendent Steer and his diabetic coma worked so maybe he could have a one hundred percent record. That was quite a step as a police officer. He hoped the smell of cheese hadn't put him off it for life, however.

Back at the station, he found himself in the CID office and Adam was just about to leave.
"Treavey, that murder, you know, the one with Sitara?"
Treavey pricked his ears up. "Uh huh?" not wishing to seem too interested but probably failing in his attempts as Adam smirked.
"Well, we seriously looked at Amoora as the culprit for a bit because she was so friendly with Sarah. We thought she may have murdered her, or maybe it was an accident, who knows, but we are satisfied it wasn't her. The motive just isn't strong enough and the forensics and circumstances don't fit. I'm afraid we are back to your girlfriend's sister, Sarah again."
"For fuck's sake, Adam, don't call her that, you'll get me in trouble if the bosses find out. I'm still unsure whether I should break it off or not."
Adam carried on packing a small bag with his lunch box and a small notebook. "I guess they could be a pain over it, but who knows. She's hardly a main witness or a suspect." He stopped for a second and looked into the middle distance as if he were thinking. "Claire is her name, right? Ah yes, Claire, could she…"
"Don't you dare!" Treavey exclaimed. "You just leave her alone. She hasn't got an aggressive bone in her body."
Adam flung the strap of the bag over his shoulder and said, "Anyone is capable of anything given the right circumstances, Treavey, but don't worry, we are back on to Sarah as the main suspect for killing Sitara. I think she

was trying to throw us off the track by saying she poisoned her, who knows?"

Adam was on his way out of the door when he stopped in his tracks and moved across to his skippet where his paperwork was kept. He reached into it and picked up a formal looking franked brown envelope and ran his thumb along the top of it to tear it open. He unravelled the folded letter inside and read it intently for thirty seconds or so.

"Shit." He read further... "Shit, uh huh, okay... shit."

Treavey watched and listened intently to him for any clues. Adam put the letter back into the envelope and threw it back in his skippet.

"Well, Treavey my dear boy. It seems that the victim had poison in her system, something like paint thinner, but not enough to kill her."

Treavey raised his eyebrow. "So, she was strangled to death but also had a non-lethal dose of poison in her? Jesus, how many people were trying to kill her? Popular lady."

The following day, Treavey was standing in a dark suit outside the front of the church at the funeral of his friend Sooty. He was proud to be at an event where so many police officers were attending. There had been a good turn out and the church was overflowing. It was a beautiful traditional church in St Columb Minor, just a mile or two out of Newquay. It was an idyllic stone building with a tower and flagpole. The weather had cleared, and a beautiful day was paying its respect to their fallen hero. Tilting gravestones framed the church which hid the stories of those who had gone before. There was so much history here, and Treavey wondered about those who were buried beneath those stones. Some had been there many decades and he marvelled at the fact people had stood at the church just like him and mourned those they loved and respected just like he was in that very space.

The scent of roses filled his nostrils, and he glanced around him to see where the sweet smell was coming from. He could hear the soft drones of the eulogy coming from within the church, not quite loud enough to identify what was being said but somehow offering a comforting tone for those present who were standing so respectfully. A large rose bush by the canopied entrance to the churchyard waved and bounced in the breeze scattering its aroma to all those around. 'How it must have been the perfect scene for a wedding' he thought as he scanned across the grave stones and up to the clock in the tower. The peace was broken by the interruption of a hymn being sung loud and clear emanating from the open solid oak wooden door showing the scars of so many years before.

Treavey was feeling a little uncomfortable in the heat whilst standing in his heavy dark suit. He felt like he needed to stand respectfully with his hands cupped in front of him and his head slightly bowed but his back was aching, and he had to move his position to clear the pain for a bit. He treated himself with a stretch by arching his back and turning his head to the far left and then to the far right and it was then that he noticed her. There in the corner of the grave yard was a familiar mound of clothes supporting a gentle soul, whose aura instantly gave Treavey a sense of peace. It was Grace. Grace had become a good friend whilst he was stationed a few miles away at another seaside town called Perranporth. She had been his confidant and he had allowed her to have the odd sneaky shower in the station on a night shift when no one was about. He had bought her some more clothes from the charity shop in Newquay and taken them over to her as there were no second-hand clothes shops in Perran. They had created a wonderful and trusting bond between them. She hadn't given too much information too early but slowly but surely, he found that Grace had been a police officer on CID in the West Midlands and her family had been wiped out in a car crash. She had turned to the bottle, perhaps unsurprisingly, and had lost her job before losing her house and turning to the streets. She'd chosen Cornwall where she had spent a lot of her happy youth when things seemed so much simpler. She was also the most perfect eyes and ears taking in all the gossip of who was doing what to who and where.

Treavey slid away from the church porch and meandered over to Grace. "I've really missed you, Grace."

Grace was a little startled. "Oh, Treavey. How wonderful to see you. It's been a few months, hasn't it? I've missed you too."

"I'm sorry I startled you," Treavey replied.

Grace smiled a warm smile which brought it back to him what a kind person she was. He initially felt deeply sorry for her and had made efforts to get her off the streets, but he soon learned to realise that she was happier than most other people. She had no permanent home, but she also did not have the stress of a job, or a mortgage. She was happy and she knew where to go when the weather changed for the worse. Maybe she had it right, and the rest of civilisation was trapped in the rat race and was miserable with it.

"Startled me? Oh yes, but I am not used to people making conversation with me. It's usually to move me on or to be abusive, unfortunately, but nothing I can't handle, you know me, Treavey."

Before he knew it, Treavey was sitting alongside her next to some gravestones with a willow tree giving them some shade. He felt comfortable to sit with her, saying nothing for a bit. They were comfortable in their own company and didn't feel the need to constantly strike up conversation. Treavey could see the irony of him being in a formal suit sitting next to Grace who was in her usual layers and that pink plastic child's bracelet still on her wrist. A memory from her past life perhaps, but he never liked to pry too much.

"Just listen to that," Grace said with her soft quiet tone. Treavey sat and listened, feeling the warmth of the sun but, also, the cool breeze from the shade of the tree. He could hear the murmurs of the ceremony from the church but much louder was the constant summer song of the skylarks in the fields beyond. There was the holiday buzz of the bumble bee and then the darting about them of the honey bee. Those skylarks, how they filled the air with sound and put a smile on his face, yet he hadn't really noticed them whilst waiting outside the church. This was a joy which Grace lived and understood. She understood the value of life.

"Are you happy, Grace?"

"Me, oh yes. I don't want for nothing. I used to be on that conveyor belt you are on, but I left all that for the better. You have an alarm clock going off when you feel at your worst, tired and maybe hung over too; should I go for promotion? Do I change departments? All of that and more. No, not for me, thank you. I may drink a bit too much but that's all. I never got into drugs. I saw what it did to people. The booze is my little bit of pleasure; my central heating if you like."

"Sounds reasonable to me, Grace. Hey, I could fall asleep here now. This is paradise."

Grace turned to him, her eyes sparkling, "You know you could go into that church and pay your respects by standing and sitting and reciting a mantra laid down by man, or instead you can pay your respects with nature.

They are returning to nature, after all. Was he a colleague? I can see by the mourners; he must have been a friend or colleague. Oh..." she hesitated and added, "... was he that young police officer who was killed on the coast road in the car crash?"

"Yes, Grace. He was backing me up getting to the head of my pursuit and he collided with the subject vehicle, you should have seen it, debris everywhere, what a disaster. It's really shaken me. He was my friend, you see, Grace. I spoke to him just minutes before he died. I didn't know he was dying. He told me to go on and go after the offenders, so I did. Then he died. I feel terrible, Grace, I feel like I left him to die with strangers."

She put her hand on his arm and said nothing. They continued to listen to the chorus of skylarks and the bees flitting about with a buzz which filled the air before gently disappearing as it sought brighter flowers elsewhere. He watched a red admiral butterfly dance just in front of them in the long grass and settle on a large yellow flower which had succeeded to grow high enough to feed off the sunlight above.

Grace pointed up into the blue sky at a herring gull gliding with its white and grey outstretched wings, using the thermals and breezes with expertise and without a flap of its wings to change its direction or even to gain height it dipped, dived and twisted to chase another seagull before dipping its wings to gain some speed and expertly adjusted their angle to gain height and within seconds it was landing on the top of the church tower with perfect timing placing its pink webbed feet on the stonework which had stood above St Columb Minor for over 500 years. It shook its feathers to settle them into some order before dipping its head below his smooth, soft white chest and immediately throwing it as far back as it could before letting out a crescendo of a squawking shriek as if to emphasise its satisfaction at its efforts.

"Treavey, my love. The world is full of regrets and disappointment. You can only do the best you can at the time and have no regrets as they will only eat into you. You have to learn from the past but live for the present. Too many people aspire for the future and forget to enjoy the past. They always live in frustration and disappointment. You can't change history so don't try to. He's gone and you couldn't have saved him. I heard the police caught those involved so surely, he'd be satisfied they didn't get away with it, at least. He's gone, Treavey. You should mourn your friend and then after a little time, you must leave him to wherever he has gone and enjoy the memories of his friendship instead."

Grace held the palm of her hand up to her face to shade her eyes from the sun which had just broken through the branches of the tree above them and gazing up at the gull on the church tower, she said, "Thirty years."

"What did you say?" Treavey asked.

"They can live for thirty years, you know. Seagulls. I'm not sure if the ones on a take away menu live that long but it's incredible, don't you think? When a common songbird lives for between three and six years. I mean, thirty years. Can you imagine the experiences it has in that time. I sometimes look at the flocks of gulls and try to find the expert flyers to see which ones are older, and which are the youngsters who have just learned to fly. Those who have those grey flecks in their feathers. It's amazing any of them survive at all really."

Treavey said nothing but slowly stood up and returned to the church porch where he could hear the service was ending. Nobody had missed him, and he knew Sooty wouldn't have minded. He had genuinely thought about him and chatted about him with Grace whereas he'd have probably shuffled uncomfortably and endured the heat in discomfort if he'd remained where he had been for protocol and convention.

As the final piece of music was heard coming from the church doorway, he knew the coffin would be following very shortly so headed towards the front gate to the churchyard. He had seen and heard all he had intended to. As he made his way through the archway of roses, he stopped to admire the blooms still bobbing in the breeze. He was learning to appreciate what was around him since he had met Grace. He was determined to begin living for the moment, not just the future.

"Steer," Treavey shouted as he stepped onto the pavement. The man turned around. "I mean, Mr Steer. Nice of you to turn up. Thank you. I know Sooty would have appreciated it."

"Hey Treavey, you scrub up alright." He turned to continue walking up the road seemingly uninterested in a sociable chat.

Treavey trotted up beside him and continued talking nonetheless. "No, really, thanks for turning up. You didn't fancy going inside then?"

The Superintendent continued looking forward and walk on purposefully. "I didn't fancy bumping into that little shit, Levey."

This took Treavey by surprise. "What does Inspector Levey have to do with anything?"

Steer's face was turning red and Treavey wasn't sure whether it was through the heat of the day or from anger. He found it intriguing. He wanted to push him for more information, especially as he felt he had a rapport with him, now.

"Treavey, there's a lot you don't know, and one of those is that that little bastard has been shagging my wife."

The Superintendent stopped in his tracks and stared directly at Treavey, his glare piercing through him. "I shouldn't have said that. Forget it. I probably made it up. I don't know what I'm saying."

Treavey jumped in, "No, come on. That's a serious accusation. I mean, I don't like the guy. I think he's a bit creepy and he was a bit slow on the uptake when he found you in your car the first day I joined the nick, but, I mean, how do you know?"

Steer sneered, "Because a woman told me. A gossiping meddling little cow who hates police did it to rub it in my face, that's how I know. She told me, my missus and that Levey slime ball have been shagging each other for months and, like an idiot, I was completely oblivious to it."

Treavey was stunned by what he had just been told. He couldn't believe it. This changed everything. They continued walking to a nearby gravel car park and the Superintendent got into the passenger seat of a new looking silver Range Rover. A woman sitting in the front passenger seat looked a little shocked at seeing Treavey. The same woman he had seen with the Superintendent in town when he'd been chasing the cash in transit robber. Steer opened the door, and put one foot on the gravel again, "Yes, I'm with someone else now, a friend from years ago and I should have done it years ago, and why the fuck shouldn't I be. For all I care, Lisa is dead to me."

He slammed the door and the Range Rover pulled away. Treavey could only imagine what was going on in the car as it sped off. His Superintendent had been emotional, and no doubt had intended to leave before anyone had seen his girlfriend but then again, he hadn't been too careful, either, or maybe he had wanted to be seen with his new partner. There was always a big chance someone else would have left early too, such as Treavey himself. So, he'd found himself a new girlfriend, he had made it clear he despised his wife, Lisa, and he didn't care where she was, and those last words ran a chill down Treavey's spine. 'Lisa is dead to me.' Did he mean she was dead to him, or dead to everyone? Had he had a fit of rage, and did he try to kill himself with a diabetic coma in the police car park to show Inspector Levey he knew? Treavey knew he had to speak to Adam.

Chapter 11
Cliff rescues and sex

Treavey was skipping up the steps to the CID office once more. He couldn't ever remember walking up them in any normal manner as he always had something to get off his chest or to find out in a hurry. Fortunately, Adam was sitting there at his desk as if waiting for him. Treavey no longer felt like a stranger there. DS Bates was at his desk and showed a respectful interest in Treavey coming into the office. It was as though he had earned his stripes. Not as a CID officer but as a uniformed officer who could enter the CID office without attracting a disapproving frown.

"Sarge." Treavey declared as a greeting and to show his respect to the rank. "I've come to speak to Adam, but you may be interested too."

Treavey repeated what the Superintendent had said to him at the funeral and after he had finished, he looked at both the CID officers awaiting their reaction. DS Bates kept tapping a pen on the table in front of him. His large physique oozed the years of experience, shifts and stress which it had endured. His bushy moustache twitched as he processed what he had just heard and he took a deep breath, pushing himself away from the desk on his wheeled chair.

"Right. Thank you Treavey. That's very useful information. Can you put it on a statement for me please?"

Treavey had been ready to get his jacket and run out of the office with Adam to arrest Steer, but that hadn't happened. He felt let down and side-lined.

DS Bates acknowledged his disappointment. "Treavey, seriously, that's some very good work, and well done for what you've done. Make sure you don't ask him any direct questions, right? That would be an interview, but you have an obvious rapport with him which is useful. Stay professional though because it can be difficult when you have befriended someone like you have. Keep reporting back like you have been, though won't you. There has been some invaluable information, and we can do some work on it."

Adam cut in. "Boss. I'd like to go to Steer's place and find some details on who this woman is he refers to. You know, the meddling one who told him about Lisa having an affair with... well you know who. It's not an interview and it's only to establish the identification and whereabouts of a crucial witness but I could do with Treavey coming along because he's more likely to tell me with him there. Ever since he French kissed him in the car park, it's like he thinks he owes him something."

The DS laughed at Adam. "Oh, he does, Adam, he fucking does owe him something; he owes him his life which is a little bit more than he owes that slimy Inspector Levey who walked past him in the car park when he was dying."

He flicked his gaze across to Treavey, "You didn't just hear me call him a slimy little whatever; you can strike that from the record."

The DS tapped his pen even louder and slammed it down on the table in front of him. "Right, okay, take Treavey along with you, Adam, and see what you can find out about this witness."

"Grab your civi stuff, Treavey, you are being seconded to CID for this afternoon." Adam shouted as he made for the bottom car park. Treavey changed as quickly as he could and joined Adam in a pale blue Ford Escort which he'd often walked past and rarely seen absent from its CID marked space. It struggled with a tiny 1300cc engine, pitiful as car engines went but it felt special to be sitting in the car that must have experienced some exciting CID jobs. He remembered the last time he was in it when he was picking up the armed robber from the post office robbery. Adam spun the steering and negotiated the car out of the car park before continuing along towards Superintendent Steer's address. It was a mere 10 minutes, and they were parked a few houses along from his.

"We don't want to embarrass the old guy, do we? This CID car is very well known around the town, and we don't want to add to the gossiping. Everyone thinks he's totalled his missus, already."

They walked up the steps to the front door and Adam knocked on the heavy wooden panel. Treavey glanced around him to see if anyone was watching on but there didn't seem to be anyone. There was a herring gull preening itself whilst standing proudly in the garden, tucking its yellow beak into its soft white chest feathers, ruffling them before taking another look around itself to look for marauding attackers. It held its head erect and stared for a moment at nothing in particular before diving its beak back into its chest to ruffle the feathers once more. The door was abruptly opened.

"Hello guys" Steer shouted. "Come in, come in... oh wait, there's two of you. Are you arresting me?"

"No, Sir," Adam replied swiftly, before following him into the house and through to the rear into the sleek white kitchen which looked out onto the garden. Treavey could see he had been busy digging the garden which would have been difficult in this heat, but he guessed he didn't have much else to do. It always raised suspicion when one's wife was missing, however.

Treavey hadn't noticed how Steer had been looking recently. He was usually a confident man who held his head high and ran the police station with the air of authority. He was tall but rotund with white thinning hair and a far too pink face. He emitted the air of a heart attack just about to happen at the best of times, but he looked even worse now and the beads of sweat gliding off his forehead and running to the end of his nose weren't painting a picture of health. The three men moved into the garden to admire Steer's handy work. Adam was looking around past the perimeter and Treavey guessed he was looking for CCTV as he had done the first time he came around and had been suspicious of the sudden digging spree. He couldn't see any but it was worth a scan around just so they could say they'd looked.

"Fancy a cold drink?" Steer offered whilst turning back towards the kitchen.

"No, no, Sir. We won't be staying long. We just came to ask you a question. Don't worry, it's more about a potential witness you can help me with."

"Oh, right," Steer replied whilst staring back at his handiwork. "I know what this is about. Our little encounter at the church, eh Treavey?"

Treavey felt it was his time to come forward and take the lead. The very fact that Adam was calling him Sir every five minutes meant it was being kept on a formal level and would remain feeling like an interview if they weren't careful.

"Yes, it is. You mentioned a meddling woman who had told you about Lisa having an affair with Inspector Levey. I don't really know how someone copes with being told that." The Superintendent remained looking straight ahead at his garden. The well dug area beside the small wooden shed had begun to sprout with something flourishing very well and Treavey found himself looking forward to coming again later to see how the seedlings were getting on.

"I was told it, though, and not for my own good, you understand. It was so she could gloat at me because she didn't much like police officers or men, coming to that."

Treavey decided to come straight out with it. "Who was she?"

The answer came back remarkably easily. "She's dead now. I think her past caught up with her.

"Oh?" Treavey was on high alert, having not expected any specifics but Steer must know who she was or how would he know she was dead? Things had started to become interesting.

"Yeah, Sitara was her name. Some Muslim lesbian who was murdered by her lover who couldn't take any more of her, I suspect. There's an Arab woman who knows more about her. Amoora, I think her name is. You may want to see her."

Adam jumped in. "Amoora. I know her. I took a statement from her about the murder of Sitara. I know all about this. So, you say Sitara came to you about you wife having an affair with that snake Levey? God knows what she saw in him." Treavey was learning fast. He was sure Adam was trying to get Steer onside by putting Levey down and made it sound like it was between friends, or colleagues at least and it was well known that police officers talked far too much when under investigation.

"Can you tell us anything else at all?" Treavey asked whilst playing with the lid on his biro.

"Only that you saved my life and I'm glad you did Treavey. It was a suicide attempt." Steer bowed his head and spoke in a much more solemn tone. "Since then, I have had comfort from an old friend, and we are getting on very well. That young lady in the car and who you saw me with in Newquay?" Treavey nodded his head. "I'd like to keep her out of it if I can."

Adam and Treavey left the house and returned to their rather pathetic looking CID car. Adam was in thought trying to pull together what had just happened.

"So, Sitara was murdered by her lover Sarah, or at least we think she was. Sitara was aware of the affair between Steer's wife and Inspector Levey and decided to butt in and tell him about it. Did Steer murder his wife in revenge and then the only witness Sitara? But then... he would still have Levey to worry about. But anyhow, he tried to take his own life until you came to work that day, Treavey."

Treavey tried to help a little by coming at it from another angle. "It sounds like Amoora may have some more information; don't you think? Worth having a go at least."

"You're right, and there's no time like the present. You free, still?"

"I think the Sarge has written me off for the shift and it doesn't sound too busy at the moment." Treavey said, but decided not to confirm it with his sergeant just in case he said no. "Better to ask for forgiveness than permission, no?"

They both giggled as they got back into their car and Adam began winding the little blue car along the residential roads back onto the main road and off again towards Pentire headland. They stopped near some garages with some flats above. A moment later they were walking into a perfectly kept modern apartment with stunning views across Fistral Beach from the lounge. Treavey ambled over to have a look through the large window and noted, with a smile, the dunes where Claire had gone topless next to him with her friend Bronwyn.

The woman standing before them was simply beautiful. She was middle eastern, he suspected around thirty, with a curvy figure but a surprisingly slim waist.

Her very straight midnight black hair streamed and flowed down to the top of her very pert buttocks like warm dark treacle. Treavey gazed straight into her stunningly dark, almond shaped eyes as Adam proceeded to ask her some questions. Treavey pulled sharply away as he found himself viewing her substantial and rather voluptuous cleavage appearing over the top of a surprisingly plain white blouse and headed towards the window again for safety as he was sure he had been caught looking by her.

The apartment was meticulously kept with everything in its place. Everything was of the highest quality with paintings and prints reflecting the local seas and landscapes and some quality local pottery ornaments sparingly displayed on the minimalist shelves. She showed off a subtle taste, but it was exquisite in its presentation. He left Adam to ask her some more questions whilst gazing across the mesmerising baby blue skies reaching across the vast and stretching lush golden sands of Fistral Beach. He watched a few figures paddle to catch a rolling wave but they misjudged their timing or the strength of the wave and they disappeared off the back of it to try again. A slight-offshore wind whipped up the face of the wave to create a thick but fine spray which rained over the back of itself creating its own little rain storm to blow into the faces and humiliate any surfer caught in its path, taunting them for their failure. Others would actively paddle to perfection and find the sweet spot just as the wave was building to its peak and the board would accelerate along the front of the shiny bluey green glass surface with the figure springing up like a statue, find their balance and turn and twist the board with the finesse of a ballerina to feel the adrenaline of the moment for as long as they possibly could. A herring gull glided above with indignant poise, no longer surprised at the seemingly waste of energy by the figures below. At the point where the wave broke its smooth glass finish to a boiling froth, the black statues dramatically but effortlessly dived into the water to begin heading 'out back' to catch the thrill of another wave of the day.

"Treavey. Oy, Treavey!" was the sound which broke the perfect day dream. Treavey wanted to stay there all day. Adam shouted once more. "Are you with us Treavey? Amoora says she knows Claire. Says that Sitara was an absolute cow and she's no loss."

"Yeah, I sort of knew that. Hey Amoora, it's great to meet you at last. Claire was grateful to you for tipping her off about the danger her sister, Sarah was in. So how come Sitara felt like she had to tip off the Superintendent about his wife having an affair?"

Adam glared at him with a frown which quickly curled into a smile. "Mate, we've just been through all that. I will fill you in on the way back, okay? Are you on a different planet today or what?"

Treavey left the apartment feeling some embarrassment walking past Amoora and offering a soft, "Goodbye, thanks." She nodded back at him and smiled with some pity. He noticed her very full lips he hadn't noticed before. They were perfect in shape for lips, almost painted on but so very natural at the same time.

"Well?" Treavey said in some anticipation.

"Are you certain you are out of your trance now mate? You looked like you were away with the fairies."

Treavey apologised and commented how he had wanted to live in an apartment like that one day. Adam ignored him, "She obviously didn't rate Sitara in the slightest which I already knew but Amoora hadn't known that she had told Steer about his wife. She didn't know herself so it's a bit of a dead end there. Sounds like she was just a busybody who enjoyed upsetting people's lives as much as she could, and especially if it had nothing to do with her."

"Do you think Sarah killed Sitara?" Treavey asked Adam.

"It all points to it which is why she's been remanded, and she says she has too. It's just weird how the method of murder doesn't quite fit."

Treavey had had enough. He wasn't getting any further with this today and the exciting finale to the shift was not going to happen. The journey was quiet back towards the station and if they'd just been a few seconds earlier, they would have made it to the sanctuary of their base. The silence, however, was broken by the thunder of a heavy turbine engine which shook the ground around them and caused Adam to twitch his steering in alarm.

"Jesus, what the fuck was that?"

They saw the low-slung grey belly of a huge metal aircraft towering over their car and then break hard to the left where it disappeared down over the cliff edge. Adam continued in the direction it had gone to see what the red and grey Royal Navy Sea King search and rescue helicopter was up to. He parked the car where a crowd was gathering at the top of Tolcarne Beach. The main road of Narrowcliff ran parallel to the sheer drop down onto the beach huts and cafe below, served by steep zig zagging steps and a slipway for vehicles via the barrow fields adjacent to it. Holiday makers were holding their cameras at arm's length towards the rocky and steep cliffs on the right-hand side of the beach. They saw the helicopter circle around the bay of Tolcarne before nosing itself into the towering cliff, but it wasn't obvious why.

"Come on, Treavey, let's get down there." They jumped into the car again and sped down the slip road to the beach and jumped out at the bottom, making their way towards the sandy beach to get a closer look.

They marvelled at the skill of the pilot who manoeuvred the great machine into position precariously near the cliffs with the breaking waves below. It raised its height, so the rotors were above the cliff edge having had a closer look below, almost as if to be able to get closer to the cliff itself to avoid the rota blades clashing against the rock face. The enormity soon became clear with the site of a person clinging precariously to the cliff some 30 feet up, and the waves having gained in ferocity throwing its sputum at the poor individual who must have realised their fate was soon to come calling. It was just a matter of which wave had the strength to pluck them from their clasp.

Treavey and Adam fed back to the station what was going on but there were little officers could do but request for an ambulance and it had probably been requested already. "Hey, Adam. The cavalry has arrived." Treavey enthusiastically pointed over to an orange streak bouncing its way through the surf and disappearing in the troughs before appearing after an agonising wait and becoming airborne before plummeting down into the trough of the swell again. The sea had gained in height and anger since that peaceful viewing across Fistral Bay some moments earlier and to an alarming effect. The lifeboat arrived on scene with a crew of four buzzed in circles, some distance off at first, and then darted towards the base of the cliffs but then driving at full throttle out of the area again before a huge set of waves came thundering in on top of them. The timing had to be to perfection to avoid the loss of the boat and its crew, but Treavey could see they knew that the person's only chance would be the lifeboat crew to save their life if the next wave was to pull them into the cauldron of strong currents and the grinding of the jagged rocks which would await them when they fell.

"It's like a fucking action movie, this," Adam said almost fixed to the spot, with the angry, grey billowing clouds accumulating above their heads. The world had suddenly become a sinister place.

The boat made several attempts to get to the base of the cliffs so they would be ready to react and pluck the person to safety. It was getting serious now, as the waves gained further height with each set coming in. The 'oohs' from the crowd were audible as the human reactions to someone else's peril became like a gladiatorial fight being played out before them. Maybe the same instincts were cutting in. Had civilisation changed so much after all?

It had become visually clear the person holding on for dear life, dressed in just a pair of blue beach shorts was weakening. With each plume of spray devouring them it was a surprise to see them still hanging on, but it was inevitable their good fortune wasn't going to last much longer. The lifeboat helmsman waited for the final large wave of the set to clear and then he threw the inflatable towards the rock face to make use of the relative calm whilst they could, before the sets began to grow again like a menacing monster licking its lips from the depths like some sort of water lizard. The helicopter was lowering a winchman towards the person who was visibly limp with exhaustion. This was the particularly dangerous bit as it was common for the casualty to relax, somehow believing they were safe already.

As the helicopter moved in with the winchman the crowd could see a particularly large set of waves building near the horizon. The clock was ticking. The boat remained at the base of the cliffs in the swirling swell in case the casualty lost their footing. The helicopter was perilously near to the cliffs with its rota blades ruffling the foliage at the top of the cliff, but the pilot was undeterred.

"Adam, look at the winchman, they are going in to grab them. They aren't waiting."

The man on the end of the wire was gliding on the wire towards the cliff at what Treavey was sure was far too fast, but the pilot had gauged it perfectly, as the winchman slowed to avoid a violent impact against the casualty and the rockface. The boat was forced to spin around and head out to sea at the last moment to avoid the monster set and Treavey could feel their frustration. They wanted to stay where the action was. At that point, a huge wave crashed against the base of the cliff and swept its violent white volcanic froth up and over the casualty and the winchman just as he managed to straddle the helpless victim. There was another gasp from the crowd and a moment of silence to await the horrific scene of an empty rock face. The lifeboat was back foreseeing the impending doom but to the huge relief, away swung both the winchman and the casualty on the wire and out over the heads of the lifeboat crew who were already spinning the boat about again, to avoid the repeated massive set of rolling waves heading towards them.

But whilst the casualty was relatively safe, being swung in dizzy circles just above the sea, and towards the sea shore where Treavey and Adam were waiting, there was another adventure unfolding for the crowd. The lifeboat was trapped at the rock face, and the rollers were powering towards them and getting larger with every metre. The helmsman opened the throttle on the boat and whilst the helicopter gently landed its cargo on the beach next to the officers, the lifeboat was at full speed heading for the safety of deep water. The crew could be seen to physically brace themselves as the top of the wave began to curl and collapse right over the top of them and the boat, having reached an almost vertical position… disappeared.

As the wave continued as if not noticing the destruction it had caused, the crowd roared in shock and disbelief to see the lifeboat resurface but upside down with its propellor still turning. This was not what Treavey was expecting to see. The emergency services were usually in full control, and this was not it. This had gone horribly wrong, and the prognoses was looking dire. One by one the four-man crew bobbed up around the upturned boat to the relief of everyone, but their danger was not over. The next wave was soon on top of them and pushing them underneath its washing machine of currents. Their suits and lifejackets, even though saving their lives also, were buoyant enough to push along on the front of a wave like a beach ball and straight into the cliffs.

There was no time with the helicopter crew unclipping the casualty at the feet of the officers and having been informed of the disaster unfolding by the pilot and with Adam shouting to the paramedic on the wire, he headed out to sea again with the paramedic still on the end of the wire and with no time to winch him up for some respite.

One by one, the paramedic picked the casualties up. One by one having to winch them up and then return down to pluck another, the last being so near to the base of the jagged rocks and weak from the pummelling of the waves they could not have been left for another minute.

Once the last of the lifeboat crew were up in the helicopter, and after a short pause, the huge thundering metal angel bowed its head before turning towards the direction of Truro hospital and was off at speed. Heavy with its belly full of shocked and exhausted lifeboat crew, and after a sudden down wash of its rota blades, it was gone, and silence returned. The crowd had disappeared as soon as they had arrived.

"You certainly gave these holiday makers a day to remember, young man," Adam said to the shivering man who had been deposited at their feet. "Come on, let's get you in the warm car and get you to Newquay hospital for a check-up, okay?"

Half an hour later, the relieved parents were with their son at the local hospital, not having believed the fuss around the coast had been caused by their 18-year-old son. Treavey was touched by his concern and relief to hear the lifeboat crew were safe.

"I could never have lived with myself if any of them had died," he said to his parents who were cuddling him like a baby. "I caused them that mum. I can't believe I did that, I'm really sorry."

Treavey felt he needed to come in. "Look, don't worry about it. Apart from an expensive boat, which I'm certain they won't be billing you for, they are safe, and you didn't do anything intentionally or even recklessly. You just got it wrong which many people do, so put it behind you now. You're okay."

The parents were relieved at his words of comfort. Treavey and Adam could see they were decent people and there had just been a bad set of circumstances. Age, experience, knowledge and perhaps being a little too much on holiday and not keeping an eye out on the tides.

Later, at the station, Treavey put his hand on Adam's shoulder as they walked down the hallway, "Usual day on CID was that, Adam?"

Adam sniggered but then hesitated and replied, "I'm going to have a chat with Levey tomorrow, Treavey. I'll let you know how I get on, but I best have a chat with DS Bates first because he is the OIC after all. Not sure whether he's a suspect or a witness at this stage. I suspect we'll treat him as a witness until he says something dodgy to incriminate himself and then we'll have to caution him and interview him."

Adam was talking as if he were thinking aloud and Treavey was flattered he was so relaxed with the confidential information regarding the investigation being discussed in front of him. Adam carried on upstairs to the CID office leaving Treavey wondering if he should apply for a CID aid to get some proper experience. No. Treavey wanted to join traffic and fire arms. That's the direction he wanted to go. Exhausted suddenly, as if someone had pulled the plug out of a beach ball, his energy left him. He had been through the mill, but what had he actually achieved today? Very little when he came to think about it. Perhaps tomorrow will be better. As he left the station to walk home to Lusty Glaze, he decided to pop around to see Claire at her flat. He hadn't spoken to her for a while and was missing her.

On arriving there, she met him with a warm, welcoming smile, hugged him tightly and kissed him provocatively on the lips which felt different from usual. He looked at her and notice she bit her bottom lip and smiled after kissing him. She looked mischievous and naughty. He was happy to be with her and felt he could fully relax, that he could take his guard down and be himself. They both went over to the settee and sat down next to each other. Claire placed her hand on his knee, and he placed his hand over hers, now feeling a little awkward but it felt good. He wasn't used to this affection with her yet.

"I needed to be here, Claire. I just want to relax here for a bit because it's been a bit rubbish today. Nothing major but I'm not making as much progress with things as I thought I would."

Claire listened intently, gazing into his eyes with a warmth which made Treavey skip a heartbeat. He was getting attached to her. Her eyes were the brightest blue and he never got fed up looking into them. They turned him on like a light switch and she would very quickly change his mood for the better.

"Is there any progress on getting my sister out of prison?" Claire asked.

"I hoped there would be some news today, to be honest with you, but no one seems to know very much. We know that Levey was having an affair with the Super's wife, and he found out because Sitara told him. I have a feeling it's all connected. I still can't see how your sister is involved with that side of things, though. I think she made a bumbling attempt to poison Sitara, but someone got there before her. I mean why else would you confess to killing someone, try to top yourself and then get the method that killed them wrong. There's no sense in it. I think she's got a good chance of getting off remand with a half decent solicitor. The only person she had a gripe with is already dead and the cause of death doesn't match, and yet there were traces of the poison in her but not sufficient enough to kill her so you could ask what she's doing in prison? Someone else must have got there first and I think it's something to do with Steer and his lot."

Claire was swirling thoughts around in her mind. The mischievous expression had changed to more of a bemused one. "You mean, because Sitara told Steer about his wife's affair and now, she's gone missing? But that's not much, is it? I hope you're right though. That would get Sarah off."

Claire gazed at Treavey and replaced her hand on his knee and stared into his large brown eyes as if trying to recover what they had lost. He could sense she was wanting to change the subject and forget all the serious stuff for a moment. "I haven't seen you in a little while, have I, Treavey?" she spoke in soft and sensual tones.

Treavey lent forward, moving towards her so, so close, he could feel her warm breath against his lips. He took hold of the soft material of her cotton blouse around her chest between finger and thumb and pulled her slowly towards him until her lips met his. The electricity ran through him and sent tingles rushing over his muscular torso and thighs. As they gently kissed, he touched the tip of her tongue with his and found her wanting more, so whilst placing his on her now rosy cheek, he gently pushed her back, so they sunk into the sofa together. She moved her thighs apart so he could lie between them. He lay motionless, staring at her fresh, beautiful young skin and the brightest of blue eyes, those eyes which had enticed him so much in the first place, and he took in the sight, not quite believing how fortunate he was to be with this girl. She smiled sweetly back at him, biting her bottom lip and staring into his eyes, their faces almost touching. She put her hand gently behind his neck and pulled him closer towards her, locked lips in a sweet kiss which he hoped would never end. He breathed her sweet fragrant perfume in and revelled in the feeling of being wanted by someone so much. Feeling affection felt so good and having someone want him as much as he wanted them felt so natural which he hadn't felt before.

All his stress left him, and he allowed his guard to slip down further, so much so, all the macho fakery of trying to impress her left him and it was more akin to imagining her and him to be two swallows dancing in the skies together, darting to and fro in perfect sync and to be partners for life. He was perhaps getting a little carried away; he knew the hormones were surging around his veins as was hers. Before long, she moved up a gear, showing more confidence with every second as he could feel her move her hand towards the buckle of his jeans and perhaps too expertly, release the top button.

"Oh?" Treavey cheekily enquired and pulled his head back to look directly into her eyes once more. Claire had accelerated things somewhat. He was happy to press his weight on top of her so she could feel him, and noticed the devilish twinkle in her eye which told him she knew exactly how turned on he was.

"Are you sure about this?" Treavey asked with some nervousness, his heart pounding as he still couldn't believe he was in this position with a girl he fancied so much.

"Like you wouldn't believe," she confidently confirmed and with some fumbling and clumsiness along with some embarrassed awkward giggling, she removed her trousers along with his jeans and they lay together in their underwear panting and giggling like two teenagers. It wasn't long before she had grabbed him by the hand and pulled him towards the bedroom and before falling on top of the duvet, she posed teasingly in front of him, pulling off her blouse and delicate powder blue bra, posing in just her small but surprisingly plain looking pair of knickers.

"Well?" she cheekily demanded, stretching her naked arms above her head interlocking her fingers and slowly letting herself fall back onto the soft, bouncy bed. Treavey moved towards her on the bed. She was looking vulnerable and exposed, but he knew she was the one with the confidence. He was going to have to find it from somewhere. Her flirting with him was just a part she was playing, and she played it well. He couldn't get his eyes off her breasts which had last teased him on Fistral Beach but were untouchable back then. He leant over her with his broad, tanned masculine frame and she reached up to touch his defined pec muscles, running her finger teasingly down his chest to a nipple. He put one muscular arm either side of her, and he held himself there so she could take his youthful but manly physique in. He wanted to tease her with what he was going to do next, but he didn't know himself. It was time, but he wanted to savour this moment too. She waited in anticipation as there was little she could do. She could feel him between her legs and was incredibly aroused herself with just their thin underwear between them. He lowered his statue-like frame towards her, kissed her breasts and then her nipples gently before looking back into her eyes again. He grinned at her with a mix of confident masculine male pride and shy teenager and so wishing to delay what was going to happen very soon, he gave her the softest of kisses whilst manoeuvring his hips and very obvious bulge across her thighs. She bit her bottom lip again and smiled like the devil herself. She ran her fingers down from his, now nervously dry lips, across his naked, broad, tanned, and sculpted chest, down his flat and muscular stomach as if it were etched in granite and then with an overpowering smile and momentary pause, into his boxer shorts. She had waited long enough.

Chapter 12
Death on the doorstep

PC Jon Goodman had been partnered up with Treavey for the night shift and he sat momentarily in the Escort panda car at the police station waiting patiently for Treavey to adjust his driver's seat.

"You quite finished poncing about yet, Treavey? Christ, you gonna do your hair next?"

A Sunday night in Newquay shouldn't be too busy even though it was the summer. The weather was looking damp so PC Rain should be getting rid of any drunk stragglers as there was nothing worse than repeated calls to drunken idiots pulling bins over and perhaps smashing a window which created a substantial amount of paperwork for a mediocre £25 fine.

"Let's go find a drink-driver, Treavey," came the gruff voice of the hulk of a man sitting beside him. "That should kill most of the night by the time we process them. Where shall we go? Maybe Crantock for any drinkers driving back to Newquay instead of getting a taxi?"

Crantock was an isolated little village on the coast, just 5 or so miles away but there was a popular nightclub there and it was known many revellers would take the risk in driving back rather than wait for a taxi at the busiest of times.

"Sounds good, Jon. That's usually good fishing ground but we'd better be quick with the pubs closing out there."

Treavey knew he was well looked after with Jon as a crew mate. He did go on about the Huer's hut a bit, but he admired him for that. Jon could see a piece of

Cornish history crumbling into the sea and was raising awareness and money to save it. The ancient white building was just above the cliff where he first met Claire, so he had some fondness for it, and he wasn't going to hear anyone say anything against it now.

"Hey Jon, if we get any fighters tonight, you can hold them all by their necks in that one hand of yours and I'll do the paperwork, sound fair?" Treavey joked, referring to Jon's bulk and pure physical strength. He knew he could joke about Jon as he was a wonderfully gentle man in reality. He was a gentle giant but was very handy when needed. Every Section needed a Jon Goodman on their side.

"Golf 31, can you attend St Austell for an immediate?"

Treavey sighed. "That puts that down the pan," he replied despondently. He pressed the transmit button on his personal radio. "Go ahead, what have you got, control?"

Some typing could be heard in the background as the dispatcher had pushed her transmit pedal under her desk. "We have a woman who is calling on a niner saying her ex-boyfriend Michael Goring, who has an injunction against him, is breaking into her house. Unfortunately, we don't have any units nearby. We need you to start heading towards St Austell and we'll update you with the exact address enroute. We are attempting to get back-up from Traffic or Armed Response units."

"St Austell?" Jon exclaimed to Treavey, "That's over half a fucking hour away, man. The only unit?"

Treavey had already spun the front wheels of the Escort out of the station car park and switched on the sirens and blue light. He could feel the punch of hot adrenaline rushing around his body soon forgetting their original plan of catching a drink driver. He told himself to keep it cool; not to panic and to get there in one piece but he had to get there fast. How was she going to hold her ex-boyfriend off for over half an hour?

The Panda slewed around the bend as he threw the steering to the right to join Narrowcliff and stamp on the accelerator wishing he was driving something substantially more powerful than he was. He positioned the car on the damp road on the opposite side to gain the most visibility across the pedestrian crossing lights which were on green opposite the Bristol Hotel and onwards out towards St Columb Minor. It was one straight road out of town and pretty much all the way to St Austell, so he was able to concentrate on the traffic and occasional pedestrians rather than getting his cornering right. He glanced across to Jon who seemed to be very comfortable in the passenger seat not fazed by the street furniture rushing by at breakneck speed.

"Golf 31, what's your eta? We have her on the phone screaming at us to come quickly. He has a machete, and we can hear breaking glass in the background. We have dispatched ARV, but they will be there after you, I'm afraid."

Jon snapped back in a cryptic tone. "20 minutes."

After a short pause, more tapping from the dispatcher's keyboard and, "Okay, we have ambulance enroute, but they are holding off until your arrival."

Treavey expertly manoeuvred the panda around a congested junction full of cars with drivers giving way to everyone but no one actually moving. The Panda drove through it in a flash no doubt leaving several startled motorists even more flustered.

He took a deep breath and checked his speed. 70mph now, as he headed out towards Indian Queens and onwards, using the railway crossing as a ramp and achieving clearance between his wheels and the road. The car bounced as it landed slightly off centre, but he maintained control whilst quickly negotiating the roundabout just ahead.

"Steady," Jon said quietly, but there was nothing more to be said.

The dispatcher was becoming more frantic. "Treavey, she's telling us he has got through the glass door and he's getting past the barricade she's put on the stairs. She's screaming he's going to kill her."

It was unusual for a control room dispatcher to refer to a crew member by name and it showed the controller was stressed. Treavey knew this was as serious as it could get. He was squeezing everything he could out of the little car. "10 minutes," replied Treavey. "Going as fast as we can."

Jon looked over at him as calmly as if he were a passenger on a Sunday drive and with a twang of sarcasm. "If you put your foot down a bit, you might get there in time."

The little Panda continued bouncing around the country lanes towards and through the village of St Stephen and into St Austell towards the address Jon had just been updated with.

"Golf 31, we've told her to stay in the bathroom and to barricade herself in with what she can. It's gone silent for a couple of minutes now. ETA?"

Jon just managed to reply, "2 minutes," before they were both startled by a car coming at them from a side junction. Treavey swerved to the left to avoid it, but it was only just enough. There was a gentle nudge at the rear as they realised the car had just glanced the rear of their car, but he had avoided a serious side on impact. The panda swayed but did nothing more. Treavey glanced into his rear-view mirror to acknowledge it wasn't serious. The car had stopped where it had hit them, so he continued. His destination was far too serious to give up on now.

"Golf 31," Treavey shouted, "we've just glanced off a car and I am unable to stop so you may get a call. Minor damage. We are arriving now."

Jon looked at Treavey, "Ready? This could be the big one mate. Casco's out?"

"Fuck yeah. Hit first, ask questions later with this bastard." Treavey continued, already having switched the ignition off, removed his seatbelt and was now springing out of the car taking the lead towards the house made up of the two flats and with an obvious devastated front door.

They got to the door. Treavey pushed it forcefully, so it swung open, and the remnants of the glass crashed to the ground making a sound like a dozen pairs of symbols. He felt himself being pulled back by an immensely powerful arm which almost caused him to lose his footing. "What the?" he exclaimed.

"I'll take this one Treavey," came the reply from the bulk of Jon squeezing by him in the corridor and up the stairs flicking debris aside as if it were nothing to him. "Michael, Michael, stay where you are you little bastard. Uncle Jon is coming to get you Michael Goring. Don't move a fucking muscle."

Treavey ran up the stairs behind him desperate to get a view of what had happened and what the state of the girl was and whether he was needed for another pair of hands but unless this guy was a monster, he would stand no chance against Jon.

The site that lay before them both was terrifying. Treavey had never seen so much blood. It was everywhere. Up the walls of the stairway and hallway, smeared to head height and with sticky globulus puddles on the carpet. It smelt putrid like death and as they moved forward towards the bathroom door, a shiver ran down his spine like a cube of melting ice running from the nape of his neck to the small of his back. Treavey feared what he was going to look at next.

Treavey glanced behind him and seeing something with caught his eye, "Jon, look!"

A body lay in the doorway of the bedroom. Treavey ran over and quickly established this had been the cause of the blood around the flat. It was as if a champagne cork of some devil worship celebration had exploded its contents. Treavey rolled the body over onto its back, which resisted at first as if held down by treacle. It was a man.

Jon didn't bother negotiating through the door to see if the young girl was in there, but instead with a tap of his foot and a shove of his shoulder pushed the door open to find the girl inside crouched beside the basin pedestal blubbering uncontrollably, her skinny frame shaking with fear and exhaustion. Her face was smeared with blood which continued down her filthy vest. Her loose dirty white cotton trousers were ripped revealing her clean pale smooth thigh.

Jon spoke softly as he crouched down beside her. "Hey, you're safe now, okay? You are safe. He's gone now." She pulled herself towards Jon and fell towards him into his arms for a hug and he embraced her with his muscular frame. Treavey stared at both of them, looking around himself and collecting his thoughts. He was taking the scene in for a moment or two.

He quickly checked the other rooms for any further injured, and for any photos of children. He hoped he wasn't going to come across another body, let alone a child. He didn't know how he would have coped with that. Jon gently questioned her on any further details but also knew he couldn't go into too much detail as she would also be a suspect for a murder. Fortunately, she had said there was no one else involved. Just them. What this poor woman had endured during her time with him must have been agony for her, but now the tyrant wasn't free to infiltrate his way into another innocent woman's life. Society was a safer place this monster had now gone.

The paramedics arrived after Treavey had given the all clear and they split up to assess the casualties. The woman medic approached the body of Michael and quickly recognised life was extinct. They would have to wait for a doctor to confirm the man was dead, although the 8-inch machete blade embedded in his head was making it pretty obvious it wasn't survivable, but that was the procedure. The ARVs arrived just as the initial fuss was dying down and made a comment about what a fine mess Treavey had got himself into when left for five minutes. Treavey knew it was meant as a friendly joke to relax the situation as one off the ARV officers patted him on the back and said, "Nice one. Glad you are all okay. Sorry we weren't here sooner to back you up; we were at a nasty accident at the back end of nowhere and came as quick as we could."

The young woman was led off with the ambulance, followed by a CID officer from St Austell who had decided to get her sorted out medically first of all before stressing her out with any arrest which may come later. Treavey knew they would need to seize her clothing for analysis. It had been a hell of a fight in there, but she was safe, that's the main thing. Treavey felt in need of a shower as his clothing had been impregnated with death, his boots were sticking to the carpet and at some point, the blood was so deep, it had curled up the side of his boots and over the toe of them. He couldn't think where to start.

Adam arrived and Treavey was impressed by the immediate control he took of the scene. No one was permitted in from then on. The place was shut down. Treavey had ensured no one who didn't need to be in there hadn't gone in for a nose, but there was quite a lot of footfall dealing with the very dead Michael and his ex-partner who seemed like she was generally unhurt apart from the psychiatric issues she would have from now on.

Adam approached Treavey and Jon who were outside the house under a lit street light emitting just sufficient light to show them trying to clean some of the blood off from their boots on some grass. "Don't do that guys. Can you take them off and wait for the crime scene manager please?"

They both looked back at him with some embarrassment at what could be seen as destroying potentially useful evidence, but probably unlikely in the circumstances, but also disbelieving that they were going to have to get back to the station with no boots.

"Is that necessary Adam? I mean, I can tell you what's happened." Jon enquired with a deep sigh, annoyed that CID were making a mountain out of a molehill.

"It's just better to do it now instead of regretting anything later Jon," Adam replied. "Anyway, what do you think has happened? Adam asked.

Treavey replied to break the awkwardness, "I think the comms tape says it all, Adam. Michael Goring, that corpse in there lying upstairs in a pool of his own blood on the carpet has an injunction not to go anywhere near his ex-missus but he did just that with a machete to kill her but fortunately she managed to get the better of him. She is petrified, that's obvious to all. That's no act, anyone can tell that."

"Right. Thanks for that, Treavey. That's the case wrapped up then, is it?"

Treavey was suspicious. He trusted Adam but he was acting strangely. "What do you mean? Isn't it?"

Adam sat down on a low wall next to Treavey and Jon, staring across the road where a couple of teenagers out too late had stopped with a bicycle and were staring on, gossiping about why all the police were about. This was the most exciting thing that had happened in their neighbourhood for quite some time.

"I'm not convinced." Adam said and then fell silent for quite some time. He remained sitting with the officers staring ahead and being momentarily distracted by the group of boys with the bike. "Haven't they got beds to go to? It's nearly 1am and there's no clubs open around here. I know I'd be in bed if I had the choice."

"Adam," Treavey shouted impatiently. "What are you talking about?"

Adam now sitting next to them shuffled his bottom on the wall as if to make himself more comfortable and glanced over his shoulder at the house, momentarily. "There's no forced entry like she said there was on the tape. She said he was breaking in. The blood runs up the stairs so he was fatally injured at the bottom of the stairs but was either dragged or managed to get upstairs whilst injured and there's no major damage to the door of the bathroom apart from a popped lock which a five-year-old could get through."

Treavey and Jon felt sheepish as they looked at each other with some embarrassment. Adam continued, "I could be wrong of course. The crime scene manager will be here in a minute, and I have only stepped where I've absolutely had to establish the basics but there's not a lot right with this job. Something is wrong. A lot is wrong."

Treavey asked, "But couldn't he have barged his way in, attacking her but she managed to get a strike with the machete somehow, but he ran after her upstairs to attack her more…"

"It's not a zombie movie, Treavey. I think she's dragged him up there looking at some of the marks. She doesn't look much but neither is Mike, her ex. And first enquiries show he's not been a bother since the split over a year ago so there's a lot of digging around to do first. It's easy to jump to the safe conclusion, as the woman being the victim and we should believe them at all costs, but I'm more interested in the facts, and women do kill, and they do lie, believe it or not and history has proven that time and again."

Treavey and Adam stood in their bare socks in front of Adam, looking like two scolded school boys. The teenagers opposite were looking even more confused at what they saw was two uniformed police officers standing in their socks. "That's probably why you are CID, and we are response, Adam," Jon replied with a snigger. "In the meantime, old boy, we are going back to the nick for a cup of tea, and we can leave it in good hands with you, okay Adam?" Jon laughed as he tiptoed his way back towards the car. "Come on, Treavey, let's go. Our work here is done."

As Treavey began to drive the panda back to the station, he remembered the car which had glanced off them. He rolled his eyes, mentioned it to Jon and they discussed whether the other driver would call in to make a complaint. Of course, he must have but how much trouble would he be in? He was relieved that he'd informed the control room about the incident straight away. A polac (police accident) meant they had to inform supervisory, and he guessed Sgt Fox would wish to see him when they got back. As they parked up and walked into the front office, he saw a very disgruntled looking man in a pair of jeans and a long-sleeved buttoned office shirt sitting in the front office.

Sergeant Fox walked past the two officers. "Sarge?" Treavey hesitantly asked.

The Sergeant looked back at him momentarily, his black bushy moustache bristled and a voice from within replied, "Not now Treavey. I've got a customer of yours to see to."

Treavey wanted to know more about the complaint and how much trouble he was in. He trusted Sergeant Fox but sometimes supervisors went for the route of least resistance and fannied around complainants who were simply being unreasonable.

They headed to the front desk enquiry officer who was sitting back on his chair reviewing a large newspaper and looking bored.

"Kevin, what's the complainant like?"

The enquiry officer straightened himself up and closed the newspaper slamming it on the desk. He was a fat man, a very fat man with a huge rotund belly spilling out of his buttoned-up shirt and almost succeeding to burst it open at the buttons. The hairy pale fat spilled over his belt buckle which hadn't seen daylight since the time he had put it on earlier that day.

"Oh, hi, Treavey," he acknowledged in a calm but friendly voice. "The man's an absolute dick. I explained from the log what job you were going to, but he keeps shouting about him being a councillor and he's fed up with police cars driving around the town like racing drivers making unnecessary noises with their sirens. I tried to pacify him, but he's determined to cause trouble and says he's going to take it all the way."

Treavey leant back against the desk next to Kevin. "Shit, that's all I need. I'll probably be suspended from driving for this. Driving school will drag their heels and I'll have to wait until someone's available to take me out for an assessment. It's a bloody nightmare."

Jon was about to say something, but he was interrupted by a loud commotion coming from one of the enquiry office's interview rooms. Treavey popped his head around the corner of the front desk reception which was otherwise empty of people. There was a lot of shouting, but it was coming from one person, that being Sergeant Fox, with the occasional short inaudible protest from the councillor, before more shouting from the Sergeant again. A brief period of silence was soon followed by a chair being thrown back against a wall and the door being swung open and an explosion of shouting emitting from it.

"Get your useless councillor arse out of my station now. You have our insurance details and that's all you're getting you selfish little prat. Perhaps instead of flaunting your self-inflated title like it's the only thing you've achieved in your short miserable life, you could try to do something useful with it like help the police clean up this town, instead of trying to threaten me and my hard working, dedicated officers with your self-sanctimonious drivel. Now get your sorry backside out of my station."

The councillor backed off with the onslaught of noise coming towards him. He came out of the room into reception swiftly followed by the skinny form of Sergeant Fox who needed no more bulk behind him to verbally evict the councillor who was considerably larger than he was. The man practically ran for the exit without a word coming from his now trembling bottom lip. He had bitten off more than he could chew this time. With a final wave of his hand behind the man who was stumbling across the walkway back towards his slightly dented car with his slightly dented ego. Sergeant Fox swung the front door shut and spun on his heals.

The three men in the enquiry office stood in shock and pleasant surprise and admiration at what they had just witnessed. The Sergeant glanced across to them as he paced quickly towards the security door leading towards his office, Kevin quickly pressing the button to release the catch in time to not cause the Sergeant to break stride. Sergeant Fox simply declared, "No complaint." and continued through the door and disappeared.

Treavey took in what he had just witnessed for a moment, looked at the other two men with him who were just as agog, and raised his eyebrows before commenting, "I'm keeping that Sergeant, he's mine."

Jon sat down on a swing chair, stuffing pouring from its cushion next to the desk with Kevin. He sighed and asked Treavey, "You making tea, mate? I'm parched and we can hardly go out without our boots, can we?"

Treavey wandered towards the kitchen door. "I'll get one for you too Kevin. White with two, yes?"

"And make one for me, won't you Treavey?" came a voice from the security door swinging open with a beaming faced Adam striding through. "Here, you two, you left these behind." He deposited two pairs of boots on the floor in the corridor.

"Don't you need them?" Jon asked, wearing a frown which quickly turned from confusion to suspicion.

"Never did want your boots, guys. Sorry, I couldn't resist it!"

Treavey shouted, "You little shit, Adam. How could you?" He grabbed the boots and threw Jon's pair towards him and adjusted the laces on his. "That's one we owe you, right, Jon?"

"Absobloodylutely," Jon agreed. "You little shit, Adam. My socks are wet now."

Adam giggled. He was looking very much the victor and soaking up his victory but was soon contemplating the potential avalanche of revenge wind-ups against himself he had unleashed. "We might have needed them to be honest, so I put it through the crime scene manager, and they took a quick look and said they wouldn't be of any use."

"Do we believe him, Jon?" Treavey asked with some suspicion.

"No, we don't, Treavey. We shall bide our time."

They settled back in the front office with Kevin to continue talking about the incident. It was too early to tell but Adam was confident the girl was hiding a lot and could even have made the whole call up.

"She was a bloody good actor if she did," Jon said.

"So, I understand. It'll be interesting listening when I get the tape from control. It's as calculated as you can get if she's enticed him there to murder him and then blame it on him. Anyway, I've some work to do, a lot, actually, and the night's getting on. See you."

There was a loud bang from the front door which caused them all to swing around to see who it was. There standing before them, looking distinctly out of breath with puffing cheeks and a bright red face was Superintendent Steer.

He stared at them all one by one before ending his gaze on Treavey. "I've seen her. I've seen the little bitch."

Jon gasped under his breath, "What else is going to fucking happen tonight?"

Steer repeated, "I've seen Lisa tonight, in a car."

Adam appeared back around the corner. "Hello Sir. What do you mean? Where did you see her?"

"In a car, driving out of Newquay. I saw her plain as day. I didn't imagine it. She's alive and well. Thank Christ, you can't suspect me anymore. She's around here now. You'll never find her body because she's not bloody dead."

He bounced with joy, almost ecstatic with excitement as he relayed to them what he believed she had been wearing, that she was on her own but didn't manage to get the registration number. "I was too excited to see her and make sure it was her. Her hair was slightly shorter, but it was her I tell you."

Adam told him they would be around the following day to take a statement from him but didn't show very much enthusiasm other than that. Treavey could already tell there wasn't a lot in it. The Superintendent could be making it up, he may not have seen what he thought he had seen, or indeed, there was a chance it was her.

"I'll take a quick statement from him now, if you like, Adam." Treavey knew that any extra time spent with the Steer may turn out useful and at least it looked as though they were taking him seriously. It would also break the back of this night shift and it would be finished before he knew it. He was beginning to get tired and there was nothing worse than being a nodding dog on night shifts. They always dragged when he felt like that.

One statement finished and Treavey was soon getting out of his uniform at his locker and standing outside to begin his walk home as the sun had come up emitting a golden glow from the east. It was a peaceful time of the day before the tourists had woken up for breakfast in their hotels. He loved his amble back towards the Barrowfields across the top of Tolcarne Beach watching the gentle waves lapping on to the fresh, clean, and golden sands, as if trying to wake the beach up gently in readiness for the busy day ahead. Much fun was to be had when the sun shone, and many a pasty and ice cream devoured by the hordes of tourists who had flocked from their busy lives up country.

He was halfway across the Barrowfields, a protected green space above the cliff and about half a mile long. He liked to walk along the very edge and glance down at the rugged coastline below. He had to stop momentarily and study the gliding sea birds who were streamlined like torpedoes with their undercarriage raised so sleekly beneath them, leaving a grey and white teardrop body heading so efficiently into the wind. The herring gulls skilfully and effortlessly danced on the thermals and currents rushing up the dark, jagged, and menacing cliffs before circling around above potential food sources, usually above a fishing boat returning from a night out over the horizon or a person doing much the same as Treavey and staring out to sea in the hope they were eating something they could snatch some cast off from. The occasional bin would be a last opportunity but there was little to scavenge from the night before.

The silence was broken by the occasional scream from the gull in mid-flight, usually reserved for a roof top to proclaim its presence. With its beak wide open, it rhythmically lets out a repetitive scream finalised by a drawn-out announcement of its dominance. Treavey couldn't think of any other reason they would make such a spectacle of themselves on an otherwise peaceful morning. 'It was all very unnecessary,' he thought as he continued along the coast breathing in the fresh salty air and admiring the dark blues and blacks coming from within the depths below him. How he wanted to be up today enjoying the sun, but how he also wished to collapse in his heavenly bed to shrug off the tension of the shift he had just completed, ready to do it all again tonight.

He watched on as an over keen jogger ran by, sweating from their morning run before they started a long day at work, no doubt, something he found he could never do himself. How they found the motivation, he never knew. They would have to get up before 5.30am and there was no possibility Treavey would do that without pressing the snooze button and abandoning the whole idea within the first three chimes of the alarm. He was far happier to enjoy the sites at a slower pace. He was young and able to get away without too much exercise and he was grateful for the genes he had which meant he was able to stay slim without too much effort. He was distracted by the rescue helicopter making its way towards Trevose Point where the lighthouse sat, almost hidden by the low sea mist, which gave no clues to what type of day was going to unfold for the tourists. He felt a pang of jealousy watching the grey and red Navy rescue helicopter thundering its way through the air above him.

How the pilots must have been the most skilled of aviators to do a job like that in the worst weather conditions. Treavey had witnessed it himself when pursuing a Range Rover on to the beach at Watergate. They were drug dealers who had driven onto the sands and along the base of the cliffs to avoid capture knowing his panda car would not be able to follow. The rescue helicopter took him to the scene where the criminals had to abandon the car before the seas engulfed it and the drugs with it, and he loved every second of the excitement. During the winter months, he'd witnessed this huge Sea King beast hover just millimetres from the cliff and pluck desperate souls to safety just in the nick of time, before their bloodied and frozen hands lost their grasp from the razor-sharp black rock which they clung on to for dear life.

He contemplated the possibilities of joining the navy but then shook himself out of his daydream realising the chances of getting what he wanted were minimal with his very average exam results, his occasional migraine and his hay fever which almost stopped him from getting into the police as well. No, he would bide his time and maybe apply for the traffic department to fulfill his need for speed and then eventually, the gun cops; the armed response units who had recently been formed instead of having to be called out on pagers which took far too long. Treavey felt a rush of excitement when he thought of the idea of going to jobs such as the robbery which had taken place earlier in Newquay. He'd decided, now he was out of his probation and making a name for himself he would apply to have an attachment on Traffic. Decision made; he would have a chat with Sergeant Fox when he was back off his rest days.

He watched the helicopter for as long as he could, watching it get smaller and smaller to no more than a spec of black against the dark grey mist beyond. Treavey was momentarily startled as he thought the helicopter was plummeting towards the sea but quickly realised its form had miraculously morphed into a seagull. Time to go home.

Chapter 13
Heroes in stockings

August was well underway and Treavey had managed to get himself quite a tan despite the night shifts and sleeping through many balmy summer days. He and Claire had enjoyed several more sunbathing days at Fistral Beach in the dunes, this time on their own so Treavey could enjoy her being topless and not pretending he hadn't noticed anymore. He was happy and she looked to be, too. Everything was going well, and he was content.

Sergeant Fox walked into the parade room. Treavey had just started a morning shift and he was ready for an adrenaline packed one which usually meant it would be as dull as dishwater.

"Police Constable Treave. I have a job for you. I don't think you've had a concern for welfare yet, have you? Can you take a look at this one that's just come in. An elderly lady whose relatives in Kent haven't been able to raise her for nearly a week now which is unusual. Here's the address. Do you want someone to go with you?"

Every sinew in his body told Treavey to say yes. He was naturally nervous about searching a house for a body. You never knew where it would be and if it were there at all. Often, with the more information saying they were dead, they were usually fit and well with a perfectly rational explanation. He hoped it would be the same this time, but he needed to prove his metal to his section.

"No, I should be okay Sarge. Is this the address?"

The sergeant handed over the piece of paper with the details of the job including the informant's name, Mrs Joan White. It contained the details of the informant who was the daughter of the elderly lady who lived in Newquay on her own. The lady was 85 years old so it didn't look good, but he would first check the hospitals to see if she had been taken there. That was a quite common reason for not being able to contact relatives or elderly friends. If it were a younger person missing, it was worth checking the prisons as well, but he didn't think Mrs White would be the sort to get herself incarcerated overnight.

The checks proved negative so Treavey couldn't put it off any more. He drove the panda car slowly, trying to delay the inevitable, but soon arrived at a creepy looking bungalow looking foreboding amongst the long grass. It was a quiet residential area of similar looking bungalows with overgrown gardens and hand rails framing the steps and worn concrete garden paths, all of which advertised the age of the occupant.

He parked outside the house which had seen better days. The green gloss paint on the window frames and doors had long since faded and was peeling from the extremes of weather over the years. He approached the next-door neighbour's house but got no response, and on the other side, a very elderly lady told him to go away. He was impressed at her attitude knowing she would be safe against cold callers. That attitude had probably saved her from many a con-artist in the past, but she inevitably picked up the odd innocent along the way. Treavey didn't mind.

He walked around the house to look through the windows, but there was little to be seen. Then he came across the bedroom window which was closed with the curtains drawn. That was never a good sign. He took out his spring-loaded centre punch he had once confiscated from a car thief. He selected a window small which would allow him to reach in and gain access through a larger window below it. He updated the sergeant on the radio.

"Sarge, there is no reply at the house, and I can see the curtains are shut in the bedroom. I intend to smash a small window to gain entry. Can I confirm I have authority?"

"Yes, go ahead... Control room, can you get onto the glazier to save a little time please?"

There was no point in hanging about, so Treavey had one last look around him to see if anyone was approaching him waving their arms at him shouting, she was safe and well, but he just saw a man walking his Jack Russell showing no interest at all.

'Crack', the window shattered and Treavey used the shaft of the spring-loaded punch to scrape the excess glass from the small window frame before jumping up onto the window sill and reaching inside to the latch below. It opened easily and he manipulated himself onto the kitchen worktop trying to avoid knocking the flowerpot off the sill. 'Crash,' the pot fell to the floor, spilling its contents of earth and plant onto the vinyl floor. His size 10 boots had been too much for the dainty manoeuvre. It crossed his mind that he hoped the lady was indeed dead so he wouldn't get into any trouble over breaking her plant but then realised the ridiculousness of his thought. He was sure she would prefer to be alive and have a broken plant to complain about.

Now for the bit he dreaded most of all. He pacified himself it wasn't night time as that could be very creepy when searching a house for a body. It beat most horror movies although the spooky atmospheric music wasn't present, it did still make the hairs stick up on the back of his neck.

Treavey surveyed the outdated kitchen with worn, yellowed Formica units before moving on to the lounge where numerous photos in frames were displayed on the mantelpiece and windowsills. Pictures of family and memories of a happier time were displayed, one presumably of her with her husband standing proudly in a black and white image in a silver frame, with the man smartly dressed in a suit outside a church doorway. He found it fascinating how women of that era still had the same hairstyles when in their 80's; the perms which he associated with only the elderly but were in fact the fashion back in the 1950's and they had just kept with what they knew. The carpet was worn and there was an electric fire in the corner, fortunately switched off as there was nothing worse than an overheated house that had had a body in it for any length of time.

He stopped in his tracks as he heard a shuffling coming from a room adjacent to the lounge. "Hello! Mrs Woods, are you here, it's the police?"

There was no response which surprised him, and he felt a shiver run down his spine. What could possibly be the explanation? A burglar perhaps? Treavey pulled his casco baton out from his belt and wracked it. He repeated his challenge and after receiving no response, made his way towards what he realised was the bedroom. As he looked through the gap in the door, he saw the corner of the mattress and as he moved through the door, he pushed it open further with the tip of his casco to reveal a cat on the otherwise empty bed, and so he rewarded himself with a sigh. He smiled at his silliness before suddenly jumping out of his skin and shrieking.

There at the far end of the bed was an elderly lady he presumed to be Mrs Woods with her tights half way down her legs, and a rather unflattering sight was laid before him. She was lying on her back at the bottom of the bed facing the ceiling with her legs over the edge of the mattress. She was dead. Treavey was pleased with himself. He had accomplished what he needed to do, and he could report back to the control room operator with the results. But first he would have a look around to see if there was anything suspicious about her death. It would be highly embarrassing if the undertakers came and found a knife sticking out of her back.

He viewed the scene with her loyal cat sitting next to her. He'd have to see if a neighbour or the RSPCA could arrange for it to be rehomed. Maybe the lady's daughter would want to have it as the last connection with her mother. He imagined how the events of her death could have been. The curtains were drawn so it was probably last night when she was removing her tights and she suffered a heart attack, fell back onto the bed, and died where she lay. Not a bad way to go perhaps but not as dignified as it could have been but then death was not respectful like that.

Treavey had been to the death of a young man with his tutor. His flat mate had reported forcing the bathroom door and had found him dead from a drug induced heart attack and surrounded by pornographic magazines. He had been pleasuring himself and must have been at the climax of the situation when his heart gave out. His tutor chose not to mention the magazines in his report to save it possibly being brought up in the inquest. That's something his parents could be spared when they had enough to deal with already.

Mrs Woods will be described as found deceased on her bed whilst getting ready for the night when she died. No more detail was required. He updated the operator in as casual a way as he could knowing other officers will be listening, probably being very pleased they hadn't been given the job. He walked into the lounge again to get out of the depressing bedroom. He knew her daughter would be waiting on the result so asked if the control room could update her. He didn't expect her to be too shocked by her mother's death. He'd decided not to ring her on her mother's phone in case she thought it was her ringing and had an awful surprise when she heard his voice instead of her mother's.

Whilst he waited for the doctor to arrive and certify death, he studied the objects left behind to discover the type of person Mrs Woods had been. She was a mother, a grandmother, and a widow. She had a photo of her standing with a group of men and women in her wartime civilian clothing and a picture of what looked to be an old and grand but not oversized manor house with a large lawn frontage, delicate pillars and ornate bay windows both on the front and either corner of the building. Why she should have this photograph displayed made him curious, so he turned the photo over and slipped it out of the frame. On the back of the photo written in pencil on the back of it. *Bletchley Park. Edith Woods April 1943 to June 1945*.

Treavey stood motionless looking at the photo and the scribbled handwriting. This was history. The Bletchley Park code breakers shortened the war without any argument. They converted the German codes to the plans sent forward for the intelligence services to decide which to act upon and which not, so as not to give the game away. How they must have wept over those poor souls they knew were going to be attacked by the Germans and yet nothing was going to be done because the Germans would have guessed they had decrypted the codes such as the enigma code, believed by Sir Winston Churchill to have shortened the war by four years. He wondered how Mrs Edith Woods would have felt deciphering the messages from the Nazis and hoping the authorities would be taking action to warn those individual allied forces, those individuals she knew were going to be attacked imminently and only hoped would be the ones saved, but she'd probably never really know.

He felt solemn in that lounge. Edith was next door and he felt bad that such a wonderful person was looking so exposed. He returned and placed a blanket over her waist to give her some dignity. He returned to the lounge and sat on the settee opposite the armchair she would most likely have been sitting before retiring for the night. It would have felt wrong to sit in her chair. What lives these people had left but it wouldn't be long before the last ones had gone, and then history would have to be read in books and not told by those involved.

It took a couple of hours before the body of Edith was removed from the house and taken away by the undertakers. Treavey had filled the form 95 as much as he could and returned to the station and faxed the form to the coroner's officers. Something made him call the daughter because he had an urge to make a connection with her, and to find out how much she knew about her mother's past.

Her daughter very much appreciated Treavey calling her, knowing he was the person who had found her, and that he 'sounded like a lovely officer,' she told him.

"Mrs White, do you know what she did in the war?" he asked her.

"The woman hesitated, as if wondering what the relevance was. "Oh, call me Joan. Yes, she was very coy about it but something to do with intelligence. We always suspected Bletchley Park, the code breakers but she never divulged what she actually did or whether she was there or not. Said she'd been sworn to secrecy."

Treavey took a breath in and replied, "I think she has divulged it now, Joan. I have a confession to make."

"Oh?"

"In the lounge there is an interesting photo of a manor house. It's of Bletchley Park."

"Is that what it is? She said she met my father there but said it was some manor house and kept the photo as it reminded her of him. He died shortly after I was born."

Treavey decided to go for it. "The bit I have to confess is, I thought it was familiar so took the photograph out of the frame and it's got an interesting inscription in pencil on the back."

Treavey read out what he had seen from his pocket notebook and waited."

"Oh, good God, thank god you found that," she answered. "That's her telling us, isn't it? I mean, if we'd just thrown the photo out, or just put it on one of our shelves, even, I dread to think. Thank goodness you had a look. Well, the little devil. She was at Bletchley and when it was all happening, too. I suspect my father had a lot to do with that as well. This is fascinating. You've got me on to something here. I'm going to do some research to try to find out more. That generation was so modest and humble, you see."

Treavey didn't mention how her mother was found. She didn't need to know.

A few moments later, after a quick coffee, Treavey was making his way to Claire's flat as she said she had some important news for him. He ran up the stairs to her flat door and it opened on his arrival.

"Treavey, love, come in. I need to give you something." She led him into her kitchen where she had another coffee on the go for him. He didn't want to tell her he'd just had one. "I bet you've been so busy, so I thought I would get one on the go for you," she said to him, whilst staring confidently into his eyes with those dazzling blue eyes which so melted him every time. He was put into a trance by her blue eyes every time.

"Oh, yes, thanks. It's been okay this morning. Interesting in fact, but I'm glad to be with you for a bit. What have you got for me?"

Claire popped out of the kitchen and ran back in again as if she were an excited puppy bringing back a toy to her master. She was visibly excited, holding out a mobile phone. He took it from her, studying it, rolling it over in his hand and looked at her inquisitively. It was a battered old Nokia, and its display was lit up.

Claire took it back off him enthusiastically and said, "It belonged to Sitara. We found it. Sarah told me where it could be, and I found it in her flat. I've had a look at the texts and, well look."

She pressed a few buttons on the phone and turned it to face him so Treavey could view the screen. He read the message out loud. "L, you know I know, and I won't hesitate to tell him, so if you want to keep the pension, you just need to give me £10,000 of it. You know I'll say otherwise."

It wasn't replied to. There was a phone number which Treavey noted in his pocket note book along with the message verbatim in case the information or the phone was lost later on. He looked at Claire intensely, "So she's sent this to someone called L. We think Lisa, right? And it won't take much to confirm the number belongs to her either, we'll already have those details. That makes a lot of sense and the date…. June 3rd, so that fits too. Adam will be extremely interested in this. This puts even more doubt on Sarah being directly involved in her murder."

Claire grabbed him by the hand, "Come with me." She pulled him towards her bedroom, but Treavey stopped her in the doorway. "Are you mad, Claire? I could be in trouble for just going out with you, let alone if I am caught in bed with you on duty, which would be career over."

Claire's eyes glinted with mischief. "Who's here to find out, Treavey? Oh, come on, I want to undress that hot police uniform of yours. This is every girl's dream, and I have you right in front of me." She placed her hand on his crotch, and he jumped back away from her.

"No, Claire, please don't. You know I want to, but we just can't do that now. What if I'm called to an emergency and they find out I didn't leave here for 10 minutes. I should be gone already. Look, I'll see you after work, okay? I finish at five, and I'll just hope you are still in the mood."

She reluctantly let him go and Treavey skipped down the stairs with the Nokia in his pocket. He wanted to get it to Adam as soon as possible. Claire said she was giving the details to her sister's solicitor to hopefully get her out of prison from remand. Both Treavey and Claire were hopeful this would finally succeed.

Back at the station, Treavey was standing in front of DC Adam Gee at his desk feeling like a proud school pupil handing over a shiny apple to his teacher.

"Wow, nice one. This is extortion. And with Lisa disappearing, this puts Sitara in a bad light, but also makes Lisa the prime suspect for her murder. If only we could find Lisa. Dead or otherwise."

Treavey tapped his fingers on Adam's desk whilst he stood in front of him contemplating the possibilities. Treavey couldn't hold back any more. "So, Sitara was controlling Sarah to the extent Sarah thought the only way out was to poison her, and she tried to but her attempts were pretty crap as it would never have killed her, but then at the same time, because Sitara was such a bitch, she was trying to blackmail Lisa to stop her telling Steer that his wife was having an affair with Inspector

Levey, but then... well... surely it has to be Lisa who has murdered Sitara by going around to her place and strangling her. She was strong enough, looking at her. She has the best motive, no?"

Adam nodded his head in agreement. "That phone number on the Nokia is Lisa's mobile number so it's confirmed Sitara was blackmailing Lisa, yes. But then where has Lisa gone? Did she panic and just leave thinking we would be after her? We now know that Steer knew his wife was having an affair so did he do Lisa in? Statistics show it's usually the close relative when someone is mysteriously murdered. No, we need to find Lisa dead or alive to give us some more information. I will ask DS Bates to re-circulate her as missing in the hope someone knows something. He won't be happy though because we will get inundated with false leads as well."

Treavey wanted to clear his head and as there was a full section of six officers working, he asked Sergeant Fox if he could go on foot patrol. He enjoyed foot patrol because it was going back to traditional policing being one to one with the public, and usually the nice public who appreciated them being there. The public were generally pleased to see a traditional police officer on the streets, walking the beat. He couldn't wait to get out in the sun. He swapped his flat cap for his custodian helmet. The Devon and Cornwall helmet was a superior quality to most other forces as it had a silver nipple on the top as opposed to a flat plate. The crest was beautiful, and it stood up to being dropped whereas the Avon and Somerset helmets in the next Force would shatter into many pieces of plastic if dropped. That's why they were called Avon and Some Kit at training school.

He wore his white shirt and tie, and of course his black heavy trousers and boots, and around his waist he wore his utility belt with his hand cuffs and his casco strapped to his belt. There was no sign of rain today. The sun was beating down hard with the crispest of blue skies filling the palette above. Just the faintest wisp of a cloud could be seen high up in the stratosphere. He breathed in deeply as he stepped onto the high street, crossed the busy road with holiday traffic almost at a standstill and headed down the tram track towards the town centre and the Killacourt. He could make substantial progress this way by avoiding the main road into town where he would have most likely been stopped every few metres. The tram track was the cut through he had ended up on when chasing after the post office robbers. It had high hedges either side full of vegetation and a break halfway along where there could be seen the stunning views of the sea and coastline, looking down onto beach or tide at high tide between the Great Western Beach and Towan beach.

There were a few benches placed there for people to enjoy the view and usually they were occupied by a vagrant or two. It may not have been the most lucrative place for begging money, but it allowed a break from the drab life many usually led. Time to appreciate a bit of nature and something the richest of kings enjoyed on an equal level with the lowliest of tramps. No one could take that away from them.

Treavey hoped to see Grace, but she kept to herself most of the time. She tended not to mix with the other vagrants who Treavey suspected she felt were below her. After all, she had a job as a police officer herself once, and it was only tragic circumstances which led to her current position of sleeping on the streets. There was a hierarchy within the vagrant community, and it was as if she was separate from it. She wasn't the top as she would have had to fight for that position and it usually meant she had been in Newquay the longest, but she had only just appeared there. His task was to try to find her. She usually had a favourite position where she could survey all around her, such as on the top of the hill looking over Perranporth Beach when she was living there. He would use his patrol time to try to find her as he would even admit to himself, he missed her a little bit. She could be back at St Columb Minor church of course, but it was something to do rather than aimlessly walking around with nothing to aim for.

He appeared out of the end of the tram track, turned right past the bus station and down towards the Killacourt again where he had parked his car to watch the storm coming in before he found himself running down to Towan Beach to carry out CPR on the girl from the landslip. He had found out she hadn't survived but he could tell it was unlikely she would have, anyway. Treavey tried not to give it a second thought. He could not allow himself to dwell on these things. Too many adding up could be the end of him. He'd heard of a police officer in Truro who had been steady as a rock but had been found hanging in his garage by his wife one morning. Treavey didn't know him, but it had hit hard within the Cornish police stations. It was thought by those Police in more crime ridden cities up country that Devon and Cornwall officers had an easy time of it with beautiful country, coastline, and beaches to work amongst, with little crime occurring, but Cornwall had its own problems and lacked the investment that many other large cities had. There was a big problem with depression, especially in the winter where people found themselves particularly lonely. Police officers had extraordinarily little back up and some were often working alone day after day, and if they were having marital problems as well, that was sometimes enough to tip an officer over the edge. Some of the scenes Treavey had already seen in his short service were going to stay with him for life. The death of the poor little boy in Perranporth knocked over in the street. Seeing his colleagues desperately attempting to save his life was pitiful to watch and the plane crash where he saw the light aircraft in pieces and the manikin like corpses strung amongst the undergrowth and in the trees was more trauma to pack away in his head. It wasn't all ice cream and sand castles.

He skirted across the top of the Killacourt and back into town to walk along the Highstreet, feeling all eyes on him as he pretended he wasn't noticing. He occasionally gave a nod or a, "Morning," to a passer-by, and winced on hearing someone bending down to their small child whispering to them, "You see, if you don't behave, that policeman will take you away." He could never understand why parents passed their poor parenting skills on to the police by threatening them with a figure of authority. He passed WH Smiths, taking a glance in the window to have a look at the latest books were for sale. He wasn't a reader himself, but some police officer had written a book called 'Firearms and Fatals' and it had pride of place in the centre. He stopped and read the front cover, discovering it was spilling all the beans of his lengthy career. He may buy it later on but would probably wait until it was in the bargain bucket first.

He intended to turn back ages ago but found himself walking along the full length of Fore Street, across the top of the harbour and out towards the place his colleague, John Goodman had introduced him to, and where he first met his girlfriend, Claire; at the Huer's Hut. As he arrived, he admired the bright white paintwork on the knobbly single storey building and imagined the views it had enjoyed for so many years. He imagined the man called the Huer, who would have stayed in it and kept warm with the fire, then climb onto the roof to look for the pilchards to guide the boats in for the catch. Treavey caught sight of a familiar bundle of clothes on the sea side of the building. "Hevva!" He cried, and the bundle of clothes moved. It was Grace.

"What on earth are you talking about?" She asked.

"You will have to know if you intend this to be your main spot to survey your kingdom, Grace."

"Oh, pray tell, Treavey, educate me," and she patted the grass next to her. Treavey took his custodian helmet off, relieved to feel the cool air. He ran his fingers through his hair and rubbed his scalp, enjoying the release of the tension and relief from the sweaty itchiness.

"Oh, that feels better, Grace." He sat on a mound of sea pinks next to her. "Something I learned only recently, I'm ashamed to say, was that the Huer used to climb on top and look out for Pilchards and when he saw the shoals, he would cry, "Hevva, hevva" which meant 'Hear they are!' so the townsfolk would drop everything and rush down to the harbour to launch the fleet and prepare for the landing of tons of fish. Proper teamwork."

Grace was genuinely interested. "I like that. Some real history. I will make this my new spot when I need a bit of contemplation. It's so important to have a favourite place to think, or to simply be, Treavey."

"It suits you," Treavey commented and before long, he was comfortably sitting in silence next to Grace feeling no need to fill the gap at all. There was never any awkwardness with the two of them. They were good friends and happy to know they could fully trust each other.

"I need your help with something, Grace," he eventually said. "I have to be careful as it's all very confidential, but I do trust you."

"Go on"

"The murder of that Sitara woman. My girlfriend... My friend's sister is on remand for it, but I am very sure she wasn't the one who did it. Long story short, we believe it could have been the Superintendent's wife who did it."

"Lisa? That missing woman, you mean?"

Treavey looked visibly shocked. "Er, yes, precisely. How did you come to that conclusion?"

Grace didn't alter her deadpan expression as she continued to look straight out to sea, focused on a little blue fishing boat bobbing on the white horses which flicked their white foamy tails in the small choppy waves below the boat's hull. The usual flock of seagulls were dipping and swooping above, and occasionally diving into the water to pick up a stray fish tossed aside by the men on board, or if they were truly fortunate, spilled from the full net as it surfaced above the waves before being hauled on deck. "I've already heard about your girlfriend Treavey. You have to be a little careful with that one. I wouldn't rub it in too many faces yet. That could get you into trouble."

Treavey said nothing and looked away and up the coastline, feeling a little ashamed.

"Don't worry, you have to follow love. It's never simple. Better to ask for forgiveness than permission, hey Treavey?"

She adjusted her position on the cliff, digging her heel into a mound of grass to gain more purchase. "Lisa has gone missing, and the chances are she's committed a very nasty crime, or she wants to disappear. I wanted to disappear. There are many reasons people wish to do that and they aren't always obvious. Maybe her husband was beating her, maybe work got too much for her, she has addictions, she was running off with another man, she just wanted to get away from the world. She could have been murdered, too."

Treavey was impressed with her wise words, putting the options very simplistically and all of which were utterly believable.

"What do you think has happened to her," he asked Grace.

"I think she's been murdered." No one disappears for that long without some trace. Your CID will have checked her bank cards and if there are no obvious boyfriends she's had…"

"Apart from Inspector Levey," Treavey stopped short as he knew he had said more than he should have.

"Interesting," Grace acknowledged. "She was having an affair with one of her husband's colleagues. A lower rank at that. Was she not trying to go up in the world?" She smiled and let out a little giggle.

Grace patted his leg and said with a soft comforting tone. "It'll all come out, Treavey, it always does. You just have to keep your eyes and ears open. Keep an open mind as there's nothing more restricting than a closed mind. Don't find the evidence to match a motive. Just search for the evidence and it'll eventually come, whatever it is, and usually when you are least expecting it."

Chapter 14
Fast and furious

Today Treavey was more excited than he had ever been. He was beginning a late shift and was being picked up in the Traffic car from Newquay station. It was unique in its stature and simply looked beautiful, oozed with power and speed just sitting on the tarmac outside. It was the much talked about Ford Sierra Sapphire Cosworth 4x4. Known to be a bit of a stallion, very quick and would grip the road like no other but could occasionally bite back.

The livery had already won awards with its thick yellow police logo go-faster stripe, almost fluorescent in its brightness framed by a thin blue and white police check. The attractive design led the admirer's eye from the low nose along the side of the car and flicked upwards towards the racing spoiler as if it had been racing to meet it. The Force crest, one of the most impactive in the country, sat proudly at the back of the stripe and the blue letters of the word 'police' announced its presence in case its prey had still been none the wiser. Treavey couldn't believe he was on attachment to traffic for the day, and this work of art had arrived to pick him up. He had to contain his school boy urges to whoop and jump with joy. Instead, he was welcomed by a refreshingly enthusiastic traffic officer, PC Paul Leyton.

"Hi Treavey, I hear you may want to join us one day. You're already getting a name for yourself, with Sergeant Olly Tayler anyway. Welcome aboard. Shall we get right to it?"

Treavey jumped into the cockpit of the car. It felt like the star ship enterprise with the coloured lights, dials, and radio displays. The car itself looked incredibly modern although it was already showing signs of wear. This car was used and abused every shift and was usually either at full acceleration or on full braking, using every millimetre of its massive brake discs to slow that mass being thrown through the country lanes and the dual carriageways of Cornwall.

The next moment, Treavey felt like he was gliding along Narrowcliff away from the town centre, towards the green lanes where the hunting ground of the Cosworth was best suited. He had to monitor the local channel around Newquay on his personal radio and the additional main set underneath the centre of the dash. A large Bakelite telephone receiver was slotted into the side of the footwell where his legs were. It felt quite an old-fashioned thing to have but served its purpose of having an ear piece and microphone available so confidential information could be passed without prying ears intercepting it from the back seat.

Paul could sense him checking the car out. "Our call sign is Tango 36, okay Treavey? That's your job to answer the radio, and you can sort the lights out too when we need them."

Treavey was using every ounce of his acting skills to portray himself as a calm, professional police officer being unphased by the car or being on attachment, but he knew it couldn't last for long.

"You have no idea how happy I am right now," slipped out of his mouth. He glanced at Paul who was laughing.

"No worries Treavey, we've all been there." Paul comfortingly replied. Treavey was relieved he hadn't got one of the stern traffic officers who had been 'lumbered' with the patrol cop attachment. There were a few arrogant ones who had soon forgotten the enthusiasm they had once shown too.

"Tango 36," came the dispatcher's voice, abruptly breaking through the relaxed chat, "Can you attend the A30, Redruth where there's a report of a car driving on the opposite side of the road towards the Truro direction? We have had multiple calls and will try to pinpoint the location for you."

Treavey had hardly put the phone receiver to his lips before he was being pinned back into the bucket seat, the scenery flying past him like he had never seen it before. He was witnessing the expertise of Paul handling the powerful car, placing it on parts of the road he would never have considered, and going for overtakes he never thought were possible. The Cosworth was effortlessly threaded through the scenery, whilst Paul astonishingly and calmly gave a commentary of what he was doing.

"I'm looking up at the horizon over there where the road comes over the brow of the hill, Treavey, see that patch of road? It's empty so I'll keep an eye on it in my peripheral vision so I will know if there is any other traffic coming towards us. I'm lining up with this car in front, accelerating for the bend so if it's clear, I'm going. I can see the dead ground has opened, joining up with the space I've already cleared, see it? Right, clear, and I'm going."

With that, the engine let out an enormous growl and the police car shot past what now could almost have been a stationary vehicle, no doubt giving the occupants the shock of their lives. One minute the road had been clear behind them and the next, they had this police liveried Cosworth beast overtaking them as if they had been standing still. If Treavey had been unsure about joining the traffic department before, any doubt had now completely disappeared. This was the job for him.

To his joy, Treavey was heading down Rejerrah hill; a famous hill in Cornwall which resembled a big dipper with clear view along its full length but was often quite dangerous when motorists misjudged the speed of oncoming traffic. Straight as an arrow, relatively wide, but you wouldn't want to risk putting a lane between the oncoming lanes. The Cosworth almost let out a squeal of delight as Paul planted the accelerator which pushed Treavey back into his seat again. His eyes were planted deep into his sockets, and he winced at the mass of information and forces on his body as Paul put the car onto the other side of the road and Treavey afforded a quick view of the speedo. 140mph and still feeling as if there was more. The impact on his senses was gaining even further, and with an added punch of adrenaline, he knew he wanted this to continue forever, if his body and mind could take it.

They continued through the twisting lanes, past the junction with Perranporth where he had spent his previous couple of years and had had so many adventures, but wow, did he feel he had moved forward. He felt excited, he felt part of an even bigger team as the police Force was, a gang who could and would do good for others and it felt amazing. Whatever he asked for, be it Traffic, the helicopter, a dog unit or more officers, it was always sent if physically possible and no matter how much it cost. He was still in his twenties, and it felt good. Really good.

"Righto, Treavey," Paul calmly spoke as if not wishing to startle him in case he had been sleeping. The control and calmness of his tone shocked Treavey. How on earth was he able to remain so calm when all this was going on? "...we need to be careful from here in case we meet it coming head on. Usually with these calls, we hear nothing more because they get the hint after they have turned down the off slip, but it may be a drink driver so, we'll see."

Onto the dual carriageway towards Camborne and Redruth, Treavey felt the blood drain from his face with what he could see in front of them. There was a lot of traffic backlog, and he knew this was unusual. "Fuck, Paul, this isn't good, right?"

Paul expertly slowed the car, forcing Treavey forward against his seat belt, but by now, he'd learned not to be alarmed.

Treavey began to speak but was distracted, "Hopefully there's no injuries, Paul, but I expect…" Paul manoeuvred the car, with sirens blaring, between the two lines of now stationary traffic. The police car was making progress through the traffic jam at a slow but progressive 20mph but sometimes, with spurts of 30mph. It was like looking at the parting of the red sea. It was almost beautiful to watch as the cars on the right nosed into the centre reservation and the traffic on the left, into the nearside. Huge lorries managed to disappear in front of their eyes to allow them passage. Treavey felt like a king. He felt the envious eyes of the occupants as he passed passenger windows, their noses pressed up at the windows just a couple of feet away from him.

Moments later and they saw smoke ahead. The sense of urgency rose, and Paul's relaxed expression became more pensive. Treavey knew this was not good news. It was exceptionally rare for a car to burst into flames and often when reported it wasn't fire at all, but usually someone putting the wrong type of fuel in, or a turbo blowing but generally cars were very reliable as far as fire was concerned. Thoughts were rushing through their heads and Treavey instinctively called on the radio, "Control, can we get fire on the way, please. We think the vehicle may be on fire. No idea of casualties yet."

There was a curt response from the dispatcher as there was nothing more needed to be said, until just a few seconds later, "Tango 36, we are getting reports of trapped persons in the car. We have fire and ambulance en route,"

There was silence in the car as they continued to make progress. Treavey couldn't get his eyes off the black plume of smoke ahead of them, rising wider and higher with every hundred metres they drove. It wasn't very long before they were on top of the scene, and it was devastating.

"Control, from Tango 36," Treavey blurted out with some trepidation confirming his arrival status, "We need everything here. This looks bad."

Paul expertly swung the Cosworth across the road to block as much view as he could from the waiting traffic. There were a few members of public out of their cars with expressions of horror and they were fixed to the spot.

Paul shouted across the roof of the Cosworth at Treavey who had jumped out and paused with his jaw dropped to take in the scene. "Mate, you get the fire extinguisher, I've got the crowbar."

The boot lid was open in seconds, and they were delving in the back of the car, Treavey recovering the extinguisher and running to the car which was well alight. It was an old green Jaguar and had been the victim of a much newer Audi coming the other way. The red Audi had spun off into the Cornish hedge and the elderly male driver remained in the seat but was talking to passers-by who felt they could cope with that particular part of the collision. There was substantial damage to the front of the car, but it had got off lightly as it had glanced off the front of the green Jaguar avoiding a full impact head on. The Jaguar must have been hit in the perfect spot affording a narrow gap where Treavey emptied his fire extinguisher into.

Flames were licking from the edges of the vast and now sculptured bonnet, and although his urge was to smash the glass and get the middle-aged woman out of the car, he knew he had to leave it to Paul so they could hit it from both ends.

The extinguisher was finished almost before it had started, but there was a huge cloud of white powder hanging in the air obscuring the car. Treavey sighed with some relief, but it was cruelly short lived as the flames teased from the edges of the engine bay again but with extra vigour, almost laughing at them as they did so.

He glanced back to see Paul looking frantic and having put the crow bar through the window and spent some time trying to pull the door open, he was now jabbing it into the edge of the driver's door and forcing his weight onto the end of it, but it just kept slipping out of the narrow gap between the car body and door. Treavey ran to assist him. "Keep it in there Paul, keep it still... now!"

He swung the empty extinguisher back and slammed it onto the end of the crow bar which, to their utter relief, sunk into the gap a good inch. "Pull now, fucking pull it Paul, we have to get this thing open."

Both clung onto the end of the crow bar and slowly the gap widened. It emitted a sound like a large oak galleon ship being pulled apart on the Cornish rocks, a deafeningly loud creak which slowly gave up its grip on keeping its prey in the metal coffin within. They managed to force it open just enough for Paul to force himself in to get to the woman in the driver's seat. She was unconscious, with a peaceful expression and completely oblivious to the danger around her.

"For fuck's sake," Paul cried. "Where's Trumpton? We need Trumpton. Her legs are trapped in the pedals. Her legs are smashed mate. What are those flames like?"

Treavey didn't want to look because he knew it was going to be bad. "We need to get her out now, Paul. I mean, now mate."

The flickering flames dancing through the gaps in the bonnet and grill had now morphed into a fuel filled welding torch like flame, not fuelled by the petrol, but by the oxygen being sucked through the engine grill as the heat emitted from under the windscreen was now sucking the flames to follow it. The situation was dire. The car was filling with black acrid smoke and Treavey was having to withdraw to take fresh gulps of air before appearing over Paul's shoulder feeling powerless to help him further. Paul was being caught out by the black smoke occasionally, causing him to splutter uncontrollably, his red face turned to Treavey; he took a long gulp of air. Treavey could see the stress on his face. It was fear. He knew he was losing this one.

"Let me…" but Paul was gone again, his head and shoulders underneath the woman's legs which resembled pieces of thick rope through being fractured by the impact. Treavey could see the determination on his face. There was no way he was going to let Treavey take over. Paul forced his torso into the footwell again, desperately scrabbling at the woman's feet and shattered broken ankles to attempt to free them. Treavey was entering a state of shock. The sense of being so useless was too painful.

Treavey's eye caught the glimpse of a sparkle in the toxic smoke to the right-hand side of the steering column. It was there for just half a second before the sparkle fizzled out and was lost in the folds of dense smoke. Something made him stare at the space to see if it appeared again and as if like a message coming through the gloom, he recognised it as a silver key ring, framing an oval photograph held within it. A baby. A photograph of a baby on her keyring. Treavey spun his head around to peer through the glass of the rear passenger seats. Nothing. He couldn't see anything there apart from a bundle of debris from the car hitting the Audi head on. It was probably a coat, but was it? He had to make sure, just in case.

There was an explosion of glass as Treavey put through the window, took a gulp of toxic smoke and with his head spinning around and feeling he was going to pass out he leant into the back of the car. The heat hit him immediately. The flames were up to the engine bulkhead and blackening the windscreen which had now crazed. Grey and black patterns covered the glass like a modern art painting, but it was merely a warning that worse was to come. How long was it going to be before Paul had to pull back. It must have been an oven in the footwell.

Treavey scrabbled about through the pitch blackness, his arms and hands investigating every lump of clothing and object. A hard piece of plastic. Maybe a toy, but it was larger than he'd expected, so he gave it a pull and found it was heavy. He yanked himself further in, feeling the edge of the jagged window on his stomach, but his clothing was thick enough to protect him from it, so he pulled himself in even further, so his feet were almost clear of the ground.

It was a baby seat. It was upside down so it must be empty right? Otherwise, it would have been strapped in properly. The collision was hard but not enough to rip a baby seat from its fixings. He pulled it towards him, and it rolled over. Still not able to see anything through the dense acrid smoke, he almost hugged it to bring it towards him and attempted to wiggle himself out of the car again. He felt a soft fleshy sensation on his bare hand as it rolled over and to his horror, realised it was a baby. Before he could think any further, he was out in the dazzling blue sky and clear air, gulping in the sweet nectar into his lungs. He cleared his vision as best as he could, rubbing his eyes, realising too late it was only going to make it worse. It was enough to see Paul pulling the lifeless looking body of the woman from the car. He had managed to get her free but was she still alive? Her face had been permanently in the smoke whilst Paul was low in the footwell where the air had been slightly clearer, and he was managing to take in gulps of relatively clean air by turning around occasionally to reach for the clearer air behind him before diving back in. Had his efforts paid off?

Treavey noticed somebody approaching him in his periphery vision and they swiped the baby from him. "We'll take this little one," and it was gone. Treavey remained dazed but slumped on his bottom not caring what he looked like anymore. His head was spinning but he felt confidence in the person who had taken the baby from him. He had done his bit, and he hadn't got the energy to check the little one for life. Maybe he didn't want to know the truth as it had been so quiet. Was it dead already? It seemed likely. He didn't even know what sex it was. He reached for his radio, then hesitated as he scanned around to see Paul bending over the body of his casualty. Treavey struggled to his feet and staggered over to him.

"Mate, how's things?"

"I'm fucked, mate, but I think she's going to be okay. Her legs though,"

Treavey glanced down at them. They were bending where they shouldn't be. They were as straight as they could be, Paul had made sure of that so at least she had some circulation still, but they were battered. It was going to take some surgery to pin them together again in any form of normality, and months of recovery after that.

She was breathing though. That made Treavey feel euphoric so Christ knows how Paul must have felt.

Looking back at the Jaguar, he could see the flames were now engulfing the cabin of the car. She had been pulled free in the nick of time. Once the flames had got hold of the soft furnishing of the car seating it was like a scene from bonfire-night. The billowing smoke reached up and across. Bystanders were stepping away and perhaps regretting they had stopped their cars so near and then, finally the fire service had arrived. This time, though, due to the traffic and the size of their vehicle, they would have arrived too late if it hadn't been for Paul's efforts. They soon devoured the flames and, before long, the black smoke turned to white steam and the fire was out.

Treavey jerked into life. The baby. Where's the baby? This day was turning out okay, but it could soon be ruined if he found the baby had suffocated in the smoke and what if it had died because Treavey hadn't looked in the back earlier. If he hadn't seen the key ring spinning in the smoke, the fire fighters would be pulling the body of the baby out of the charcoaled car interior right now, and then how would he have felt.

He strained his ears, desperate to hear a baby crying but he couldn't. He was frantic to find out, but, at the same time, he wanted to walk away and not know. He wanted to blank it out of his mind, but he found himself walking over to the ambulance, nonetheless, which was abandoned on the hard shoulder. He knocked on the side door. It opened and he was relieved to see a smiling face of a paramedic beckoning him in.

"Well done you. The baby's fine. She's in good form. And I hear from our colleagues in the other ambulance, her mother should be fine as well. A good day's work for you two. Well done."

Treavey almost fell back off the step of the ambulance in relief. He felt ecstatic but did not have the energy to celebrate. He was exhausted. The paramedic followed him asking if he felt okay but he waved her away. "You look after that little one. I'm fine, honestly. I'll be fine."

The area where Paul had been was clear. Looking around, he could see he was talking to some other traffic officers who had their clipboards out. Treavey began walking towards him to see if he could be of some use, but Paul was coming towards him and said with some assertion, "Come on Treavey. They've kindly taken this on. We are free to go."

They made their way to the Cosworth, still sitting there, its sleek looks, as if it were driving a hundred miles an hour. Treavey appreciated the beauty of the car, and he marvelled at the fact he was able to not only sit in it, but to actually be driven at speed in it. They both got in the car and sat in silence. Then Paul spoke.

"Well, how are you enjoying your attachment so far, Treavey?"

Treavey glanced across to him trying to find something appropriate to say but caught the sight of Paul grinning. His white teeth shone out through his blackened face, and he laughed, and said, "Fuckin hell, mate. That was pretty fierce!"

It made Treavey feel as if he had been fully accepted within the team of that car. He felt he belonged and was proud of what he had managed to do, but he knew he had got away with it by the skin of his teeth. If he hadn't seen that key ring, there would have been a very different feeling within the car. He sat there and bathed in the atmosphere. He wasn't going to feel like this very often. It was like a drug, and he liked it very much. God knows what that baby will achieve now. How many children and grandchildren will come of it, and it was all down to him. Down to Treavey. What a feeling that was.

"Come on mate. Let's head back for a cup of tea. The boys have got it from here."

Treavey noted he was now a mate. They had been through an experience together and he had passed the test. He shuddered with satisfaction. The Cosworth worked its way around the smouldering gravesite of cars and headed on towards Redruth to turn around and head back towards Bodmin where the traffic units were based. Very soon, and with the help of the windows open, Paul was accelerating the Cosworth again. Nowhere to go but what else was there to do with an empty dual carriageway which was still cordoned off. At top speed, heading into a relatively tight bend felt safe to Treavey. He felt like he was an old hand to traffic, and nothing would phase him, even though it had only been a few hours. He sat back and tried to relax, glancing the needle on the speedometer dancing around the 140mph mark, then settling back to watch the blur of the world rushing by.

He absorbed the surroundings around him. Lands' End was ahead of him, at some distance, granted, but he could see the same blue sky with white fluffy clouds the locals and tourists would be enjoying. He could smell the fresh, sweet air and hear the deafening wind rushing past the windows before Paul had decided it was quite enough and closed them. And then there was the oasis within the racing car he absorbed before him. The dials and switches were designed with speed in mind. It was a pleasure the police hadn't decided to dumb things down and get a sensible car for their traffic department. In the end it was found the more hot hatch the car looked, the less likely the bad guys would be tempted to run. No one escaped a police pursuit, no one. It was an unwritten rule that you'd have left traffic if you'd met someone who had outrun you. That was a walk of shame back into the traffic centre no one wished to make.

Watching the skills Paul displayed showed Treavey that getting into traffic wasn't going to be simple. He was going to have to pick up these skills and be constantly assessed under immense pressure. There was no fooling about and many traffic officers and armed response officers who needed the advanced driving ticket fell by the wayside and had to quickly rethink their whole career plans. It was going to be tough, but he knew it was what he wanted to do eventually. He was going to have to make a name for himself in the meantime and, fortunately, it looked like it was mapping out for him so far.

The car wound down its speed, coasting from within a mile from the junction, with Paul expertly assessing the speed to approach the off slip without having the need to apply the brakes or accelerator. He must have done that a few times before.

The drive back towards Newquay was somewhat more sedate. They cranked the windows open again which filled the car with the scent of warm cut grass and wildflowers. Wild birds flicked about the hedgerows, expertly dodging the traffic to look for the insects flung from the car grills and windscreens. The kings of this scavenging were the crows who judged the speed of the cars expertly, and occasionally tugged at the great prize of a rabbit carcass, but otherwise the larger beetles would do as a stop gap.

The drive back was heavenly smooth and even relaxing even though the suspension was harder than the average car. The summer was in full swing, and life felt good. Paul was controlling the vehicle as if it were a well-behaved beast, doing exactly what was demanded of it. Very little input was needed by him to control it, and Treavey marvelled at his ability to judge when to come off the accelerator as they approached the rear of another car, requiring no need to apply his brakes before waiting until the bend opened and smoothly accelerating past it. Having had the adrenaline dump subside, he felt he could very easily have dropped off to sleep, especially as he hadn't had too much sleep the night before in anticipation of his day ahead with Traffic and the humdrum of the road surface being so hypnotic.

The blue lights were switched on and Paul pulled over a grey Volvo car in front. Treavey waited in the car whilst Paul walked forward to have a chat with the driver. Treavey was embarrassed and hoped it hadn't been something too obvious he had missed, and he suddenly felt awake again. He watched Paul carefully, ensuring the conversation was cordial and, in the meantime, Treavey got onto the radio asking for a vehicle check. He watched Paul walk around the car checking the tires and then tapped one of the back light lenses before looking satisfied, waving at the driver, and walking back towards the car.

"Brake light?" Treavey enquired.

"Yes, it's working now, but her toddler keeps undoing his seatbelt and is kicking off when he has to put it on. I mean, we aren't here to bring up their kids, are we."

"A Mrs Andrew Morris, yes?"

Paul looked at him with a little surprise, satisfying himself that Treavey was not just a passenger but would find something to do to help. "Yes, Mrs Morris, that's the one, with a stroppy little kid cos she gives in to him all the time. Usual problem."

Treavey climbed out of his bucket seats, said, "I've an idea," and made his way to the car in front. He knelt by the passenger side of the car but adjacent to the toddler.

"Right little man, I am a police officer and Mummy has told us you don't like wearing your seatbelt and it's very important to keep you safe, so... I have fitted something to your car which is connected to this belt clip here. If you undo the belt, the car will come to a stop at the nearest safe place, won't it Mummy," He looked directly at the woman who was enjoying the deception. "... and the car will stay there until the belt gets clicked back in, won't it Mummy?"

"Yes, righto, officer, thank you. It will get very boring if we must stop in a layby for hours, but I suppose that's what we will have to do, won't we Jack?"

Jack, the toddler was looking bemused, slightly stunned, and was very much taken in by the event. It would be something his mother could tease him over for many years to come when he was older.

"Tango 36, we have a single vehicle on its roof at Trafalgar Roundabout. No injuries believed, but it is blocking the road."

"Enroute," Treavey replied, running back to the Cosworth and just a few moments later, Paul was swinging the traffic car past the mother and toddler and accelerating hard towards Truro. It wasn't going to take very long to get there.

He could see Paul wasn't going quite as fast as he did to the first collision. This one was said to be less serious with no injuries reported but it was causing chaos with it blocking the road, so they needed to cut through the traffic. Anyway, it was more fun that way.

Twenty or so minutes later they were pulling up to the roundabout and the scene of the upturned car. "There it is," Paul acknowledged. "Lying on its back with its legs in the air."

Treavey chucked, making note of that one to use in the future sometime.

"Control, can we have recovery on the way please. A full lift is required or if they have the ability to right the vehicle, a slide on will be fine," Paul requested, before opening the rear boot lid and grabbing a broom before throwing it to Treavey. "We'll need this later."

The roundabout was a large one with five roads leading from it. It was very much a central part to the city of Truro and the upturned car was indeed causing some chaos. An elderly woman, gaunt and frail, was looking somewhat sheepish standing next to it with a sympathetic bystander wrapping their arm around her shoulders. Broken glass was scattered across the lanes which passing cars had scattered even further. A trail of dark liquid was running from under the car into a nearby gutter. Someone had scattered some earth from a nearby flower bed across the sticky line to attempt to absorb the majority before it disappeared into the drain. The car looked a bit sorry for itself lying on its roof, but it was almost still in one piece. It wasn't obvious how it had got to its resulting position at first, but an examination of a few scuff marks and some witness accounts told the story.

The car was being driven down the road at a very average speed, but the driver had not recognised the traffic had slowed in front of her, and so over reacted. She had pulled the steering over to the left to avoid a collision in front and mounted the pavement narrowly missing a young couple before simply driving up the wall and gently rolling over onto its roof. The old lady was well, but shocked. Treavey peered into the car to survey the mess which lay before him. It was surprising what people, particularly women, kept in a car. Men were far more minimalistic as a whole but a woman's car was her home and her office, with all sorts of vital equipment and ever so necessary lipsticks, tissues, oils, and lucky charms, and as with this one, a small car bin which had scattered its contents of banana skins and sweet papers across the roof lining.

He walked around to the rear of the car where the boot lid had shattered, spilling its glass over the road along with a grey ash powder which was now being blown over the several lanes of traffic. He knew that heroin could be off white in colour, and this suited that description very well. He skipped over to Paul like an excited puppy, surveying the woman with suspicion. She may have been a drug dealer all her life. What a perfect cover, after all. He was going to impress Paul one more time.

"Er, Madam... Hi, I'm PC Treave. I need to ask what that powder is on the road which has come from your car. I need to caution you first. You do not have to say anything..."

The old lady looked ashen. Her wrinkles deepened with a tight frown. Her grey hair waved like strands of corn in the breeze as she began to speak.

"Oh, that's Gerald. Is he escaping? Oh no, we must stop him, quickly."

She begun hobbling her way over to the car looking somewhat distressed as Treavey was finishing his rehearsed caution.

"...Gerald?" Treavey asked.

"Yes, it's my Gerald's ashes. I keep him with me. Oh no, it's him, he's getting away, quickly we must stop him, dear. I don't want to scatter him on this roundabout."

Before they knew it, both officers and the elderly lady were scooping what felt like handfuls of Gerald into a shopping bag, the only convenient container being available. Treavey hoped that Gerald wasn't too fussy about his accommodation. He must have already lost at least a leg worth of ash, so it was all hands-on deck to recover the rest of him.

It was an hour or so later when the road was clear, and they were making their way back to Newquay. They had had an eventful shift and Treavey was shaken out of his deep thoughts by Paul. "What are you thinking, Treavey?"

"Genuinely? I was wondering whether we managed to find his dick. A man shouldn't be buried without his dick, right?"

Paul remained composed, and with the same tone he would have used when talking about politics or some other serious subject, he replied, "I think you have most of his bell end on your shirt, mate."

Treavey glanced down to notice some dust remaining behind and brushed it off. "Oh my God. I reckon Gerald is getting everywhere at the moment. Bloody hell. Are we being followed?!"

Chapter 15
Synchronize your watches

The summer was showing some signs of fading. There was a slight nip in the air which hadn't been there before, and the tourists were beginning to thin out a little. Treavey had decided to walk into town and meet Claire in town for a coffee or maybe go for a walk depending on how the mood took them. He enjoyed walking along the impressive steep and craggy cliffs, along the Barrowfields gazing out to sea and the beaches along the coast. He enjoyed the soaring and swooping seagulls often despised by the locals for ripping dustbin bags open and dropping their copious amounts of seagull poo over anything and anyone they could find.

  He paused a while to admire their display so often taken for granted by those who moved below them. Watching the seagulls was a guilty pleasure for Treavey. He marvelled at their flying skills, never misjudging, and hitting the cliffs, telephone wires or buildings if they ever timed their flight wrong or got caught out by their inexperience or overzealousness or the power of the wind which could be considerably gusty on the cliff edges. He was even more impressed with the newly hatched and maturing grey mottled seagulls with their whistling cries, still relying on their mother for most of their nourishment. He would watch the youngsters tapping on the orange spot on their parent's beaks to encourage them to regurgitate some food stored in their mother's throat for just the occasion. Yet they also flew like expert spitfire pilots ducking and weaving the thermals, often using little effort to make their progress across the width of the beach. By approaching the cliff edge of Lusty Glaze, they would gain height just through gliding alone, as the strong uplifts pushed their outstretched wings and they drifted upwards. He never got bored with watching their sleek arrow head bodies, and their perfectly formed gracefully outstretched wings tilting and tipping with every sudden change in the breeze. He knew it would be a much duller world without them.

As he got to the end of the Barrowfields he glanced over Tolcarne beach where he had witnessed the rescue helicopter saving the person on the cliffs. He could continue along the top of the path into town and past the police station and into the tram track, or proceed past the tram track towards the post office where he had witnessed the armed robbery when he had first arrived in Newquay. After that very first day he thought there would be an armed robbery every day in Newquay but soon realised it was just by pure chance it had been an unusually exciting day when he started. He found himself trekking down the driveway for Tolcarne Beach and before long was across the soft sand with the occasional hardened sunbather and on to the solid damp sand where the tide had crawled in and ebbed back to its low level again.

He breathed in deeply, bathing his lungs in the fresh salty air from the Atlantic. He knew he was so lucky to live in Newquay, a place so many others could only wish for. It had its draw backs, of course, especially in the winter when everything was closed, but then there was a calm to the place, and the few more hardened local surfers continued to surf through the winter months but with thicker suits, gloves, hats, and boots to protect them from the bitter temperatures.

The sand was as flat as a pancake and compacted hard, so it was easy for him to slip his shoes off and walk bare footed along the water's edge. This was a way he could commute to town when the tide was out and walk back from the nightclub in the middle of the night whilst very much worse for wear.

He was going to meet Claire in a cafe along Fore Street which was the far end of the town, and he was relieved to see the low tide still allowed him to reach the steps up the harbour wall and onto the street above. Before he knew it, he was hugging his girlfriend in the cafe and ordering another cup of tea.

"Hi Claire, you okay?"

Claire had something exciting to tell him. She was finding it difficult to contain herself, her cheeks were almost bursting with excitement.

"She's out. Sarah, she's out!"

Treavey sat down with a slump. "Wait, what, Sarah, she's out of prison?"

"Yes, they've released her. Her solicitor argued it was more like a half-hearted attempt to kill Sitara, and it wasn't her who killed her anyway. There's quite a difference between poison and strangulation."

Treavey contemplated what Claire had said. "I suppose it's a bit like someone making a threat to kill. The law says, 'an idle threat will not suffice,' so in other words me laughing and saying, 'I could kill you,' is not an offence. I wonder if it was the same with an attempt to kill. If it was so feeble and would never work, that must be the same."

"Who knows, but I'm just glad she's out now. It's not the right place for her in that prison."

"She was in Exeter Prison, wasn't she? That's a nasty prison, but she wouldn't have wanted Prince Town either. That one's in the middle of Dartmoor. Really spooky, damp, and cold." Treavey shivered at the thought and took a sip of tea.

An hour later, they were making their way towards the Huer's Hut. Treavey had explained about it and explained how this police officer in Newquay had educated him on it. PC Jon Goodman was knowledgeable about it and had almost taken ownership of it making it known if any of the local youths defaced it, he would come down on them like a ton of bricks, and they could even find themselves at the bottom of the cliffs instead of going to court. Claire flicked her hair from her eye and strode on next to Treavey. She was wearing a casual navy-blue vest and some denim jean shorts which showed the cheeks of her buttocks. Treavey tried to get the odd glimpse of them, but it was becoming obvious. He lagged behind and she caught him looking at her.

"Oy!" she exclaimed laughing and giggling.

"What, who me? I just needed to do something back here. I'll be with you in a minute. Hey Claire, can you touch your toes whilst you are there? I bet you can't!"

Claire wasn't having it even for a second. "Yes, I can but I'm not proving it to you so you can look at my bum, thank you very much." She giggled mischievously, "You should know better, PC Treave."

They climbed the slight incline towards the Huer's hut and stood there looking out at the vast canvass ahead of them. So much sea and sky stretched out before them. They could see fishing boats pulling in their nets with a flock of sea gulls taking their chances to snatch fish from the nets and smaller fish thrown back into the water. They could see fishermen relaxing on the rocks, surfers in the waves and the little red and blue blobs of sailing dinghies bobbing their way out of the harbour towards a yellow flag, marking nothing in particular in what seemed to be the middle of nowhere.

"Look Claire, I mean look at that." Treavey stood mesmerised at the view before him.

"We met here, didn't we. This is our place, Treavey. This is our place." Claire grabbed his hand and walked him around to the front of the hut. The scene where many a 'Huer' would have looked out upon the ocean looking for pilchards to call the boats out to.

"There's that old tramp friend of yours, Treavey," Claire hesitantly pointed to a bundle of clothes facing out to sea at the same view they had been enjoying.

"Shush, Claire, she could hear you. That's Grace. I'll introduce you."

Claire didn't seem to be too keen on the idea. "No, you're okay, I'm sure she's okay."

"Don't worry, seriously she's fine. She doesn't even bite, I promise you." Treavey grinned at Claire who was looking sheepish having realised what she had sounded like.

They both sidled down the grassy verge towards the edge of the cliff where Grace was taking in the view. Treavey took the lead and with a nod of acknowledgement, he moved sideways up to her along the narrow path and sat down on a spongy cushion of thrift, next to her.

"Don't do it, Grace, step away from the cliff."

Grace glanced across to him and broke into a smile. "Oh, stop it, you rotter. I'm not going anywhere. I bet I'm the happiest girl in Newquay."

"Oh really," Treavey replied, "that's quite a claim. Happier than my girl here who happens to be with me so has to be the happiest, right?"

Grace shrugged her shoulders and ignored his statement. Claire sat nervously next to Treavey but leant forward very awkwardly and held her hand out in a hesitant wave. "Hiya Grace," she said in a sweet soft voice. Treavey was proud to be showing her off to Grace. He was still concerned with her attachment with Sarah and whether it was being frowned upon by his bosses, or even worse, the complaints department, but there was no way he was going to split up from her and so would just have to hope for the best. They were doing no harm, after all.

"But can I trust her?" Grace said to Treavey whilst remaining staring out to see. Treavey confirmed she could.

"I heard a conversation you may just like to hear about, that's all. It involves your ex-Superintendent. Steer's his name, isn't it? I've seen his photo in the local papers with that wife of his who's gone missing. You'll want to know this."

Treavey glanced across to Claire noting her expression had gone from nervousness to concentration. Her slender fingers had been playing with some grass, twisting them into a grass rope effect but she'd stopped in mid twist and put her hand on her bare knee, to concentrate on what was being said.

"Go on," Treavey replied whilst trying not to sound too interested. He wanted to keep this casual to coax Grace into saying as much as possible.

Grace was milking the moment for all its worth. She shuffled her bulk on the grassy verge she was sitting on, before settling herself comfortably again before running her fingers through her matted, grey, and scraggly hair. She glanced at Treavey with strikingly blue eyes, which looked just as youthful as Claire's eyes which had first attracted him, just a few further feet further down the cliff where she had been talking the woman away from the edge. Grace was in her early seventies and looked a lot older, of course. Her frame was large and battered and her skin damaged from not only the sun, the cold, and the rain, but the years of alcohol abuse since losing her whole family in a road accident. She hadn't been able to cope as a detective in the West Midlands police any longer. She had lost all control of her life, had no family or income but had found her bit of heaven along the coast of

Cornwall here amongst nature and she knew where to find shelter and protection from the Cornish storms which smashed into the rugged coastline with such ferocity. Not even a seagull felt it was safe to venture out at times like that. She could hide in plain sight watching the tourists bustling around so busily like honey bees rushing here and there from shop to shop yet going nowhere in particular.

"It was yesterday evening, and I was staying up here later than usual, waiting for that orange sphere of sun to disappear over the headland over there. I heard a couple arguing. A man and a woman, it was, and they walked up here from that direction." She waved towards the ancient and disused old lifeboat station at Little Fistral.

"I didn't take too much notice at first, but it got quite threatening. I mean really threatening. The guy knew it too. He was saying she had to give herself up because she was making him look like a killer. She was laughing at him saying that was his problem and not hers as she was with someone else far away and would be gone for good."

Treavey excitedly butted in, "So you can say you saw Lisa, can you? You saw her, and you heard her winding him up and taunting him? I mean, did she say why she had disappeared?"

Grace hooked her hand under her vast bosom and adjusted herself before realising what she was doing before brushing some imaginary crumbs off her lap and formally crossing her hands in front of her.

"I can't say on oath I saw her. I was staying out of the way. People tend to ignore me sitting amongst them, but they won't if I pay too much attention. No, I'm sorry, I can't say it was her. She was taunting him though and I don't know if it was a real threat or not but…" she hesitated before going on. "… he said that if she was going to disappear for good then he may as well make sure it was done properly and 'don't think he wouldn't do it.'"

"Whoah," cried Treavey. "He threatened to kill her?"

"Nothing that would hold up in court. Especially from someone like me. Can you imagine anyone taking my word for it?" It surprised Treavey how matter of fact she was as he expected her to be annoyed at people's prejudices against her. She could tell he was thinking something along those lines. "Oh, I'm not bothered. I would have thought the same when I was collecting evidence for a murder. You have reliable witnesses and then you have the homeless drinkers. I wouldn't want to go down for murder on the say so of some of my fellow homeless witness' accounts."

This is why Treavey was so fond of Grace. She was a realist. She never complained about her lot yet had many reasons to do so. Life had been cruel to her and she had had some torrid times, and even though some would have said she was presently at her lowest, being homeless, Treavey felt she was the richest person in Newquay without the constraints of modern society, and she had the knowledge and experience to find the basics in life. He was surprised how content with life she seemed to be.

Grace went on as more information came to her mind. "Steer sounded desperate. I thought she was walking a tightrope by laughing at him. He told her his girlfriend had left because she couldn't take the stress anymore and he had nothing. He sounded desperate, I tell you. I felt sorry for him. She sounds like a right bitch. One of those users, I reckon. You know their house is rented, don't you?"

Treavey pricked his ears up. "You what? Rented? How on earth do you know that, Grace?" Treavey felt very comfortable chatting to her, what he felt was a friend he could trust completely. As she spoke, he studied her face, marked, and scored like a Jordanian red desert landscape. Valleys, creases, and undulations with many imperfections on the service. Her elderly face had been weathered just like those middle eastern desert landscapes over millions of years but over her short seventy years instead.

"Because the woman said he had nothing she wanted. She'd got her revenge and got away with it. She was out of there and if it created a little trouble in the meantime, then so be it."

Claire sat in silence and looked in some surprise at the direction the conversation she had just heard, had taken. She added, "Treavey, what's happened with that phone threat from Sitara to Lisa? Isn't Lisa the main suspect now?"

Treavey hesitated before answering but he felt it was safe ground to comment. "I did hear from DC Gee they are keen to interview her over it. It does give a motive, yes, but they are keeping their options open still. There are a lot of people who didn't like Sitara for one reason or another. I wonder what she meant by 'she had got her revenge.' That sounds sinister. I'm glad Sarah is free now. She had a lucky escape."

Treavey and Claire said their goodbyes, leaving Grace at the hut whilst they made their way back towards town. As they passed the harbour in Fore Street, Treavey tugged on the hand of Claire, "The tide's out, shall we go back to Tolcarne via the beach?"

Claire excitedly grabbed his hand and pulled him down towards the steep steps which led down to Towan Beach. "Yes, let's do that, sweety. In fact, let's head all the way to Lusty and we can have some fun at your place if you see what I mean." She radiated happiness with her dazzling blue diamond eyes beckoning him to follow her down. He was more than happy to follow.

What a treat it was to walk, run and chase each other along the tide line. The vast expanse of damp sand stretching all the way to Porth was an incredible site, as flat and smooth as a billiard table, the only disturbance being someone else's footprints before they faded and disappeared forever. Treavey ran after and caught Claire who was giggling hysterically, and she screamed as he scooped her up in his arms and mimicked throwing her into the water. A little brown border terrier cross scampered past with a green tennis ball in its mouth, still managing to bark with excitement as its owner shouted his name some considerable distance off. "Arthur! Come on boy, this way."

Both of them were very happy hand in hand in the most idyllic setting, which was right on their doorstep, walking on the carpet of wet sand which stretched from the waves rolling in, to the dry soft sand at the foot of the cliffs where the previous high tide had failed to reach.

The draw of the city was strong, when living in Newquay, but the paradise they lived in did not go unnoticed by them either. Perhaps when Treavey was younger, he was bored of the cliffs and ached to have a busy social life in a bustling city but that soon passed by when all he heard from the tourists was how they would have loved to have lived in Cornwall. Some were overheard discussing buying a place to retire in, many ignorant to the storms which come in from the Atlantic and ripped up anything which was not bolted down. The locals soon got to know what to do when a storm was brewing. Even the seagulls would know it was time to hunker down and not take on the beast that was coming from over the horizon. His wish for an active life as a police officer in London soon subsided when he realised it was simply different in Cornwall. No, there wasn't the level of serious crime here but there wasn't the backup either, so he had to think on his feet a lot more and dangerous moments were not rare. He was on his own with no one instantly at hand, only the comforting voices on the police radio to remind him he wasn't alone.

He felt happy, hand in hand with his girlfriend. She was a comfort to him, very soft in nature but also a strong woman who would protect him and support him. He knew he could rely on her. He loved the way she tried to help her sister, Sarah, where she could, and was probably the main reason she was now out of prison. They clasped their hands together tightly and rocked them forward and back befitting the lovers they now were. Treavey sensed a pang of embarrassment and grinned at Claire to release the tension he was feeling, but falling under her trance once more as she returned his glance with glowing cheeks framing the widest of smiles with soft pink lips.

Claire tugged on his hand and flashed her blue Cornish whirlpool eyes at him. She admired his athletic frame and well-groomed blonde hair, almost military like after his latest haircut. She thought he was looking sharp and Treavey could see it in her face. He felt proud and confident and put his arm momentarily around her shoulder as if protecting her from the world. He could see she was completely devoted to him, and he knew she was willing to do anything for him right now. As they walked further along the beaches, they passed Tolcarne where she would normally have left him to go home, herself. She was heading with him to his place, and Treavey knew what was going to be happening there. Maybe the kettle would be boiled, and the coffee put in the cups, but that was probably as far as the niceties went. They were going to enjoy each other's bodies in his bed, and he hoped for some time with her. This was as good as it had got, so far, and he was loving his life.

Two days later and as Treavey headed into Newquay station, he was feeling a buzz of anticipation around the place. The austere grey block building's corridors had its familiar concrete prison block smell about it, but it was also a business-like smell, a motivating smell of dankness and mustiness but why was it not despised? Why did Treavey think, if anything, it was motivational. In a strange way, it wasn't a bad smell, perhaps because it was associated with excitement. Many an adrenaline filled event had happened or a narrow escape was followed by walking into this station for a cup of tea or a debrief, or with slinging on his civilian jacket and passing through those corridors to make his way home, which was another good feeling, tired and with a head spinning with the events of the shift.

    He ran down to the cloakroom hoping to find someone there, but he was slightly late, so his colleagues had already made their way for the briefing. A few hurried minutes later, he hastily approached the door to the report room, checking the top button on his white shirt before clipping on his tie and slowing his pace to an almost stop to give the impression he had been unrushed.

    The room was full of officers and staff. Some he had never seen before. Adam was at the front of it standing next to an overhead projector with a stern looking DS Bates sitting in a worn grey plastic seat like a headmaster perusing his students in assembly. Adam and the DS played with the paper work and clasps on their clipboards that rested on their laps. It was very much their time to shine. There must have been developments and Treavey couldn't wait to find out what they were.

Adam stood up and asked a colleague to turn on the light on the overhead projector. The noise and bustle lowered to a murmur which shortly dissolved into silence.

"Right, welcome everybody and thank you for coming here today. For those who don't know me, I am DC Adam Gee, and this is DS Geoffrey George Bates."

A restrained cheer went up from the back of the room from a couple of older response officers who knew what heritage was sitting before them. The DS's reputation had gone before him. He was already considered somewhat of a legend as he was a no-nonsense man, banging criminal's heads together and getting results. He had a number of reliable informants and above all else, he respected the officers below him. He was kind and supportive and quick to praise, which was often a surprise coming from a gruff voice under a thick bushy moustache and bulky frame bursting out of the front of his Harris tweed three-piece suit. The officers loved him and would often refer to him when discussing the more physically streamlined CID officers who were more into running marathons than going to the pub. Character was everything. It meant so much when walking into the CID office which was like entering hallowed ground. They had been working on this job for some time and were about to tell the response officers along with those imported from outlying areas what they needed them to do to get the job done.

Adam made it clear that the information he was going to give should not leave the room and he insisted the form of attendance going around had to be signed by everyone before leaving. It was imperative that confidentiality was maintained. Treavey felt the hairs along his spine raise. He slowly glanced around him to take in the atmosphere of the room. There was a strong air of excitement and much shuffling on seats. There were at least 15 officers of all departments, ages, and experiences all of whom had paper and pens poised on their laps. The lights were switched off allowing only a little daylight to push through around the blinds. The screen lit up. The title in capitals on the top of the screen said, 'Operation Cove' and under the title were three photos. The top photo, slightly larger than the other two was of Sitara. The two below were of Lisa Steer, the woman who had gone missing but believed dead, and beside her was a picture of Superintendent Steer with a very ordinary heading of 'Andy Steer' with the title underneath of 'Suspects."

There was an audible gasp in the room. Treavey took in who was either side of him and observed a neighbourhood officer next to him raise her eyebrow before looking down to her pad to scribble something down. Suddenly, the room filled with a blast of light from the door opening and a rather dishevelled police officer walked in with scruffy auburn hair flopping over his bowed head as if trying to make himself invisible. Treavey recognised him immediately.

"Oh Christ!" he sighed. "It's only bloody Ken Ford," from his time stationed in Perranporth. "It's only bloody Rambo."

Rambo had not been a very popular officer and Treavey had not missed him since moving to Newquay Station. Treavey slumped further into his seat hoping he wouldn't spot him. He was still that gaunt, skinny man he remembered and by the way he had sauntered in late without a care in the world, he hadn't lost his arrogance either. Rambo shiftily glanced around him in the darkness of the briefing room as the door closed behind him, before opting for jumping his backside up on a desk running alongside the room to take in the rest of the proceedings.

The briefing was as Treavey had expected, but he had been surprised at the frankness of Adam and the DS. The confidentiality of the investigation was unfolding in front of them. This operation was to arrest the Superintendent, Andy Steer and to search the house and garden for the body of his wife Lisa Steer or material, including a computer which may lead to the disappearance of Lisa and of course the death of Sitara which they admitted may or may not be linked in some way. DC Gee explained that they suspected Lisa had murdered Sitara before being murdered herself by her husband but there was nothing tangible to link them yet.

Treavey carefully took notes on his pad, realising it was more the plot of a book than a genuine investigation. He could see where his input had helped and felt proud of his contribution. Putting it simply, the evidence showed that Sitara had been extorting Lisa Steer, the wife of Superintendent Andy Steer because Sitara was aware of Lisa's affair with another man. The details of the other man were kept from the board, but it was wildly known to be Inspector Levey, who was conveniently missing from the briefing. It was heavily believed that Lisa had murdered Sitara by strangulation in her flat where her partner Sarah, had found her dead and assumed the poison she had been giving her over the past few weeks had finally taken effect. She was no longer a suspect because toxicology post mortem reports had shown the levels of poison were known not to have been sufficient to kill her. In the meantime, as Lisa had disappeared it was suspected that Andy Steer was more aware of her whereabouts than he was letting on and therefore was being arrested to obtain more evidence from the house.

Treavey had known that by treating her merely as missing, the Superintendent's house could not be searched for anything more than a person with his consent, and therefore after this amount of time, it was decided to step things up a bit. Treavey's report of what Grace had witnessed had come to nothing. She had been right about a vagrant's witness account not being believed, especially when she hadn't physically seen her. He scanned either side of him at the rows of officers and saw that all in the room were completely transfixed on Adam giving the briefing. The room was silent apart from the strong harsh words clattering against the walls given by Adam.

The intelligence and information part of the briefing had been given, including a photo of Sitara's phone with the pink ribbon and the letter 'S' displayed with the text on it threatening extortion to Lisa, and now the method of how officers were going to be deployed was given in great detail. Officers were reminded that Superintendent Steer will be well aware of forensics and so every care should be taken to not miss a thing. The officers selected to knock on the door or force their way in if necessary were from outside the Newquay area and were made up of the Tactical Aid Group, TAG, a formidable tough group of officers who suffered no nonsense from anybody. Treavey's heart slumped. He now knew he wasn't going to be involved in the main bust and he could feel the job running away from him. As the jobs were divided up, he slowly realised the only two people left were him and... Rambo. The day had just got worse.

The briefing finished and Adam walked over to DS Baits to be congratulated, before shuffling some files and making their way out of the room. Most of the officers got together in their small groups with the sound of screeching of chairs dragging on floors. Rambo sat where he was taking in the scene, before catching the eye of Treavey who raised his eyebrows in acknowledgement. It couldn't be ignored any longer, and sensing everyone towering above him anyway, he slowly dragged himself out of his chair and made his way over to Rambo who uncharacteristically smiled at Treavey.

"Hello Treavey. You look nicely settled here in sunny Newquay. A little bit busier than Perranporth, no? I was quite happily doing very little over there dealing with the odd deer in the road when I was very rudely requested to come over and help out here. It looks like it's you and me on patrol whilst this lot have all the fun, right?"

"Right," replied Treavey with an exaggerated reservation in his voice which he, himself, felt embarrassed about. He thought he had better recover the situation a little. "How are things, Rambo? You doing okay over there without me?"

Rambo didn't wait to answer but slipped off the table onto his scuffed heavy Dr Marten Boots and shuffled his way towards the door. "Come on Treavey, you can show me this Newquay place. Show me where everything's at, will you?"

Moments later, both Rambo and Treavey were sitting quietly in the panda car looking through the windscreen at the railway station opposite. A few tourists were dragging their bags behind them out onto the pavement and being taken away in taxis one by one. There was a hive of activity for ten minutes or so before the taxi rank was empty again and not a person was left behind. The two officers continued looking straight ahead and nothing was said until Rambo broke the silence, whilst switching the ignition on and putting the little Escort car in gear.

"Why so quiet, Treavey? It's not like you."

Treavey squirmed in his passenger seat. He was being forced to account for his silence and it was going to be awkward. He wasn't expecting to be exposed like this. He had an idea how to deflect his ill feeling about him.

"I'm sorry mate. I guess I'm a bit gutted I'm not on the job seeing as I've been involved so much."

Rambo slipped the clutch, and the panda slowly made its way towards the junction of the main road. Rambo flicked the indicator to left. "Why? What involvement have you had?"

Treavey already felt much better. He could feel the awkwardness ebbing away. "I nicked the woman called Sarah, on a nearby beach, who was first suspected of murdering her partner, Sitara when in fact it turned out she hadn't murdered her at all, but it was that woman called Lisa on briefing because Sitara was black mailing her…"

"Yes, I know, I was at the briefing you know," Rambo cut in, "Lisa was having an affair with that Inspector guy Levey, and they think the ex-boss of this place, Superintendent Steer has murdered his wife Lisa because she was having an affair with Inspector Levey. Is this place East Enders or what? But what part did you have other than arresting the wrong suspect?"

Treavey grimaced at the suggestion his only contribution was a red herring. "Someone I know, Sarah's sister, Claire, found the victim's mobile phone in her sister's house when she was on remand, and found the text which showed Sitara was blackmailing Lisa."

Rambo looked to his left at Treavey, and the car slowed as it crawled along Mount Wise towards the far end of town. "So, you arrested a woman for murder, she was remanded in prison, and she wasn't the murderer? Wow, I can see the positive contribution you had to the case."

A dreaded thought came into Treavey's head. Perhaps that's why he had been left out. Did DC Gee and the DS think he was a fool? Could they trust him?"

"I suppose I didn't think I had a choice when I found the body of her girlfriend in the boot of her car when she had been trying to walk into the sea herself, and when she told me she had poisoned her."

There was silence in the car for a more than usual period of time before Rambo replied curtly... "Fair enough."

"Golf 31, are you free?" They were going to their first job of the shift. Ten minutes later, they were walking up some overgrown steps to a weathered wooden front door with the green paint peeling off. They pushed it open and walked in. Rambo took the lead. "Mrs Hooper. Mrs Hooper? Are you there my darling, it's the police."

There was a faint cry from a nearby room and the two of them quickly walked towards the lady's moans. "Mrs Hooper, hello, my love. What have we done to ourselves now, eh?"

The woman was lying on the floor, she was incredibly frail. Her white straw-like hair was scraped back into a bun and probably hadn't been released in months. She had tuffs of white beard sprouting from her chin. She smiled broadly showing off her stained yellow teeth which had seen many a better day and raised her arm gesticulating a wonderfully jovial wave. "Hello dear," she said, "Have you come to help me?"

Treavey stood by as Rambo went into action carefully helping her up and propping her up against the bed which was in what used to be her sitting room. She sighed with relief. "Thank you so much officer. How silly of me. I reached up for that curtain over there and before I knew it, I was on the floor. I didn't know what to do. I had to shout in the end and thank goodness someone heard me."

Treavey was awestruck how Rambo, this gruff, cumbersome, seemingly unprofessional officer who used to disappear to see his girlfriend on shift when he knew him in Perran, was showing so much compassion towards this lady he didn't even know.

"Now Mrs Hooper. You just stay there for a moment. I'm going to make you a cup of tea for you, my love. Do you take milk and sugar, and do you have a secret hoard of biscuits around here?" He disappeared into the kitchen and Mrs Hooper shouted her instructions after him.

Having sorted her out with a cup of tea and a couple of rich tea biscuits, Rambo skilfully established what social services help she had, or rather didn't have, found the details of her GP and had forwarded on the information to the Control Room who would be forwarding on her predicament to the local health centre for a GP visit. Mrs Hooper was going to be in safe hands. As the officers walked towards the front door to leave, Rambo shouted back to her, "Mrs Hooper, Treavey here is going to come and pop in next week to see how you are, okay? Aren't you Treavey, that's alright, isn't it?"

Treavey at first taken aback that he'd been volunteered for such a task, quickly relaxed, and replied enthusiastically, "Yes, of course, you try to stop me. Especially knowing you have those biscuits, Mrs Hooper."

Treavey shut the door behind them, and they returned to the police car in silence. Treavey was confused. He couldn't work Rambo out at all. In Perranporth he had come across as lazy, who would disappear without warning for an hour or two and would never account for his whereabouts. Treavey had covered for him on several occasions, but it had happened too many times, and it was highly suspected he had a girlfriend.

"You were really sweet with that old lady, Rambo. Nice one. I liked the way you handled her."

"Practice," Rambo almost dismissed the acknowledgement with one word. "Practice, that's all."

"Go on?" coaxed Treavey.

It was clear Rambo didn't want to say much more, but Treavey was determined. There was more to this man than he had thought. The past thirty minutes in the car with Rambo had completely changed his opinion of him and he was determined to find out more about him.

Chapter 16

The silent hero

"Rambo, sorry mate, I have to ask. You disappeared off many times in Perran, and I'll be honest with you, it did piss some people off. You surprised me a little back there, cos I thought you didn't really care much about your job, and then you go and do that?"

"Oh, yes," he replied, sounding more sheepish than Treavey had noticed him be previously. "I heard the sarcastic remarks, but I thought it was none of their business, so I kept it to myself. I know you all thought I was seeing someone on the sly."

Treavey could feel himself blushing a little. He was intrigued, however, and so hoped he would continue.

"I was visiting my mother. She was just like Mrs Hooper there. That old lady reminded me of her. She was annoyingly independent but couldn't maintain it anymore; should have been in a care home really, but that would have destroyed her."

Rambo negotiated a car on the roundabout, the driver was confused for a moment as to which junction to come off before clearing the way and Rambo slowly manoeuvred across the roundabout towards Pentire Headland without a second glance at the muddled tourist. Rambo was going nowhere in particular but Pentire was a beautiful part of Newquay with views on all sides once you were up on the top and at the end of the headland.

"So, I used to pop in whenever I could. I had to make sure she was up out of bed, and she had had breakfast, although she rarely ate much then so I could risk it until lunch time. I was worried if I hadn't seen her by then, though, and I would just have to leave what I was doing. I'm sorry, Treavey, I tried to be as quick as I could, but she had dementia, and it was always at the worst times when she needed me. Vascular dementia, fortunately, not that disgusting Alzheimer's that sends you to a world of fear and frustration."

Treavey felt himself welling up with tears. He pinched his leg to stop himself from shedding the tear which was determined to embarrass him in front of Rambo. He had no idea why it had affected him so much.

"I hope you don't mind me chatting to you about it, Rambo."

Rambo was quick to reply. Treavey was surprised how open he suddenly was. It was almost as if a cork had popped, and he couldn't stop Rambo from telling him about his mother. It was often during a double crewed shift with someone you really got to know who they were.

"No, mate. You know, now, anyway. There's nothing more to it really."

"Is she still with us?" Treavey dared.

"No. I found her dead in her bed last year. I was relieved to be honest. She had stopped eating and drinking. Well, sometimes she surprised me. I think that was about the time you were there, so I was a bit irrational, I admit. Mum would refuse to get out of bed except to go to the toilet and she was very unsteady on her feet then. She relied on her frame, but I hoped I was there each time she did it. I had a carer come in for a couple of hours a day in the end. She would wash her and stuff, but I would have to do everything else." He looked across to Treavey and asked, "Which way?". "Left," replied Treavey.

"I knew Mum was getting worse as she imagined seeing things. She would get into her organising mode when there was nothing to organise, but I'd find her bed clothes all over the place. She would even ask me to get the number of her mother because she said she wanted to phone her. I mean, she died 30 years ago."

"What did you do when she asked you to do that?"

"I'd say I would get the number for her later. She'd forget and things would continue as before. I told her once her mother had died thirty years prior and it was as if she had to go through the grieving process again. I only did that once. I felt terrible."

"So, you… careful," Treavey pointed out a pedestrian not paying the attention they perhaps should, as they headed across the road in front of them. Rambo slowed and waited for them to cross. A teenager with his Walkman and in a world of their own.

Treavey wanted to keep him going. He was fascinated in this man who everyone had completely misjudged, had cursed, even, when he disappeared and sometimes officers weren't even too subtle about doing it so he could hear. He felt awful.

"I'm sorry mate. That's a lesson to us all. You never know what's going on in people's lives, do you?"

Rambo shook himself out of the heart-to-heart moment they were having. "Oh, don't bother yourself about it. If I'd done the right thing, I'd have told work and maybe got some help, but I'm glad I managed to help her as much as I did. She died in her own home and even though it was a little more dangerous that way because she could have fallen like Mrs Hooper there, I knew it was the best for her. To coin a cliche, it was what she would have wanted."

They sat in silence for the next five minutes or so. Treavey could tell it must have been a release for Rambo to talk about his mum like that and may have been the first time he had done so. Treavey was flattered he had been able to trust him with his most personal thoughts.

"Now we are here, Rambo, I'm going to introduce you to a girl I know called Amoora. She lives around the corner, and she was the one who told my girlfriend, Claire, her sister was getting controlled by her now dead girlfriend. We may not be directly involved in the bust today so we need to keep schtum about everything that's happening at the moment, but you should see her view from her flat. It stretches across the whole of Fistral beach. I mean, from one side all the way over to the Headland Hotel on the far side. It's absolutely stunning."

"Do you know her well, then?" Rambo enquired thoughtfully.

"Not really, but I feel a connection because of what she did for Claire and her sister, even though it didn't work out very well for anyone, and we tend to bump in to each other in Newquay, anyway. Don't worry, she's got a clean record too. I'm not getting you into anything awkward."

"Sounds like a good place for a coffee, then," Rambo replied enthusiastically.

Just three minutes later, they were walking up the steps to the flat of Amoora, the Middle Eastern Arab woman who Treavey wanted to secretly show off to Rambo. She always looked extremely glamorous with perfect makeup and although only 5'3" tall, made a huge impression on those around her with her jet black long straight hair which flowed down to the base of her curvaceous buttocks. She answered the door, and they were welcomed with a broad beaming smile with the most perfect of white teeth.

"Come in, come in," she welcomed them. Treavey glanced at Rambo who looked ever so slightly shocked by the encounter, and he caught him glancing at her olive toned and perfectly plump cleavage gently bouncing in front and below his eye line. He had lost himself for a moment before collecting his thoughts.

"Er, hello Amoora, I've heard so much about you," Rambo said somewhat nervously, glancing around the flat to divert his gaze from where he knew he shouldn't be looking but couldn't help being drawn towards. Amoora giggled, being very used to the reaction. She enjoyed dressing well, wearing perfect makeup to enhance her middle eastern almond shaped eyes and dazzling eye lashes. She was proud of her bosoms and her cleavage was not going to be hidden but tastefully shown off. Her whole persona was she was all woman, and she was immensely proud of it.

The three of them moved into her lounge in a somewhat awkward silence, Treavey rescuing the moment with, "I'm sorry Amoora, I just had to be cheeky and bring Rambo here to meet you and selfishly look at your view. You are so lucky to live here, honestly. It must be the best view in Newquay. I mean, look at that, Rambo."

"Rambo? Did you say Rambo," Amoora asked in a very, not so believing she had heard, manner.

"Yes, it's our Rambo. He may not like it but he's good in a scrap, aren't you Rambo?" Treavey thought he would leave out the fact he was considered a bit off the scale with eccentricity.

Amoora accepted the explanation and tossed her hair forward over her shoulder, so it draped over her left breast, so long it almost reached her navel which was just visible under her tight and cropped top. She stared directly at Treavey and smiled at him broadly. Treavey couldn't move for a moment being stunned like a rabbit in headlights. He turned back towards the view of the beach feeling some guilt. Why had he come to Amoora's flat after all? Was it only the view he had come to see? He felt embarrassed and ashamed before turning his attention back to the beach and commenting on a man playing ball with his little brown dog.

"I think I remember those two on the beach walking back from the harbour to my place the other day. He's called Arthur I bet. Such a cute dog. Border cross I think." He could feel himself rambling on. Rambo joined in.

"We are lucky aren't we. I mean, some of the guys go surfing before a late turn, or they go after a hot early turn. How many police officers across the country can do that except if they pay good money to come on holiday to a place like this. We really can't complain."

Amoora disappeared into the kitchen to put the kettle on. "I expect you want a coffee whilst you are here, yes? Oh, I was thinking, Treavey, what came of Sarah's phone that Claire found."

"Phone. Sarah's phone? We didn't find Sarah's phone, or if they did Claire didn't say anything."

Amoora appeared around the door frame and leant against it, frowning. "You know, the one with the pink ribbon and the letter S on it. I popped in and it was on the table, and she told me it was Sarah's phone. I told her you may need to have that, seeing as she had been arrested the night before."

Rambo pricked his ears and turned away from the window; his brow raised as the conversation had suddenly got interesting. His attention was fully with Amoora now, and so was Treavey's and both directed their attention on Amoora. Treavey was trying to sort the confusing thoughts in his head. "No, that was Sitara's phone, and yes, Claire said she found it in Sarah's flat a few weeks after. But yes, Claire did hand it over."

Amoora stood motionless taking in what she had just been told and looking very confused. She was an intelligent woman and Treavey knew he could believe what she said she had been told but it was easy to have misunderstandings with anyone.

"Some time after?" Amoora enquired with disbelief. You mean the morning after, not sometime after, right?"

"No, Amoora, I mean about two or three weeks after. That's when she found the phone and handed it over saying it was definitely Sitara's and Adam confirmed it was, too. It had the text on it extorting Lisa."

Amoora walked over to Treavey very slowly and in deep thought. She ran her slender fingers along the top of the Settee before putting her delicate hand on his arm and stared directly into his eyes. This time, there was no flirting, no, she was serious, as if getting ready to pass some desperately sad news. It was an expression Treavey had not seen her have before. "Sweet heart," she took his full attention, "I can tell you now, that phone, with the S on a pink ribbon was in Claire's hands a day after Sitara's murder, not two or three weeks. I know it was the day after because I purposefully went to visit Claire to give her some support as I knew she would be devastated. Claire distinctly said it was Sarah's because I commented on it when I saw it on her lounge table. She looked a bit startled; I grant you, but I guessed that was because she was still upset about her sister being arrested."

Treavey felt the blood drain from his face. Rambo stood silent listening to all what was going on in front of him. The small talk about dogs and beaches had ended. This was getting remarkably interesting. The penny had dropped for Rambo.

"Treavey, in the briefing, the text on Sitara's phone was about extortion Lisa. It was on the day of her murder, right? She was demanding £10,000 wasn't she, and then Lisa went around there and strangled her, right or that's what we thought, I've got that right, haven't I?"

Treavey nodded his head. "That's exactly what was said in the briefing, yes Rambo. Yes, my fucking girlfriend is not a girlfriend after all. She's a murderer and she's had me this entire time." Treavey paced around the lounge looking pensive. He was stressed and desperately looking for a way out for his girlfriend to be innocent, but this was damning evidence. She'd kept hold of the phone for several weeks knowing it belonged to Sitara and would be vital for the police, and when Amoora saw the phone, Claire must have thought quickly and said it was her sister's, Sarah's phone.

"But we met on the cliff with the jumper beforehand, so she didn't track me down to use me then. No, wait, she..." Treavey was wracking his brain. "The dunes... she went topless in front of me," He glanced around realising he had said it bit more than he had intended, but then dismissed it. It didn't matter anymore. "That was all before the murder, so did she genuinely like me or was she preparing to murder her sister's girlfriend and needed a cop onside to pass her fake information to and maybe get an idea of how the enquiry was going?" He quickly glanced up at Rambo, his furrow creased with concern, "I didn't tell her anything, Rambo, I don't think so, anyway, no I know I didn't."

Rambo sighed deeply before making towards the door. "We need to tell Adam immediately, Treavey, come on, I'll get him on the radio, and we can meet up. I think they've already done the raid, though. I think we've missed that boat, and who knows, Steer may have done away with his wife anyway. It could all be a coincidence."

Rambo paused at the door, before turning around to look at the two following him. "It would be a perfect cover, don't you think? Know of Lisa and Insp Levey having an affair, and make it look like Lisa has murdered Sitara to stop her extorting her, especially when you are

Sitara's girlfriend's sister so will have full access into the flat to their phones. It would take some organising, mind you."

Both officers ran down the steps towards their car. Rambo was on the radio arranging a meet and Treavey tried to process what was going on in his mind. He was in shock but knew he had to confront Claire about it. It could jeopardise any evidence, but the urge was too strong. He had to get to her.

They headed back to the station where Adam had asked them to meet up. As they walked into the reception area, Treavey said, "Hang on, Rambo, you go up and start telling DC Gee what's happened. I've left something in the car. I'll just be a second."

Moments later, Treavey was spinning the front wheels of the car and heading towards Claire's flat. He understood he wasn't thinking straight but he didn't care. He had to speak with her.

He was soon jumping out of his car and leaping up the steps to her flat door and he briefly composed himself before knocking on it, trying not to make it sound too urgent and therefore alarm her. She shouldn't be suspecting anything.

The door opened and Claire welcomed him, smiling with her perfectly white teeth. "Hey, you. This is an unexpected surprise, what… what's the matter?"

Treavey pushed past her and marched into the lounge. "That mobile phone. We need to talk," he growled abruptly.

Claire hadn't followed him all the way but had stepped into her bedroom. "Hang on sweetheart, I'll be with you in a minute. I must switch something off in here."

Now Treavey was in her lounge, he had time to think as he surveyed the nick-nacks she had collected from around Newquay in an attempt to make the place look a little more homely. It could show a lot about someone's character, but he was struggling to get any feelings from it. The surfing bits and bobs were displayed either side of an uncharacteristically ornate clock, possibly left by a relative. It stood on the window sill next to a joss stick which had been burned to almost nothing.

He already knew he would be heavily criticised by his bosses and CID in particular for going to her and tipping her off. He wanted to do the right thing, but his head was a fuzz of confusion. Many scenarios were spinning around his brain, but they were all leading to one outcome. One he didn't like. Should he arrest her on suspicion of Sitara's murder? Was he himself a suspect, now? Had he missed a perfectly rational explanation, perhaps? After all, Claire was so composed about things, and he was sure she wouldn't have let her sister take the blame and be remanded in prison for something she herself had done. Would she?

He waited a few more moments before feeling an uncomfortable shiver run down his spine. Things had gone noticeably quiet. He approached the corridor and saw her bedroom door was left ajar, and perhaps not surprisingly, the front door was open as well.

Treavey flung the bedroom door wide open to see clothes hastily flung around the bed and abandoned on the floor. It was very much in haste by the looks of things. Claire had exposed her guilt by running from the flat and how she chose what to take with her, nobody would ever know. Did she really think she was going to get away with murder?

He was out of the flat in a flash and jumping several steps before sprinting out onto the main road, his heart was pumping with adrenaline as he glanced up and down the road to see which direction Claire had gone but she was out of sight already. He felt exceedingly gullible and was not looking forward to confessing to Adam and even worse the DS on how he had completely messed things up. He could lose his job over this, or worse. Could they think he was a co-offender? He hesitated before getting on the radio and pressing the transmit button. He noticed his finger on the button was shaking. He was in pieces. He released the transmit button. Nobody knew he had attended the flat so he could keep it to himself for now. He had time to find her but where would she go. She didn't have a car. Did she get a taxi? Is she walking? Would she have found some solace with her sister? No, too obvious, what about Bronwyn, her friend on the beach, but he had no idea where she lived. The Huer's. What about the Huer's. He hoped not because there wouldn't be a safe reason for her to be there. It was where they first met and where she was attempting to talk a woman off the cliff. Yes, the woman had jumped but she had survived, plucked out of the sea by the lifeboat in the nick of time.

      He opened his panda car door and slumped into the driver's seat not sure what to do next. Surely, she wouldn't go to the Huer's hut if she had taken clothing because it would show she was attempting to escape. He glanced up at the clouds above which had turned an ugly grey, and further hostile looking black clouds were coming from the horizon. A breeze wafted through the window he'd just opened as he'd felt a flush of faintness run over him, but the breeze offered no solace with a bitterly icy bite, far too cold for this time of year. It was as though everything was hunting him down. A speck of rain appeared on his windscreen, and he watched it sit there static for a few seconds before another joined it. He could hear the police radio in the background, but he wasn't listening to it. It was white noise. His attention was elsewhere or nowhere, he didn't care which.

He found himself driving towards Tower Road which led towards the Huer's hut. He hoped she wasn't there but there was nowhere else to look. The car was almost driving itself as Treavey wound his way around the top of the Atlantic Hotel, a huge white beast of a cubed building sitting proud on top of the headland facing off the worst elements from the North Atlantic. Just below it, the Huer's Hut was like a newly hatched chick nestled beneath its mother's wings. The car came to a stop and Treavey stepped out and sauntered over to the edge of the cliff where he could see the spot where he had first met Claire talking the woman off the cliff. There was a person sitting on the ledge. It was Claire.

What to do. He should step away and get someone else to deal with this. He's too emotionally involved but he couldn't do it. She was alone and she had nothing with her. No bag or personal belongings that he could see. She was a little way below him. He decided to make it a casual approach, to hopefully not raise her alarm too much. "Claire?"

She didn't look around at first, but on hearing Treavey approach down the slippery bank of heather and thrift, she spun her head around to face him. He noticed her piercingly bright blue diamond eyes and fell in love with her all over again. Why did this happen to him? Why could he not have a normal relationship? Why did it all have to go so wrong for him?

She was off like a dart, scampering past the place she had spent so much time trying to talk the suicidal woman off the cliff, and along the cliff path towards the headland. What was she intending to do, where was she intending to go? Treavey ran after her shouting at her to stop, but Claire continued to pick up speed, skipping and jumping over rocks and heather along the path. The rain had begun to fall quite hard, the clouds were building, heavy and angry and the sea was rising and falling from the rocks below, as if lying in wait down below them. One mistake by either and he knew this sea was never going to give them up. Claire was reckless in the way she ran, and had to save herself a couple of times from falling over the edge, as she adjusted her direction from left to right, over a rock set deep in the path and then down into a dip before climbing up towards the road and the large and looming white old lifeboat house set in the dip of the headland. The concrete slipway running down into the sea had been one of the steepest in the country when built over a hundred years before. The enormity of the building hung over them, foreboding in its stature, steeped in the history of the life boats had launched to save the desperate souls in the century before. Claire stopped and turned at the head of the slipway. Treavey paused a few metres away and put his hand out flat ahead of him to calm her.

"Just stop, Claire. This isn't as bad as you think it is. You had reason to kill her. You had reason to look after your sister from her abuser. They will understand."

Claire's once dazzling blue eyes had dimmed to a dullness he hadn't seen before. "You can't have any idea, Treavey. I can't go to prison. I just can't."

She was distraught, blubbing into her hands. Her world had fallen apart around her. Emotion had completely taken hold of her, and he needed to try to gain some form of control himself. He desperately looked around to see what options he had. Maybe to grab her if he couldn't win her around, at the very least, but it would be risky. He'd only get one go at it.

He glanced down towards the bottom of the slipway and at the waves lapping the bottom of it. The water was black and menacing. It purred and scoffed, awaiting any prey which may fall into its lair. The rise and fall of the water was more extensive than usual. The rain had let go completely and both Treavey and Claire had been soaked in seconds. Claire's normally perfect hair was draped down the front of her face, sticking to her forehead like strands of seaweed. She tried to brush it aside, but rivers of rain continued to run down her face pulling her hair down with it. She stepped back, her face turned ashen with a sudden expression of shock wiping across it in an instant. There was a momentary panic as she stepped back and tripped over the lip of the slipway behind her, her body twisting as she flung her arms out to break her fall, but then almost a sense of acceptability upon her face. Had the decision been taken from her? He stepped towards her to vainly attempt to stop her falling but she was gone, tumbling down the slippery surface, rolling and sliding before hitting the water below with a slap and a shriek.

"Claire!" he screamed, stepping on the concrete slipway above and leaning over as far as he dared to stare down towards where she had fallen only to see her gently being pulled into the depths away from the concrete and rocks and into the shadows. That same black water gently kissed her as she sunk deeper into it, only to disappear as a final wave caressed and folded over her head, and then nothing. She was gone.

Printed in Great Britain
by Amazon